The Murder Of Manny Grimes

Angela Kay

Copyright © 2020 by Angela Kay, all rights reserved. No portion of this book may be reproduced in any form (stored or transmitted) without written permission from Angela Kay and/or Stained Glass Publishing. An exception is granted to the use of brief passages for review purposes.

This book is a work of fiction, and all characters are products of the author's imagination. Any resemblance to real people, living or dead, is purely coincidental.

First printing, September 2016
Second printing October 2020
Cover design by Hayley Faye

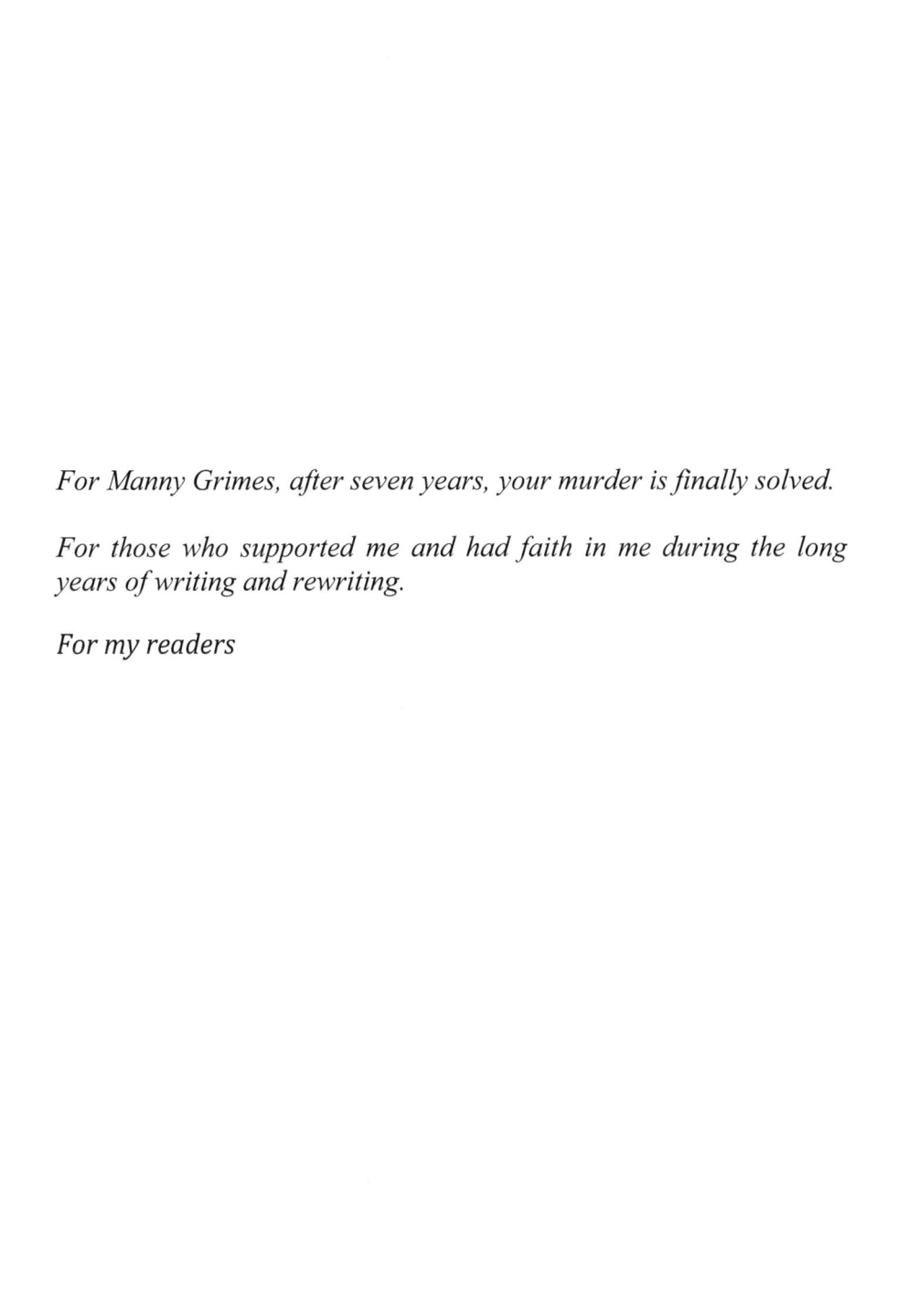

For Manny Grimes, after seven years, your murder is finally solved.

For those who supported me and had faith in me during the long years of writing and rewriting.

For my readers

Chapter 1

"We're gonna get in trouble."

Ten-year-old Bobby Walker fell to his knees into the thick snow and ice with a groan. The wind bit at his face, triggering a violent shudder between his words. The ski jacket and gloves he wore barely protected the skin underneath.

He shook his head, finding himself wearier than when he'd first climbed into bed.

Bobby struggled to keep with the pace set by his brother Tommy and their cousin George. It wasn't easy when it was so cold, and all Bobby wanted to do was crawl into bed and sleep. The thought had him yawning as the wind enveloped him and a shiver rushed up his spine.

He wondered if his lips had already turned blue.

They passed a couple of cars that had at some point skidded along the slick ice. The ongoing wind blew against the traffic lights causing them to swing wildly.

Bobby looked at the sky, overcast but now clear of the freezing rain it dispensed earlier in the afternoon.

That was a plus.

The few times Bobby dealt with the snow, he had hated it. It was too cold.

However, he decided when Tommy and George began climbing out the window earlier, he'd rather suffer the snow than be ridiculed for staying behind.

It seemed as if they had trekked through the frozen white landscape forever. For the thousandth time, Bobby began to wish he had stayed in bed—where he should be—where they all should be.

He tripped and fell, his knee grazing a rock hidden in the snow. He released a small whimper.

Tommy looked behind him to roll his eyes at his brother. It was hard to tell in the dark, but Bobby was sure his brother scoffed and rolled his eyes toward George, as if to say, "Look at that chicken. Can you believe we're related?"

"You didn't have to come," Tommy yelled over the wind. His voice let out the same cold-inspired shudder as his younger brother, but unlike Bobby's, his eyes showed signs of excitement.

Tommy looked at his cousin.

George, his face red and frigid, tugged his own coat tighter around his bulky frame as if it would further protect him from the wind. He remained silent, looking ahead toward the shadow of the schoolyard.

With shaky legs and a hesitant sigh, Bobby scrambled to his feet.

As if it were a signal to continue, Tommy trudged on through the snow, one foot sinking after the other.

They didn't stop again until they reached the edge of the school parking lot.

It was like a mirage against the thickness of the fog. The dim moon was the lone source of light on the building, creating ghost-like sparkles.

Again, Bobby shivered, but this time, it wasn't from the cold. The scene of the school gave the appearance of a building from an old black-and-white horror film his dad used to love.

"Where do you want to start?" George wondered, breaking into Bobby's thoughts. Breath escaped his lips, evaporating into the wind. He popped open his can of spray paint.

"I think the gym," Tommy suggested, an unmistaken sneer in his voice.

The Murder of Manny Grimes

Bobby shook his head with anxiety removing the spray paint he had stuffed in his jacket.

The two older boys began to engage in a conversation, which Bobby ignored as he lagged behind.

Amidst the fog, he spotted movement on the playground by the swing sets. He squinted, trying to use the little light he had available to make out the distorted shadows.

"Hey, Bobby, you comin'?"

"Look!" Bobby said. His hand quivered as he pointed. "What do you think that guy's doing?"

The other boys followed his gaze.

"Can you see who it is?" Tommy's voice had become hoarse.

Bobby shook his head again. Something wasn't right. His dad had always told him to trust the small voice in his head.

Get out of here now.

The voice was soft but clear.

"Let's get out of here." The hair on the nape of his neck stood at attention, and he felt like his nose was going to crack off from the cold.

Now seeing whoever it was by the swings—an adult with his luck—fear took permanent residence within him. "Please? Tommy? George?"

He saw Tommy take a step toward the figure.

"T-Tommy," Bobby stammered. "I want to go home."

Tommy ignored his brother as he slogged through the snow.

In hurried movements, the figure stopped whatever he was doing and stumbled in the opposite direction.

"He's jetting! I think he was doing something. Come on!"

Tommy was quick to push on through the snow before either Bobby or George could respond. When they managed to catch up with him, they realized he was staring at the ground, mouth open.

"Who is that?" George asked. He pressed his body close to Tommy's, shielding himself from the freezing wind.

A body lay on its side, one arm over his chest and the other outstretched above his head. The man's eyes stared into the void. His glasses hung, broken, off his left ear. His face was blue. Blood had settled, seeping into the white ground.

Thick snow flurries descended onto the body.

The wind pulsating against their faces made it difficult to see, much less breathe.

Tommy knelt to get a better view. "I can't tell, but..." He stood upright, grabbing George's wrist. "Hey! That's Mr. Grimes!"

George leaned in and swallowed hard before righting his body. "Ugh, let's get out of here!" He clambered away, stumbling backward into the snow.

"Is he dead?" Bobby asked from a few feet away. He had never seen a dead body before. After seeing this man, he decided he never wanted to see another. He resisted the urge to cover his mouth despite feeling as if he was going to throw up.

"It looks like it."

Tommy kicked the body with his foot and the boys jumped back as if expecting the man to grab hold of them.

Grimes fell to his back, head turned, facing their direction. His eyes remained open, pupils rolled to the back of his head. His clothes were torn, and blood pooled on the ice resting on the body.

"What do we do?" George wondered, panicky.

"I wanna go home," Bobby muttered. He wasn't sure if he even said the words out loud. His voice sounded far away. Somewhere in the distance, a dog barked, echoing against the whistle of the wind.

"I think we should find help." Tommy looked at the others.

Bobby could see the fear in his eyes. Glancing at George, he saw his cousin's mouth hanging open, his breath rising and falling with quick movements.

"We can't just leave him here." Tommy looked back at the body.

"How are we going to find help, doofus?" George demanded in a soft voice. "We're alone!"

Bobby was sure he heard the tears in his cousin's words.

"We'll walk to the police station," Tommy replied. "It's not far and they're always there—night shift or whatever. They have to be."

Bobby tried to stuff his spray paint in his jacket pocket. When he failed, he allowed it to slip from his gloves and sink into the snow.

"I don't want to get in trouble," George whined.

The Murder of Manny Grimes

"We can't leave him here," Tommy repeated. "You know that."

Bobby shook his head.

Tommy looked at his brother and cousin. When they didn't say anything, he started walking.

Bobby looked at George, who was still lying in the snow, tears sliding down the corner of his eyes. George was slow to rise but then hurried after Tommy. Once again, Bobby faced being alone, left behind by his brother.

He chose to follow.

Follow to the police department.

Follow to trouble no one could ever expect.

Chapter 2

Outside the Columbia County Sheriff's Department, someone had draped Christmas lights along the railing and roof. A *Merry Christmas* wreath lay flat on the ground in front of the entrance, with a few spots of green visible above the blanket of snow.

The cement steps were few but thick with ice. Rock salt had been scattered on the ground, and a yellow *caution when wet* sign stood below the walkway.

Bobby grasped Tommy's jacket. Tommy glanced over his shoulder at his brother and saw George had grabbed hold of Bobby's shoulder. Both boys' eyes were wide and glassy.

George let out a shudder as the wind whistled by. Their eyes met, and Tommy could tell what his cousin was thinking: "I agree with Bobby. Let's get out of here while we can."

Yes, they could take the easy way out and leave. Maybe they would be able to climb up to their room and into bed before their parents knew they'd left.

No, leaving would be wrong.

The state of Manny Grimes' body flashed through his mind.

The Murder of Manny Grimes

What if someone saw them? Saw they'd found his body but kept quiet?

Going home would be wrong.

Before he could change his mind, Tommy grasped the frozen handle of the door, sucked in a chilled breath, and dragged it open, pushing away the snow blocking the entrance.

They stepped inside.

Behind them, the door rattled as it banged shut.

The boys stood, gazing around as their eyes adjusted from glaring white snow to fluorescent office bulbs.

A fake Christmas tree rested in the corner, decorated with lights and ornaments, wrapped presents piled around the trunk. A blinking star sat on top.

A woman sat behind a glass window, head buried in paperwork, her rectangular glasses on the tip of her nose.

At the opening of the door, she looked up and her eyes widened in surprise. Removing her glasses, she waddled to the door of her stall and stepped out.

"Now, boys," the rotund woman began, green eyes narrowed as George and Bobby hid behind Tommy, each clutching his arms, "Why you out and 'bout in this kinda weatha?"

Nervous, Tommy glanced at his brother and cousin, then back at her.

"We need to make a report, I think," Tommy spoke, his voice small.

"It's important."

"Yeh, wha's that?"

Tommy looked again behind him with inquiring eyes. He swallowed hard, his throat raw.

"Just wait 'til they take a look at ya," she grumbled. She herded the boys down the hall and into an office where a few officers sat laughing and engaged in light conversation.

The room quieted when the boys entered.

The woman waved a hand at the officers. "Go on then," the desk sergeant said. "I'll fix ya some hot cocoa while ya explain what ya doin' outta bed. Ya look blue and icy. Ya boys should be in bed. It's afta nine o'clock!" She stepped away, still muttering.

The boys fixed their eyes on the five men dressed in regular street clothes. Tommy guessed they were policemen dressed in normal clothes because of the storm. Somehow, they seemed more frightening than they would be if they were in uniforms.

"What can we do for you boys?" one of the officers said.

Again, the boys took turns glancing at each other.

Well, no turning back now.

They began talking, overlapping. When another officer stammered and raised his hand, they stopped and took a step back as if he had threatened to hit them.

"One at a time, boys. One at a time." He scrutinized the boys and his eyes rested on Tommy. He gave a quick nod. "What's your name, son?"

"Tommy. And this is my brother Bobby, and our cousin George," he answered in a hoarse voice.

The woman from the front returned, holding one Styrofoam cup in her right hand while balancing two in her left. She handed one to each boy. Tommy took a sip of the steaming hot chocolate.

He let out a gasp as the cocoa burned his throat.

"I don't suppose your parents realize you're out this time of night, do they, son?"

"No, sir, we..." Tommy paused before answering. He didn't want to admit to their intent on vandalizing their school. "We, um, snuck out to play in the snow."

"You realize it's dangerous out there, don't you?"

"But, there's a man. He's hurt real bad, sir," Bobby interjected. He gulped and chewed on his lower lips. "I think he's dead."

"Do you know this man?" another responded in a deep voice. He had been leaning back in his chair, listening. Now he leaned forward.

"Yeah," Tommy whispered. He jammed a hand inside his pocket to fiddle with three marbles.

The officer waited for a moment, and when Tommy didn't reply, he cleared his throat. "And?"

"He's our assistant principal. His name's Manny Grimes," Tommy told him. "And...and he's got blood all over him." The dark realization of what was happening swept over him.

A man was dead.

Moreover, it was someone he knew and knew well.

"I see," the man with the deep voice said. "Where did you see him?"

"By the swing," Tommy told them. "At Columbia County Elementary School."

"Is there anything else we should know?"

The three boys shrugged and hung their heads.

After a few seconds of silence, the man nodded. "All right, why don't I go have a look? The boys can remain here until I get back, then I'll drive them home."

"Sure you're up for it, Lieutenant?" the first officer asked.

The second shrugged. "Why not? You boys get to stay all warm and cozy."

The other officers exchanged amused glances. "Sounds good to us, Lieutenant. Go have at it."

"Right," the lieutenant replied, the corner of his mouth curved into a smile. "Take care of our young guests won't you, Nancy?"

"A'ight," the desk sergeant said, again narrowing her eyes at the boys.

The lieutenant grabbed a heavy coat from his chair, removed a cigar from a box resting on the desk. Without another word, he set out.

Nancy instructed the three boys to sit. They complied, staring at the other officers who studied them with care.

Tommy watched as Bobby started to bite his nails and focused on a small manger scene that sat on top a short filing cabinet in the corner by the door.

* * *

When Lieutenant Jim DeLong arrived at the parking lot of the Columbia County Elementary School a few minutes later, he turned off the ignition to his truck and pushed open the door. He started to bite the end of his cigar off when he caught sight of the wind blowing debris across the schoolyard. With regret, he returned the rolled tobacco to his jacket pocket. He stepped into the fierce wind, closing the truck's door.

With slow steps, DeLong made his way toward the swing set, his boots sinking into the snow with each stride. His breath lingered against the wind as he stumbled through the thickness of the winter scene.

When DeLong reached the frozen solid swings where the boys claimed to have seen the dead body, icicles hung on the hinges, sharp as knives with a layer of ice welding the links together.

He observed the possible scene of the crime. No footprints were visible, but since the flurries had picked up again, he considered enough snow may have already fallen to refill what the kids left moments before.

DeLong knelt and dug his hand into the snow. He found nothing except a can of orange spray paint, which he shook without thinking and found the contents were frozen.

Rising, he circled around the swings, careful of where he stepped. He stopped and looked around again from a fresh vantage point.

A tree had fallen onto the roof of the school, demolishing a piece of the building. A stray dog sniffed along the ground near the back entrance, stopped, stared DeLong's way, then darted off in another direction.

DeLong watched, deep in thought. Something seemed to be missing.

He had good instincts and always trusted them. As he stood surrounded by the falling flurries, those instincts told him something wasn't right.

He looked around again and knelt, a heavy sigh escaping. There was no trace of a body. There was no blood, broken glasses or anything else to validate the kids' story. DeLong walked around the swings once more, digging, checking for evidence he may have overlooked.

Nothing.

Forced to conclude his instincts were wrong, and he was on a wild goose chase, DeLong returned to the truck. After prying his door open, he slipped inside. He could still see his breath climbing the stagnant air as he turned the key, hearing the roar of the engine.

DeLong's heart skipped a few beats when Elvis cried out that he would be home for Christmas. He waited until the heater warmed his fingers, then he turned the music down, put the car in drive and U-turned out of the school parking lot.

When DeLong returned to the sheriff's office, he spotted the boys sitting in the chairs, heads held low, knees bouncing. His colleagues were chatting amongst themselves until they noticed his presence, and the chatter ceased.

Curious to know what he'd found, they looked at the lieutenant but knew to wait until he spoke.

However, the boys seemed a bit more eager.

"Did you find him?"

"Is he dead?"

"What happened to him?"

DeLong gave each of them a look of warning and they fell silent.

"There was no sign of a body." He sighed, looking from the boys to his colleagues and back again. He felt sleep drawing him in. More so than usual. He rubbed his eyes.

"Boys, you do know it's against the law to make a false report, don't you?"

"But he was there!" Tommy insisted. He looked at DeLong and the other men.

"And he was dead!" his cousin added.

"If he were dead," a young officer stated, "then why didn't Lieutenant DeLong find him?"

"Maybe he was buried," Bobby suggested with a shrug, "by the snow."

Tommy nudged him.

Bobby's cheeks reddened.

A chuckle escaped the young officer who diverted his eyes when his comrades glared at him.

DeLong set the can of spray paint on a desk. He noticed the youngest swallow hard.

"Now, I won't be asking you boys if you know anything about this," he said. "I'd say you're already in enough trouble."

Tommy and George exchanged glances. Bobby bit his bottom lip and crossed his arms over his chest.

DeLong tilted his head toward the door.

"Come on. Let's get you home."

DeLong nodded to his buddies. "I'll see you tomorrow." He turned to leave and heard the shuffling of feet as the boys kept up. They argued in hushed voices. After DeLong shot a quick glance behind him, they silenced.

When they arrived at DeLong's truck, the two youngest climbed into the backseat while Tommy, as the oldest, took the front seat next to DeLong. DeLong slid behind the wheel and turned on the ignition.

Chapter 3

When they pulled up the driveway of a two-story house, it was after eleven. It seemed quiet and dark, except for the light of a lamp in one of the downstairs rooms. DeLong wasn't able to tell whether the parents were asleep or not.

Tommy climbed out of the truck, with DeLong following. They each folded their seats for the other boys to climb out.

A woman opened the front door, slamming it behind her.

Lightning seemed to flash in her eyes.

"Thomas Eugene Walker!" She sounded as angry as she looked.

"Where have you been? Do you have any idea how worried I was? It's eleven thirty! All of you march in that house, right now!" She jabbed her finger in the direction of the door.

Bobby was already running up the walkway.

Their mother crossed her arms over her chest, shielding herself from the cold as she turned to face DeLong.

She swiped her hand at the strand of snow-dampened blonde hair that fell in front of her eyes. "Thank you so much, for bringing them home. I'm Claire Walker." She extended her hand, palm faced down.

"Lieutenant Jim DeLong, ma'am," he replied, accepting her

hand. "And it's not a problem."

She flashed him a smile. "Please, Lieutenant, come inside, I'll make you some coffee for your trouble."

Not waiting for an answer, she turned and disappeared into the house, leaving the door ajar.

DeLong removed his cap as he followed.

The fireplace made shadows dance across the living room walls while filling the house with warmth. In the other room, the boys attempted to convince Mrs. Walker that they found the body of Manny Grimes.

"That's impossible," she told them as she opened and shut cabinet doors. "Tommy, I've had enough of your tales, and dragging your cousin and little brother with you."

"But it's true!" Bobby exclaimed.

As the conversation continued in the kitchen, DeLong focused his attention on the surroundings. There were pictures of a man in a Navy uniform, his arms draped around Tommy's and Bobby's shoulders.

Something about the photo was familiar.

But, what? DeLong couldn't put his finger on it.

He continued to scan the living space.

A few photos of George, standing with whom DeLong assumed to be his parents, decorated the end tables.

DeLong took a seat in the leather chair by the fireplace, tossing his cap back and forth between his hands out of habit.

He heard Mrs. Walker insist the boys get straight to bed and stay there.

As he waited, a gray tabby cat came out of hiding and purred, winding in and out of DeLong's legs. He reached down and scratched her neck. She stretched her head toward him, purring with contentment.

Mrs. Walker appeared with a tray of coffee, cream, and sugar. "Her name's Abigail. She is—was—my husband's cat."

DeLong rose, and the cat dashed out of sight. "I apologize, ma'am, for the intrusion," he told her. He took the tray and set it on the coffee table.

She shook her head and closed her eyes. "Please, Lieutenant.

The Murder of Manny Grimes

Call me Claire."

DeLong put on a half-smile. "Okay, but you have to call me Jim."

After she poured his coffee and handed him the mug, he dumped a spoonful of sugar and stirred, careful not to spill any.

Claire's cell phone rang, and she snatched it from the end table, putting it to her ear.

"Yes...oh, yes, Lieutenant DeLong is here with me now...yes. Really? Yes, I know...okay, I'll call you later, you're beginning to break up, and the lieutenant is still here...I'll call you soon."

Claire tapped her screen to end the call and leaned back into the love seat. "I'm sorry. That was a friend of mine. I've been calling everyone asking people to keep a lookout for my kids. He wanted to see if they were okay." She twirled her fingers in her hair and flashed him a small smile.

"It's quite all right," DeLong reassured her as he lifted the cup to his lips. "I'm sure it gave you a fright not knowing where they were."

"As a matter of fact," Claire said, "if you'll excuse me for one more second, I should call my brother-in-law. He's out there right now trying to find them."

He waited as she made the call.

After she finished, she placed the phone on the end table with a shake of her head. "I'm sorry for the trouble my boys caused you. The past couple weeks have been so difficult on all of us," she explained.

"I'm sorry to hear that," DeLong replied. He nodded to the photos on the mantel above the fireplace. "Is their father in the picture?"

Claire shook her head again and sighed. "Alan, my husband, he..." A tear escaped as she trailed off. "He killed himself not long ago."

Then it dawned on him, the man in the picture.

"My apologies," DeLong said with sincerity. "I think I remember the case. I didn't work it, but I know the story. They said he left a note, right?"

Claire nodded.

"I'm having such a hard time believing it. My brother-in-law, Jonathan, is out of his mind about it. My husband, before killing himself, killed Jonathan's wife. The boys, well, you know, they're young. They try substituting tragedies with other things, and Tommy's always been the sort to be in trouble."

"I am sorry for your loss," DeLong said. "I can only imagine."

He stared into the three smiling faces on the mantle, remembering the talk about the case. Alan Walker left a cryptic, unsigned note. He couldn't remember what the note contained.

DeLong cleared his throat, setting his almost-empty mug on the tray.

"Mrs. Walker?"

She looked over at him, using her index finger to wipe a tear underneath her eyes.

"Claire," he said with a consoling nod, "your sons and nephew came to the sheriff's office claiming a man was dead by the swings at their school."

She nodded. "Yes, they told me. I know Manny Grimes. He's a friend of Jonathan's and the assistant principal at their school. He's not dead, I can assure you."

"There's no doubt in your mind that he isn't?"

Her eyes changed expressions as she leaned forward. "Did you see him? Were they telling the truth? Are you sure he—."

"No, no," DeLong interrupted. "Although I did investigate, I didn't find evidence to corroborate their story. I only wanted to follow up with you."

Claire shook her head again. "No, but Manny did mention the other day that he might go to Alabama and visit with his sons." She let out a scoff. "I'm sorry, Lieutenant, Tommy's cooked up these kinds of stories before. It's gotten worse since his father died. I just don't know how to control him."

"We all deal with pain in different ways," DeLong offered. "He just needs to find his balance, cope with it in his way."

She leaned against the sofa, frowning. "No matter, I'm so sorry to have caused you all this trouble in weather like this."

It was his turn to shake his head. "No trouble, ma'am." He let a soft laugh out to ease the tension. "It got me outside for a bit." He

The Murder of Manny Grimes

placed his hat on his head and rose.

Delong extended his hand. "It was a pleasure meeting you, Mrs. Walker."

"The pleasure was all mine, Lieutenant DeLong," she replied. "I do hope we'll meet again soon."

"And under better circumstances," DeLong agreed as the front door opened, then snapped shut.

A man entered the living room. DeLong sized him to be five-foot-four, a good two and a half inches shorter than he.

He unleashed his tie as if a snake were trying to choke the life from him. He looked pale and drained.

"Jonathan, this is Lieutenant DeLong. He was kind enough to bring the boys home."

He glanced toward DeLong and let out a weary sigh.

"Thank you, Lieutenant. I appreciate everything you did to make sure the boys made it home. I'm surprised you didn't call us into the sheriff's office. Trust me when I say I will be speaking to them about sneaking out."

DeLong put on his disarming crooked smile. "Well, boys will be boys."

Walker glanced at his sister-in-law. "What did they do?"

"They decided to play a prank," Claire explained. "They told the police Manny was dead."

Walker's face drained of the little color it had left.

He looked over at DeLong, his eyes shining with disbelief.

"Manny Grimes? It's not true, is it?"

DeLong shook his head. "I investigated it myself. I imagine Mr. Grimes is fine."

Walker narrowed his eyes and nodded. "I'll give him a call to be sure. Thank you again."

"Well, I should get going before my wife calls in a missing person report," DeLong told them. "She'll have my head if I don't return home soon. Makes her jumpy since it's been so bad out there."

"Thank you again for bringing the boys home," Claire said.

He nodded. "My pleasure, Mrs. Walker. Mr. Walker."

"Thank you," she repeated as he began to head out.

"Are you going to find him?"

DeLong looked toward the stairs at Bobby, now dressed in *Iron Man* pajamas. "There is no evidence Mr. Grimes is hurt in any way, son," DeLong said.

"But he is!" Bobby insisted. "He was there!"

Walker pointed to the second floor. "In bed. Now!"

"But Uncle Jona—."

"Don't make me get my belt," Walker demanded, glaring at the young child. Bobby's face fell as he lowered his head and sulked back upstairs.

His uncle followed behind. "When your mother tells you to..." The voice drifted away as they ascended the stairs.

"I'm sorry," Claire said.

"That's quite all right, Mrs. Walker. I don't think the boys meant any harm. Have a good night, ma'am."

He returns to the coldness of the outdoors and walked slowly to his truck. Climbing behind the wheel, Delong turned the key in the ignition and switched on the wipers to clear the snow. As he put the car in reverse, he took a few seconds to glance at the second-story window where he noticed the three boys gazing down at him.

With a sigh, he backed out of the driveway, leaving the three children behind as he left to face his own problems.

Chapter 4

As DeLong stepped into his home, he pressed the button next to the kitchen door and the garage door rumbled shut.

Inside was quiet, as well it should be. He imagined Samantha and their five-year-old daughter were sound asleep upstairs. He found he was glad he didn't need to explain why he was out so much later than he'd expected—not yet, anyway.

DeLong flicked on the light and found a plate of food in the refrigerator. Next, he grabbed a can of Coke, popped it open, and chugged it, only then realizing how thirsty he was.

His eyelids grew heavy and his stomach growled with hunger. DeLong released a yawn as he placed his late-night meal of chicken and broccoli in the microwave. He punched the numbers, waited almost the full minute and stopped it before it beeped so as not to cause any more noise than necessary. DeLong stood at the counter and began eating as he thumbed through past-due bills resting on the counter.

Cable, electric, two credit cards...fantastic. The US Postal Service made it through again.

"Where were you?"

Startled, he glanced over his shoulder to find Samantha leaning against the refrigerator, arms linked over her chest. She wore a thick, white robe and her long, black hair was rumpled and loose behind her slender shoulders. The dark circles underneath her bloodshot eyes told him she hadn't been sleeping well...if at all.

She continued to stare at him, obviously waiting for him to explain why he was late.

DeLong turned to resume thumbing through the bills. "I didn't mean to wake you. I just got off work."

She was slow to begin talking, her voice in a low growl. "I spoke to you *five* hours ago, and you said you would be home by ten. It's after midnight. Where were you, Jim?"

DeLong clenched his teeth, then relaxed, willing his voice to come out without provoking anything further. "Sam, I told you, I was working. I couldn't just abandon my duties."

He turned to face her, holding the unopened envelope of their electric bill.

"Something came up. A few kids came in claiming to have seen a dead body at their school. I had to go investigate. I didn't see anything, so I went back, then took them home. After I had a talk with their parents, I came home."

For a second, it seemed he made a breakthrough. Samantha unraveled her arms.

Then came the scoff.

Underneath her breath, but loud enough for him to hear, she said, "You are such a liar! You expect me to believe that?" She blinked at him. "After the nights you've spent not coming home? Do I have 'stupid' written on my forehead?"

DeLong slapped the stack of bills on the counter with an incredulous laugh. "Oh, right. I'm a liar!" He lowered his voice, remembering his daughter was asleep. "I don't get it, Sam. I don't get why you're punishing me for doing nothing to you—nothing at all. You married a cop. I work whenever I have to work. When did you wake up and decide to hate me? I am so tired of dancing around this, Sam."

Samantha's eyes began to fill with tears. She turned from him, an obvious attempt to hide them.

He grabbed her elbow and pulled her close to him as gently as he could.

DeLong put his lips close to her ear. "I'm tired," he whispered.

Despite every effort, his voice sounded weak, like a small animal begging for its release from a snare.

As they stood in the kitchen, as he smelled the fresh scent of her hair, he felt his heart bleed open. He couldn't help but wonder if she felt the same way.

Her body quivered.

Samantha jerked out of his grip and started up the stairs. "I can't take it anymore," she replied, her voice on edge, her face hidden from him.

"Then why don't you just leave?" DeLong taunted. As soon as he said them, he regretted the words. Samantha's head snapped around, black feathers swinging in the air. For a second he saw the pain pass through her face, for just one second.

When that second passed, she glared at him as if she were shooting ice pellets through his heart. "You're sleeping down here tonight," she said, before disappearing onto the second level.

He'd been sleeping downstairs for a while...it was nothing new. He'd run out of lies to tell his daughter about why Daddy wasn't sleeping in his bedroom with Mommy.

DeLong pounded the refrigerator with his fist. He scanned the kitchen for something to throw. Grabbing his uneaten chicken, DeLong chunked it into the trashcan. Although his stomach still grumbled, yearning for food, he'd lost his appetite.

DeLong tried to calm his anger, but it didn't work.

Unopened bills, the Coke can, a towel and everything within arm's length scattered across the kitchen floor as he swept his arm across the surface.

Delong placed his palms on the granite counter and leaned over, his eyes shut, trying to draw slow, deep breaths to lower his heartbeat, but it had already lodged itself in his throat.

He headed upstairs and considered begging his wife to open the door. For almost a year, their lives had been exasperating, and they'd wasted time and energy blaming each other. Deep in the pit of his stomach, the guilt was like cancer eating away at him. He knew Samantha felt the same way. However, DeLong couldn't help but wonder if she held guilt for the same reasons he did.

Instead of knocking on the door, he peeked in Bella's room. He watched as she slept through the night in peaceful slumber. Oblivious to the surrounding drama. Dreaming whatever dreams she had.

Leaving the door ajar, DeLong returned downstairs to the living room and sprawled on the couch. He rested against the pillow, wrapping his body in the quilt already waiting for him. Always waiting for him.

He rested against the cushions, trying to forget his troubles, when his thoughts drifted to the Walker children. He saw no evidence at the swings to confirm their claim.

Then again, it was possible the snowfall destroyed the proof. Still, there wasn't a body. He would have seen that without a doubt.

DeLong remembered Claire Walker had said the boys made up stories before.

However, was this one of their stories?

He wasn't sure. It seemed real to them. Young Bobby Walker was so adamant.

Despite feeling tired, his mind wouldn't shut off.

DeLong bounced off the couch and snatched the phone book from underneath the phone in the kitchen. He searched the G's for Grimes' phone number. When he found it, he used his cell phone to call him.

By the fourth ring, DeLong had grabbed his jacket, scrawled the address on a notepad, and headed for the door.

He was no longer tired.

He had new resolve.

Pocketing the phone, he reopened the garage, revved his truck, and then backed onto the road, his tires skidding over the icy asphalt.

DeLong followed the directions of the GPS which led him to a long, curvy road in the midst of the woods. He couldn't see more than two feet in front of him. He switched on the bright lights so the misty glow would better show the way.

When DeLong reached the dead end of the road, he stopped to take in the view of Manny Grimes' home. A row of well-trimmed

The Murder of Manny Grimes

laurel hedges grew on either side of the drive as a makeshift gateway. The snow-covered road had tire tracks, which looped around in a half-circle with a willow tree resting in the center, its cold branches reaching for the white ground.

He counted eight windows on the front of the two-story house. Attached was a two-car garage on one side and a stone fence on the other.

It appeared dark inside, but DeLong detected a light flicker in the small attic window.

He parked, reached into his glove compartment for a pair of gloves, then climbed out of the truck, and padded to the window to peer inside. His view blurred by the frosted-over glass.

A shiver crawled up his spine to his neck.

The silence enshrouding him was almost deafening.

DeLong made his way to the front door and knocked, using the brass lion sculpted knocker. The door opened slightly, releasing air even colder than the winter storm. He raised his eyebrow slightly.

That was strange, he mused.

DeLong knocked, peeking his head inside.

"Mr. Grimes?"

No answer.

"Manny Grimes, my name is Lieutenant Jim DeLong. I'm with the Columbia County Sheriff's Department." He listened. "Are you home?"

Nothing.

He stepped farther into the cold house. "Hello? I just want to make sure you're okay. We had a report you might've been hurt. Please answer if you can hear me."

Still no response. DeLong felt another chill pass through him as he listened intently to the stillness. He tugged at his jacket as he continued farther into the depths of the house, his flashlight guiding the way.

DeLong went through the living room. There was a fireplace with an alcove adjacent to it, fitted with a large flat screen television. Above the TV were two rows of shelves where Grimes kept what appeared to be first editions of old books. Underneath the oversized French window sat a flowered loveseat. A matching couch faced the television.

On a rectangular coffee table lay an opened *Smithsonian* magazine next to a can of beer. Four white columns helped hold the second floor.

An office was in the room past the living area while the kitchen was open and inviting to the right side of the entrance.

DeLong made his way across the cherry wood floor to the stairs. He took one step, then another, the stairs creaking underneath his weight. He heard faint sounds upstairs that sounded like footsteps.

"Mr. Grimes, are you inside this house? I'm Lieutenant Jim DeLong from the Sheriff's office." His breath, as he spoke, evaporated into the air.

He flexed his cold, stiff fingers, frozen, even through the wool material.

The footstep-like sounds continued, but there was still no answer.

With apprehension, DeLong removed his Smith and Wesson .40 caliber from his small-of-the-back holster and held it tight in his palm.

It wasn't protocol for him to enter the premises without a warrant, let alone whip out his firearm. However, with a man reported dead, or at least missing, he had probable cause to be cautious.

Moreover, with the footsteps and after calling out for Grimes without a response, DeLong felt safer with his revolver in hand.

He continued to ascend the stairs, as silent as possible, trying to locate the sounds. But it had become quiet.

The base of his skull tingled as if the air was electrified. Something wasn't right.

From the second-floor landing, the layout of the floor was open enough for him to have a clear view of the living room and kitchen.

An oval window was set in the cathedral ceiling, showing off the starless sky. As he continued his expedition, he glanced in each room.

They were small and almost empty, ready for renovation. One room had its walls primed, with paint supplies resting on a silver cart and no furniture. A few had cherry wood floors and large boxes.

Some had furniture pushed to the center, draped with dusty tarps.

The master bedroom was a touch larger than the other rooms. The king-sized bed centered against the sidewall didn't appear slept in. A large brass picture frame clung to the wall above the bed, protecting the smiling faces of a family. The man was short and stout, his arms around the waist of a blonde woman, about an inch taller. Two young boys stood in front of the couple, looking at each other with a smirk.

Nightstands sat on both sides of the bed with a single glass lamp for decoration. The dresser sat next to French double doors, leading out to a deck. Two chairs and a table were outside. DeLong could see a large body of water, the light of the silver moon glistening against the lake as though millions of tiny diamonds were dancing on its surface, just enough light for him to see the trees on the border.

DeLong left the bedroom and found himself under the opening to the attic, with the ladder-like steps already pulled down. Weapon in hand, he ascended with caution.

The attic was dark, with the faint moonbeam shedding light through the small window. A lamp had fallen, and papers were scattered across the floor. The desk by the window had its drawers removed.

DeLong found the contents spread along the floor.

He shook his head slowly as he studied the mess.

Somebody had been here, and he was willing to bet it wasn't Manny Grimes.

So if not Grimes, then who were they and what were they looking for?

DeLong wanted to search Grimes' things in more detail, but without a crime in progress or a warrant, he had no legal grounds. A judge would throw out anything he might find, claiming it was an unlawful search.

His thoughts buzzed in his mind.

Where was Grimes?

He was not home, the house was cold, and DeLong hadn't found his body at the schoolyard. A snowstorm was going on outside. If he was in town, he should have been at the school or home.

Claire Walker mentioned Grimes' sons in Alabama. Did he go to visit them?

And, if the noises he heard didn't belong to Grimes, then who was in the house? Whoever it was must have managed to slip by him, maybe when he was looking out at the lake.

DeLong took a step to plant his foot on the top step of the ladder.

Hearing a noise, he turned to find the source of the sound, in time to be smashed hard on his left temple.

Light flashed behind his eyelids.

He groaned and plummeted down the attic hatch, trying to grasp anything but all he came up with was empty air.

His right arm and shoulder smashed into the hardwood floor.

DeLong's weapon skidded across the floor into the darkness. His flashlight went dark.

Hearing the ladder creak, DeLong clambered to his feet, his side sending waves of pain through him, making him nauseous.

He searched for his weapon, but didn't see it.

On the stairs, DeLong turned at another sound. His right leg became unbalanced, and his ankle twisted underneath his body sending him tumbling into the wall, with his left shoulder crunching on impact from all his weight. He toppled down the final steps to the floor below.

Who was it? Manny Grimes, thinking he was a burglar?

No, that didn't sit right.

Pain sliced through his head.

Get to the truck. Get help.

He staggered the rest of the way out of the house and into the snow to make his escape.

The sharp wind bit at his face. The pain in his jarred body seemed to sharpen against the cold as he limped toward the vehicle. At his truck, he fell to his knees, sinking into the snow. All DeLong wanted to do was lie down for a few minutes—ease the pain. He just wanted to close his eyes.

No, a voice in his head echoed. *You have to keep going. You need to get out of here.*

With a groan, DeLong heaved himself to his feet, fighting

against the weariness, against the pain.

His breathing was shallow. The earth spun on its axis like a top.

His blood pumped in his ears, his brain performing its own marching band. The pain sparked through his body, forcing a deep scream that seemed to echo in the distance.

DeLong realized he was losing consciousness.

The fall from the attic had jarred his body more than he thought.

He wondered if this was how Samantha felt that night—all alone—in pain while he was on night shift. Her face entered his mind.

Samantha.

He needed to get home. He wanted to get to her—be with her.

DeLong struggled to get the heavy truck door open. His left shoulder have become dislocated while his right arm and side felt as if there was more damage than he cared to think about, but he managed.

Falling into the driver's side he pulled the door shut just enough not to swing open. He didn't care about cold air coming through. He needed to get home to Samantha.

As DeLong fumbled with the key, he saw movement in the front doorway. The shadows swallowed the person's size and shape, but he noticed the moonlight reflecting off the weapon pointed straight at him. DeLong saw the flash and heard the sound of the gun firing. Reacting, he ducked out of sight. He turned the ignition, and without hesitation, sped toward the end of the road.

The cool wind whistled through the small crack of his door.

Help me.

Between the hedges, leading from Grimes' house, DeLong slammed on his brakes.

He strained to listen.

The voice and its words were fleeting.

DeLong shook his aching head. It was his imagination. It had to be the excruciating pain making him hear things.

Once again, pain shot up his leg, past his arms and through his head.

It was making it almost impossible to breathe. DeLong forced himself to put the car back in motion. He needed help.

He needed help fast.

Chapter 5

DeLong somehow managed to drive home. He didn't remember how he got there, but he came to, parked in the yard close to the front door, freezing, and it was still night. He slid out of his truck, landing on his knees as his left ankle gave way.

Stumbling toward the front door, he began calling, "Sam," too low for anyone to hear. He pulled himself up using the doorknob and fumbled with the keys until he managed to unlock the door and push it open with his body.

"Sam!" he exclaimed, breathless. When he made it to the couch, he fell to the cushions, wheezing. "Samantha!" he shouted, his voice scratchy and distant.

With relief, he heard the bedroom door opening and Samantha mumbling in anger. She darted into the living room, ready to spit fire, but her instant reaction upon seeing her husband was to run toward him.

"Jim!" she gasped. "What happened? You need to get to the hospital!"

"No," he insisted, shaking his head. "I can't go to the hospital."

"But—."

"Listen," DeLong interrupted. The pain was beginning to

weaken his mind. The freezing cold wasn't helping matters. "I-I can't waste any time. S-Someone shot at me. I fell down some stairs." He pulled in a wheezy breathe, forcing it out. "Think I've broken ribs. You're a nurse, you fix me."

"I can't—o-o-okay," she stammered, her hands making sit-still motions. She turned and rushed away to get supplies.

When she returned, she handed him some pain pills, and a bottled water. "Take this," she ordered. "It'll help with the pain."

He obliged as she began doctoring him.

After his muffled screams from attempts of removing his shirt, Samantha used scissors to cut it off. DeLong wasn't sure whether it was because of the pills or the pain of his aching body, but he soon drifted to sleep.

* * *

When DeLong woke a few hours later, the sun was shining through the sheer curtains, revealing a new day. Through his eyelashes, he saw his wife in the rocking chair by the fireplace. He heard Bella whispering something from another room. He assumed she must be playing by the stairs because every once in a while, Samantha glanced from the flashing pictures on the muted television to the little hall leading to the kitchen.

DeLong studied his wife for a few minutes. She looked a few years older. Her eyes were red and blotchy, and it didn't seem as if she'd earned much sleep.

She had pulled on a pair of jeans and a green sweatshirt, her hair wrapped in an unkempt bun. The sunlight illuminated her as if she were an angel.

Maybe she was, DeLong thought in awe as he took in her ordinary, yet extraordinary, beauty. Over the past year, he'd been amazed she'd stayed. Despite their switch from lovers to strangers, he'd seen that glimmer of hope. He wanted to hold on to it for as long as he could.

He proceeded to sit up and ask her what was wrong when pain shot throughout his body.

The events from last night came rushing back.

The Murder of Manny Grimes

He moaned, laying back down. His left arm and both legs had scrapes; his right arm and side competed for the most pain.

Samantha kept her eyes on the flickering television.

He cleared his throat in case Samantha didn't realize he had woken.

When she remained silent, he decided to make the first move.

"Thanks, you know, for last night."

For a long time, he watched her watch the TV.

Samantha continued to stare at the television. "So, when are you going to tell me what's going on?" she asked, her voice impassive.

"Manny Grimes," he told her. "That's what I was trying to tell you last night. Now I know something's wrong with him. I believe them. There's something going on."

"Believe who?" She looked at him for the first time.

He tried to read her eyes, but they stared back at him, unblinking, unwilling to share their secrets, their pain.

"You know those kids I was trying to tell you about last night...they claimed to have seen a body," he told her. "Someone named Manny Grimes."

"Wh-what are you talking about, Jim?" Samantha stammered. "You aren't making sense."

"Last night at the station, three boys came in," DeLong explained, "They were claiming to have seen Grimes' body. I went to look around at the school, but found no evidence to corroborate their story."

"And?" she pressed.

"And like I said last night, I took them home to their parents, then came straight home," he finished. "It turned out the father of two of the boys was Alan Walker. Remember the man who killed himself after killing the woman with him?"

"Jim, get to the point where you almost got yourself killed," she demanded.

"Well, last night I couldn't sleep. Something was nagging at my mind. To get rid of any doubts, I decided to go to Grimes' place and see if he was there. As I pulled up, I didn't see anyone, but I thought I saw a light in the attic window. Then when I went to knock, the oddest thing happened. The door opened, so when I went inside, I went up to the attic, but there was nothing, except a ransacked attic. What was the suspect looking for?"

DeLong's words trailed off as he drifted in his thoughts. He shook his head as if to better concentrate.

"I was about to leave the attic when all of a sudden, someone hit me. Then they took a shot at me as I was leaving in the truck."

"And you didn't see who it was?" Samantha asked.

"No," he said, disappointed. "It was too dark. Too bad they missed, a bullet would have been something to trace." He looked at his bandages wrapped around his waist and frowned.

She released a weak sound as if she didn't know whether to laugh or cry. "Don't even joke about that, Jim. I worry about you enough. You were lucky. If you had fallen the wrong way, it could've been your neck broken instead of cracked ribs. And you were shot? What do you think were you doing?"

"I'm sorry, Sam. I'm just being stupid, dealing with it all." He lifted himself off the couch. "I have to go back. Look for evidence. Look for my gun. I need—."

"Whoa! Whoa!" Samantha exclaimed. She rose, laid her hands on his shoulders to prevent him from moving. "You're not going anywhere. The weather is still bad and in your condition, you could get yourself hurt more, even killed."

"It's my job, Sam. Whether you like it or not, I need to find answers."

"Jim, right now, your job is to heal."

"Daddy, you're awake!" Bella exclaimed, rushing into the room.

Samantha caught her before Bella could jump into her father's arms.

"Honey, go play upstairs for a little while and let Daddy rest. He's real tired from working so late."

Bella frowned and crossed her arms tight over her chest and pouted.

She proceeded to obey her mother, but not before DeLong caught her to place a kiss on her cheek. "Not so fast, Princess. You know what?"

"What?" Bella giggled.

"Daddy loves his princess so much." He kissed her forehead.

"Right now, Mommy and Daddy have to talk before I dream about catching bad guys, okay?"

Bella hugged her father's neck. "Okay," she said and kissed him on the cheek before skipping out the room.

Delong waited until Bella was out of earshot. "Samantha, listen. Just hear me out. If this Grimes fella is dead, then there's a murderer on the loose. If I find his body or evidence to corroborate their story, then we can open an investigation. If I don't even try to find his body, then the killer might do away with Grimes and we'll never know the truth." He groaned, his vision spinning. "The longer I wait, the more time it gives them. My being shot at makes me believe something is going on. It's obvious someone doesn't want me to find out what happened to Grimes."

Samantha opened her mouth to speak, then shook her head with a sigh. "Where are you going first?"

He hesitated. He wanted to go back to the house, but he needed to go by the book from now on, the best way he could. However, he needed to get as much information as he could, before doing anything else.

"I need to speak to those boys."

"I don't suppose it'd be worth it for me to suggest you give this investigation over to somebody else?" she questioned.

DeLong shook his head. "Without a body, I'm sure the captain won't consider this a priority. I doubt he'd even listen to me. And if I let him know I trespassed inside Grimes' place, he'll have my head on a platter for Christmas dinner."

"Fine." Samantha spat out the word. "But I'm going with you."

DeLong rubbed his temple. "I don't suppose there's any way to talk you out of that?"

"No." She appeared set on her decision. "In your condition, you shouldn't be driving, not in this weather. I'll call the neighbors and ask them to watch Bella 'til we get back."

DeLong nodded, knowing it had to be this way or no way at all. He cleared his throat as he recalled the events of last night. "You know, I don't know if it was my imagination or what," he started as Samantha headed for the stairs, "but when I was leaving, I could have sworn I heard a voice. It said, 'help me'."

She laughed a little as she ascended the steps. "And what, you think it's this guy sending you messages from the grave? Here's what I think: you've been watching too many thrillers and you've fallen on your head too many times."

She disappeared on the second-floor landing as DeLong forced himself to sit up slow and easy. When Samantha reappeared, she helped him slip into the downstairs bathroom to clean up and then slip into fresh clothes and a heavy jacket.

Samantha slipped into her own jacket and called up the stairs, "Come on, Bella, you're going to stay with the neighbors for a little while."

Bella skipped down the steps and Samantha leaned over to help her slip into her pink coat.

"I can't believe I'm going along with this," she muttered as they exited the house.

DeLong dragged his feet to their SUV. "I can't believe I'm letting you," he called out as Samantha went next door to the neighbors, said a few words, and then hurried back. The dark sky that had taken over the city had at last lessened, allowing a few thick, white clouds to show face.

DeLong surmised the worst of the weather was over.

Not a moment too soon.

Chapter 6

Once Samantha pulled out on the road, they fell into a tense, uneasy silence, until DeLong decided it was time to break it.

"I'm sorry, Sam, about last night."

Samantha didn't respond. He looked at her, trying to figure out if she was listening. She kept her eyes focused on the road.

"Sam?"

"Yeah, I heard you." She paused. "It's not just last night. It's..."

"The miscarriage," he finished. He closed his eyes as he faced the passenger window. A lump formed in his throat, making it difficult to swallow. "We haven't spoken about it before. It's like it never happened."

For a few minutes, they dropped back into another uncomfortable silence.

"Turn here, then left at the second light."

She followed his instructions. "No," she said. "It's like *we* never happened."

He allowed the conversation to die away for a few minutes, his mind reflecting back to the past. So many regrets overshadowed his life. They say one must pick up the pieces and move forward, but it was a piece of advice DeLong could never grasp.

When they arrived at the Walkers' house, she pulled into the driveway and parked the SUV.

"I really am sorry." DeLong was solemn as Samantha looked at him.

"I should have gone to the store for you. And I shouldn't have been..."

He considered what he wanted to say, not wanting to open deeper wounds.

"I shouldn't have been angry."

She attempted a weak smile and opened the door. "That's another story," she said and left it at that. "And it could have happened to anyone."

DeLong noticed the curtains had opened in the third bedroom on the second floor, and the three boys peered out. The youngest shouted over his shoulder. With the help of Samantha, DeLong clambered out of the vehicle and they walked across the pathway. The door opened, and Jonathan Walker stepped out.

"Lieutenant DeLong," he remembered. Walker brushed away the thick snow piled at his doorsteps.

"Mr. Walker, how are you doing today?" DeLong asked.

"As well as can be expected," he replied, letting his shoulder rise and fall.

Claire Walker's smile was bright and full of the sun as she peered over her brother-in-law's shoulder. "Oh, Lieutenant DeLong," she called out. "Come in!"

DeLong waited for Walker to move aside, and then he stepped over the threshold with Samantha at his heels. She looked around, obviously uncomfortable in the situation, hugging her coat to her body.

"This is my wife, Sam," DeLong stated.

"I'm happy to meet you. Claire Walker." The women shook hands and then Claire led her guests into the living room.

"I have to say, Mrs. Walker, I just love your earrings!" Samantha exclaimed when she noticed the diamonds dangling from her lobes. "They're so breathtaking. Exquisite!"

"Thank you, Mrs. DeLong," she said and turned her earlobe for Samantha to have a closer look. "A very dear friend of mine once

The Murder of Manny Grimes

gave them to me. One of my most prized possessions. I never take them off."

She looked over at DeLong, eyeing him. "What in the world happened to you?" Claire questioned, noticing his limp.

"That's part of the reason I'm here, Mrs. Walker." He groaned as he fell into the soft chair.

DeLong focused his attention on Walker. "Have you had a chance to call your friend? Mr. Grimes?"

Walker shook his head. "I tried earlier this morning, but he didn't answer."

"Well, I'm afraid I'm beginning to think there may be some truth to what the boys were trying to tell us last night. Is it okay if I speak with them?"

"Boys, get down here, please!" Walker hollered up the stairs.

"What makes you think that?" Claire wondered.

"Last night, to satisfy my intuition," DeLong explained, "I went to Grimes' home. I didn't see anything out of the ordinary in his house, but I did hear something, then as I was leaving, someone took a shot at me."

"That's awful!" Claire exclaimed as the boys entered the room. She clamped her hands over her mouth, eyes wide.

"When was the last time you heard from him?" DeLong wondered.

Walker shrugged. "Uh, it's been a few weeks."

"Do you believe us now, mister?" Bobby asked.

"Did you find the body?" asked Tommy.

"Not yet, boys," DeLong replied. "But I am trying to find out what's going on. Why don't you run by me everything that happened at the schoolyard? Who saw Mr. Grimes first?"

"I did," Bobby said. "Then I told Tommy and George and we ran up to him."

"Tommy kicked him to see if he was alive," George put in.

"What happened then?"

"Nothing," Tommy responded. "He wouldn't move."

"Is there anything else you can remember, anything at all? Was there anyone else around? Did you hear any unusual sounds?"

Bobby went to sit by his mother, his knees propped underneath his chin. "I remember something. But it was snowing a little, and it was super foggy." He stopped, trying hard to think. "I think—I thought I saw someone standing next to Mr. Grimes. But he ran away."

"I remember seeing someone run off too," Tommy agreed. He exchanged looks with the others.

"Yeah, but we couldn't see that well 'cause it was foggy and dark," George interjected.

After a pause, DeLong assumed the boys had nothing new to tell.

"Okay, boys, that'll be all for now. Thanks for your help." DeLong looked at his wife. She appeared as though she had no idea what to do or say.

"So, do you believe us now?" George asked.

"Well, I'm not ruling out the possibility something happened to him, but I'm not saying anything did," DeLong admitted. "Without a body, I just can't prove a crime has been committed. However, I do have to admit, this whole thing is making me curious." He paused to rub his aching temple, a new habit. "It'll be hard to convince my captain to open an investigation, and because of the snow we've had, if there was ever any evidence, I doubt it's there any longer."

"So, what are you going to do now?" Claire asked, putting her arm protectively around Bobby. "Could the boys be in danger?"

"I don't think so, Mrs. Walker," DeLong assured her. "If they were unable to see his face, then I doubt the suspect saw them. As for what I'm going to do now, I suppose I can ask around."

Again, he looked at Walker, who stared into the blazing fire. "Do you have names of his friends and coworkers?"

Walker nodded. "I'll make you a list."

"I'd appreciate that. And if you happen to have a recent photo of him, that'd be great."

"Give me just a second," Walker muttered as he disappeared up the stairs.

"Is there anything you may know about Grimes you can tell me?" he asked Claire.

"I didn't know him that well, but he was close friends with my husband and Jonathan for many years. I think they went to school

The Murder of Manny Grimes

together. Something happened between them not too long ago. Jonathan won't talk about it much. But I knew it was upsetting him."

Walker returned with a page of notebook paper and a photo. "He's an assistant principal at the boys' school. I wrote some of his coworkers' names and addresses, but I don't know them all. He kept to himself and didn't have a lot of friends. Also, I wrote down Sarah Benson's phone number. That's his ex-wife. And this photo was taken about a year or so ago. It's the most recent I have."

Accepting the photo and list, DeLong rose, Samantha following suit. He shook the boys' hands, nodding at Claire and her brother-in-law.

"Thank you for your time once again."

"Let us know what happens?" Claire asked.

"I will," DeLong promised.

Once they were outside, they walked in silence to the SUV, DeLong deep in thought.

"Jim?" Samantha began as they climbed into the car. "Will you do me a favor?"

DeLong gave her a sidelong glance. He'd known her long enough to know what she was thinking. And he had to agree it was a good idea.

"Okay, I'll call Russ."

Chapter 7

Once they returned home, DeLong searched his phone's contact list for the one man he trusted most: Russell Calhoun.

Calhoun was a retired criminal investigator for the Navy, and DeLong's oldest friend and mentor.

"Hey, buddy!" DeLong said when his friend answered.

"Jim!" Calhoun exclaimed. "How are ya, kid?"

"Good," DeLong told him, attempting to mask the groan escaping his lips. He put his hand on his aching side as if it would ease the pain.

"Ya know, I sure am," Calhoun snickered.

"Yeah? What are you going for this time?"

"A reddie," Calhoun said in a hushed voice. "She lives in the apartment two doors down."

"Still keeping them coming, huh? Well, I hate to bother you, man," DeLong told him. "But I'm calling because I need your help."

"You know I'm there. What's up?"

He explained the events so far regarding Manny Grimes and the incident at his house.

When Delong finished, he let the story sink in. As he waited, he twisted his body so he could punch the pillows, then lay down,

The Murder of Manny Grimes

finding a comfortable position.

Calhoun released a whistle. "Tell me what you need me to do."

Samantha entered the living room and handed DeLong a glass of tea.

"I need you to help me come up with something. Help me find Grimes. He's got to be somewhere, dead or alive."

"Shouldn't you be talkin' to the captain about this?"

"I should, but I'm not," DeLong replied. "Not yet, anyway. I need to find out if this is even worth dragging in my guys or not. As it is, the captain will have my head when he hears I helped myself to Grimes' house without a warrant—and then got shot at in the process."

Calhoun released a loud sigh. Though DeLong was unable to see his old friend through the phone line, he pictured him nodding in agreement.

"Yeah, sure. You know I'll help. Whatever you need."

"First, begin at his home. I didn't do any thorough investigating. My head might have been playing tricks on me as far as the voice went, but I know I heard someone shuffling around in the attic. And from the looks of it, they were looking for something."

"If that's true, they probably found it if it was to be found."

"True, but it's possible I scared them off, so be careful. They might show up again."

"All right," Calhoun replied. DeLong could hear the rustle of paper. "What's the address?"

After he told him, DeLong said, "Listen, I've got to go. Just go as soon as you can."

"Will do."

They ended the call and DeLong rubbed his hand over his face, closing his eyes. He needed to call his captain to inform him he wouldn't be able to make it to work. Even if he wanted to, there was no way he'd be able to pretend he wasn't injured.

Still holding his phone, he punched in his boss's cell number.

However, it wasn't his captain's voice on the other end of the line.

Help me, a harsh voice whispered.

"Hello?" DeLong lifted himself off the couch. "Cap?"

Help me, the voice repeated.

DeLong let out a curse. "Who is this?"

"Is that any way to speak to your superior, Lieutenant? You called *me*, remember?"

DeLong's heartbeat against the rib cage as he pushed air from his lips. "Captain. No sir." He shook his head to clear it. "I'm sorry. I thought I heard—never mind. It's crazy. I just wanted to inform you I won't be making it in today. I took a bad fall on the stairs last night. I pretty much broke my body."

"I'm sorry to hear that," Captain Stewart said, "Those stairs can be a killer."

DeLong released an inward chuckle. His boss had no idea. "Yes sir, they are."

"Okay. Thanks for checking in. Get some rest. Come on in when you're able. I'm sure we'll be able to manage without you for a little while."

"All right, Cap. I should be well enough to come in tomorrow," DeLong said, ending the conversation. He tossed the cell phone on the coffee table.

"I put Bella down for her nap," Samantha said as she knelt by the couch to check on his bandages.

"I'm sure she's all fussy after being around the sitter's noisy kids."

"Yeah," Samantha muttered. She hesitated a beat. "Are you sure you'll be able to go in tomorrow?" Her voice was full of disapproval and concern.

"I have to, Sam. Too many things I've got to do."

"Yeah, but..."She trailed off, shaking her head.

Samantha didn't speak again until a few minutes had passed, and she rose to sit in her rocking chair. "Will we ever get back to where we were, Jim?"

He gawked at her, shocked by the out-of-the-blue question. He had to admit he'd wondered the same thing many nights. As he looked at her, at the mixture of concern and pain etched on her face, he began to remember the Samantha he married. She was different back then. Now she was grown up, but he still could see the Sam he used to know peek around the wall she had built.

The Murder of Manny Grimes

It was painful, but he rose from the couch to kiss her cheek.

"We will," he assured her in a soft whisper. DeLong moved away and lifted the corner of his mouth with a crooked smile. "It might take a while, but we will. I want us to work. Maybe we should go for some counseling. It's helped others. Maybe it'll do the same for us."

"I'm so sorry," she whispered. "You have no idea how sorry I am."

"Don't be," he muttered. "Please don't be. I'm the cause of all this. I know I'm not always easy to live with. And being a cop doesn't help matters much."

She shook her head, stifling tears.

"Sam, I put so much work into blaming myself when you had that car accident," he continued as he lowered himself on the couch, "That I ended up blaming you for it all and I shouldn't have. I was late getting home that day. I should have gone to the store when you asked me to. End of story."

A tear fell from her eyes. "Not quite, Jim."

"What do you mean?"

Samantha gave a slight smile and shook her head. "Nothing. You should get some rest."

She handed her husband the television remote and left the room. A few minutes later, she returned with the tea pitcher and refilled his glass.

DeLong didn't refuse the pain pills his wife held in her palm.

She sat in her rocking chair. The chair made soft squeaking sounds as she rocked with a slow, practiced rhythm.

"Maybe, once things get better between us, we can try again," DeLong suggested, "for another baby."

Samantha didn't respond, and when he tilted his head her way, he saw her eyes closed. She looked peaceful, reminding DeLong again of an angel.

"Sam?"

She didn't answer him, and he didn't press on.

He tried to focus on the storyline of *Miami Vice*, but the pill didn't take long to do its job. Within a blink, he was out.

Chapter 8

Russell Calhoun, a graying man in his fifties, set his phone on the table and glanced at the sleeping redhead next to him. He hated the thought of leaving her. His eyes skimmed over her body, at the sheet outlining the curves of her figure. When he lay next to her, it was as though she had been molded to fit perfectly into him.

So warm.

So graceful.

But, when his friend called and told him the story, Calhoun's interest peaked. It hadn't been too long since he retired, but in his mind, it was a lifetime ago and he wanted to get back in the game.

So, as not to wake her, Calhoun slipped out of bed and dressed.

Since he didn't own a curtain, the sun shone through the window enough for him to throw on a tee and jeans without overhead lights.

Checking his reflection in the mirror, Calhoun fluffed his hair with a comb.

Some men don't like it when their hair begins to turn gray.

Calhoun used to be one of those men.

Thinking he was getting too old was one of the reasons which prompted his retirement, but he quickly learned over this past year and a half that a lot of young women thought the gray was sexy.

Such as the redhead neighbor who slept soundly in his bed.

He scribbled out a note explaining to her that he was called out for important business and he should only be a few hours. He also told her to help herself to anything in the fridge.

Calhoun paused, staring at the note. Then he added, "I hope to see you when I get back."

Satisfied, he left the note on his pillow, took one last look at his latest affection, and grabbed his coat.

He locked the door, nodding his head at a neighbor stepping out to retrieve his newspaper. The neighbor reciprocated and returned to his home, leaving Calhoun alone in the hallway.

Calhoun made his way to the elevator at the end of the hall and pressed the button to the lobby.

Seconds later, he stepped out of the lobby doors. He sucked in a chilled breath, shuddered and tugged at his jacket.

The sun had finally shown its face, revealing the severity of the winter storm from the days before.

Residents of his building were scattered outside, helping to remove debris from cars and out of the roadway.

Calhoun passed by a blonde and flashed a smile in acknowledgment as he skimmed his eyes up and down her body. The sharp wind disheveled her hair, sweeping it in her face.

He didn't remember seeing her around before and thought to himself that he would like to see her again.

She returned a shy smile as she dragged a branch from under a car.

The new girl looked as though she was holding her own, so Calhoun continued for his truck, which by some string of faith was left untouched from the thick tree limbs. Snow covered the hood and roof. He removed the tarp covering the trunk bed, shaking it free of snow. Then he climbed behind the wheel and turned the key. As his engine roared to life, he replayed last night's lovemaking in his mind. He could still feel her warm, silky skin gliding across his.

Calhoun sighed heavily as he began to drive in the direction of Grimes' house.

As he drove, he allowed himself the excitement that maybe he might become involved with something else for a change.

Of course, he loved the company of different women every day. It made him feel alive. Needed. But he was human. He wanted a change of pace. Especially since he'd been cooped in his stuffy apartment for the past few days. There was a void in the center of his heart that could never be filled.

Maybe a little detective work would help him fill some of that empty space.

Calhoun easily found Manny Grimes' house tucked away in the woods. After he pulled up to the door and set his gear into park, he checked to make certain his Smith and Wesson was loaded. Then he slipped the gun in his pants and climbed out of the truck.

It wasn't easy stepping through the snow, but when he made it to the door, Calhoun knocked and then turned the knob. He called out, listening for *any* sound of life.

His flashlight filled almost the entire living room.

So far, the house seemed to be in a deep sleep.

Calhoun went around the sofa, admiring the Greek look of the columns and the alcove which fit the television nicely.

The room past the living area looked to be Grimes' office. Calhoun lifted the lid of the laptop and tapped the mousepad with a pen from his shirt pocket. A password prompt appeared.

Still using the pen, he opened the drawers, where he found a burgundy book in the third one down. The edge was old and ratty and the pages were hanging by a thread.

Using the camera option on his phone, Calhoun took a photo and then reached into the drawer to open the book, skimming through. It appeared to be a man's journal. He returned the book to the drawer and left the room to go to the one across from the office.

A large pool table, with two pool sticks leaning against it, stood in the middle. Calhoun ran his fingers along the green surface until he touched an eight ball on the verge of sliding in the side pocket.

An unfinished game, he mused. Being a pool shark himself, Calhoun respected Grimes' table, which must have cost him big bucks. Walking around, he made a mental note to invite DeLong to play a game of pool with him for old time's sake.

Calhoun opened the drawers of a small desk sitting underneath a

The Murder of Manny Grimes

life-sized picture of *Mona Lisa*. He skimmed through thin notebooks, which had few, if any, writings. As Calhoun turned to leave, he spotted a torn piece of notebook paper lying on the floor by the table. Snapping a picture, he knelt to pick it up and read what he assumed to be Grimes' messy handwriting.

MC at Columbia. Dec. 2, 9:00 p.m.

"Hmm," he muttered to himself. "That was the other day. MC…"

Calhoun glanced out the double French doors leading to the backyard. The deck overlooked a vast lake with patches of floating ice. A white-tailed deer sprang from the woods in the distance, glanced around, then dashed out of sight.

Calhoun left the billiard room to check the kitchen.

He opened the cabinets and refrigerator, seeing that Grimes had a multiple of almost everything in stock.

"Seems you've fully prepared for this storm, Grimes," Calhoun observed. "Doesn't look to me like you were planning a trip."

A note on the fridge read *get house ready for Sarah and boys' visit December 16,* the date circled in red ink and beneath the writing was a list of tasks left to do.

"No, Grimes, I don't believe you were going anywhere," Calhoun stated. "So where are you now?"

On one side of the kitchen was a small bar room and on the other side was a door leading to the two-car garage.

Empty.

He closed it to go up the steps to the second-floor landing. Quickly seeing there wasn't much to check on in the rooms prepped for remodeling, he found the master bedroom.

Inspecting the space where Grimes slept, he saw the bed made. As he went to open the first drawer of the dresser, his boot hit something under the edge of the heavy piece of furniture and skidded noisily.

Kneeling, Calhoun's flashlight glinted off something metallic.

A gun. He removed a handkerchief from his pocket and pulled the revolver out for a closer look. Yep, it was DeLong's. Calhoun

Angela Kay

had seen it enough times on the firing range to know it by sight. Putting the gun in his jacket pocket, he rose and inspected the dresser.

He felt underneath the neatly folded garments but found nothing to tell him where Grimes may have gone.

Inside the walk-in closet, his shirts and pants were pressed and evenly spaced by one finger.

"Talk about a neat freak," Calhoun mused. "But it doesn't seem like anything's missing."

Calhoun pulled the ladder leading to the attic and climbed. He looked around the chaotic space. He had to agree with DeLong. Someone was definitely on a mission for something.

Did they find it?

Hard to tell.

Rummaging through the papers, he found a check for five thousand dollars made out to cash, signed by Jonathan Walker.

"Why was Mr. Walker giving you a personal check for five grand?"

Calhoun added the evidence in his phone's photo gallery.

The bottom drawer was locked. The keyhole was scuffed around the edges as if someone had attempted to force it open. Calhoun searched around for the key.

He looked under coats, in files, and in old jewelry boxes stuffed with paperwork. Finally giving up on the key, he took one last look around and climbed out of the attic.

He closed the hatch behind him and went back downstairs, heading for the truck.

As Calhoun slid behind the wheel, his grumbling stomach reminded him he skipped breakfast and lunch. He reached behind his seat, opened the cooler and grabbed potato chips he was glad he had forgotten about. Eating hungrily at the stale chips, and licking his fingers, he turned the ignition and drove around the semi-circular driveway and away from Grimes' home.

Calhoun drummed his fingers against the dashboard, humming with Andy Williams telling him it was beginning to look a lot like Christmas. Calhoun glanced away from the road to lower his heater setting. When he looked back, he slammed his foot on the brakes and skidded along the road, his truck spinning in fast circles.

Earthly colors swirled in blurs before the side of the truck jarred against a tree. His head slammed against the steering wheel on impact.

Calhoun gripped his forehead, groaning in pain. After several seconds passed, and he realized he was still breathing, he clambered out of the vehicle to look around. The collision with the tree shook all the snow and ice off the leaves and onto the bed of his truck.

He didn't see the black dog that had darted in front of him. It would be a miracle if he didn't hit him. It all happened so fast, Calhoun wasn't sure.

He let out a harsh groan. He decided it was too snowy and too cold to worry about a stupid black dog. Looking his truck over, he checked to make sure there was no damage. Everything checked out except for the ding on the passenger side where he rammed into the tree.

Getting back behind the wheel, he turned the ignition a few times before it finally rumbled back to life. He pulled away and resumed his course to DeLong's, half expecting to see a black dog with its black eyes lying on the side of the road.

Chapter 9

Calhoun pulled into the driveway of DeLong's house, parking behind the SUV.

He walked to the front door and let himself in with his key, announcing his arrival.

"Yeah, in here," DeLong called out.

"Hey, kid." Calhoun stepped into the living room, eyed his friend lying on the couch, two pillows propped behind his head. He was shirtless, revealing the bandages wrapped around his ribs.

DeLong reached for the remote and muted the television. He didn't bother sitting up.

Calhoun let out a friendly tease. "You ain't too bad. I half expected Sam to have covered you in a full body cast." He plopped himself in the rocking chair by the fire. "How you feelin'?"

"A little achy and tired, but I'm good. What happened to you? You look like crap."

"Thanks." Calhoun gave a sarcastic laugh, rubbing his forehead. "Had a little accident on the way over here. Nothin' serious, though. Dang dog ran right in front of me. Should've hit him instead of swerving into a tree, bangin' up my truck."

"Don't say that to Samantha," DeLong said. "You know as well

The Murder of Manny Grimes

as I do she's big into those animal rights movements and the humane society."

"Yeah, don't I?" Calhoun responded. "She once dragged me to one of those picketing things when you were out of town. Not my idea of a good time."

"Imagine being married to her," DeLong said, pointing his index finger at his friend. "I must've gone to a dozen of those things with her. They aren't all bad, but don't tell her I said that."

On cue, Samantha walked into the room, followed by Bella, who helped carry a box of first aid supplies.

"We thought we heard voices," Samantha said with a soft smile.

Bella ran to Calhoun. "Uncle Russ!"

He wrapped her in a big bear hug and then sat her on his lap.

"You're getting so big! You're all grown up now. I better put you in a bottle so you'd stop it."

Samantha shook her head. "You don't know the half of it. Would you guys like some coffee?"

"That'd be great," Calhoun replied. He focused his attention on Bella.

"You know, you're gettin' prettier and prettier. Thank goodness you don't have your old man's ugly mug."

She giggled.

"How old are you again? Thirty?"

"No!" Bella tilted her head back with laughter.

"Ah, okay. Then forty?"

She giggled again. "I'm five!"

"Five? No way," Calhoun said in mock surprise. From the kitchen, Samantha called for Bella. "Uh-oh. What'd you do?"

"Nothing," Bella replied with a frown. Samantha called her again, and with a groan, she gave Calhoun another bear hug and then ran to her mother.

A few minutes later, Samantha returned with the tray of coffee.

"Here," she said, handing the mugs to her husband and Calhoun. "I'll be in the kitchen cleaning if you need me. I'll let you two talk business, then I'll change your bandage."

"How're things goin' with you two?" Calhoun asked when Samantha was out of earshot.

51

"We're workin' it out. There's a lot of mess to clean up." DeLong paused, looking toward the kitchen doorway. "There's just something she's hiding. I can't figure out what it is." Clearing his throat, he added, "But I guess we both have skeletons in our closets." DeLong shook his head slightly. "Well, let's get to talkin' Grimes. I want to hear what you found." He slowly righted himself to a seated position.

Calhoun took a sip of coffee.

"Well, there was nothing I found that's definite for one thing or another," Calhoun began.

"But you did find something?"

"Depends on what 'something' is. I found this." He pulled DeLong's revolver from his pocket and passed it to him.

"Thanks. That could have been bad if the guy had gotten hold of it," DeLong said.

DeLong inspected his gun as Calhoun continued.

"And then I found some other things. Here." Calhoun tapped the screen on his cell phone so he'd be in his photo gallery. He proceeded to tell DeLong what he found, starting with the check.

"This is curious," DeLong said as he enlarged the image. "It was made out less than a week ago. Walker told me he hadn't seen Grimes for several weeks."

"Maybe he didn't think about it," Calhoun suggested.

"How can anyone not think about writing a check for five grand?" DeLong countered.

"Good point," Calhoun agreed.

"Always so optimistic," DeLong teased, as he swiped the screen and read to himself.

"MC," he muttered thoughtfully.

"Found that on the floor in the billiard room. Grimes was supposed to have been somewhere or met with someone two nights ago. I also found a journal in his office, but only skimmed through it. We can go back and get it if we open the investigation. He has a laptop that's password-protected. We can have someone in to crack it. In the kitchen, the cabinets and fridge were stocked full of food and crap." Calhoun scratched the back of his head. "Jim, it seemed to me that he was getting ready to be staying in for a few weeks.

Must have gone shopping when the news first said they were expecting a major winter storm. If he left, it was either an emergency or not by his own choice. Either way, he's vanished without a trace."

"Well, that's hardly enough to begin an investigation," DeLong muttered.

"There was a note on the fridge," Calhoun remembered. "I almost forgot about it. It said, 'get house ready for Sarah's and the boys' visit December 16.' He had circled the date and made a long list of things he needed to do and get, such as more paint, carpet, furniture. It goes on."

"There still could be many reasons for Grimes disappearing," DeLong mused. "But if he circled the date, it likely means that it was important to him." DeLong paused. "It's a big house, you know."

"What are you thinking?"

DeLong gazed at him.

"I'm thinking it's a big house. Much too big for one man. He could have been trying to prepare it, make it just right so his sons could visit more often. Maybe even permanently."

"That sounds plausible," Calhoun said thoughtfully.

"It's still nothing but conjectures," DeLong reminded him. "But I'll see if Captain Stewart will allow us to treat this as a missing person."

Calhoun downed the last bit of his coffee and placed the mug on the table. "Actually, I've been plannin' to swing by there one of these days, anyway. I'll go with you for backup. Maybe with the two of us, he'll be willing to listen."

"Nice job, Russ," DeLong commended. "And thanks."

"Anytime, Jim. How 'bout I meet you here tomorrow morning. I'll drive."

"Fine with me. Now, you go on home and get back to that reddie of yours." DeLong flashed him a wide grin.

Calhoun reached toward the couch to give DeLong a firm handshake.

"Take care of yourself and I'll see you tomorrow."

Chapter 10

"We don't have the time to go searching for a missing person that hasn't yet been reported missing."

Captain Stewart listened intently to DeLong's story before shaking his head in annoyance.

"But, sir," DeLong protested, "the kids reported him at the school and—."

Though he likely already knew the answer, Stewart asked, "When you investigated, did you see Grimes at the school? Or any evidence that corroborated these children's claims?"

"No," DeLong admitted.

"I'm sorry, Lieutenant, but I'm not going to allow you to run around town, searching for a man that more than likely got out of Dodge. I don't appreciate that a member of *my* team," Stewart jabbed a thumb toward his chest, "and entered another person's home without permission. And convinced a civilian to do the same." The captain glared from DeLong to Calhoun and back again.

"Captain Stewart," Calhoun put in. He had been seated quietly, listening as the lieutenant recounted once again what had happened the day before. Now he rose to put in his two cents. "I believe something happened to Grimes. I went to his house on my own

The Murder of Manny Grimes

accord. Everything Jim just told you, I stand by. Something happened to this man. We have a duty to find out what. Captain, if we come up with nothing, or we find out we've been chasing our tails, then I'll eat my jacket."

Stewart narrowed his eyes in Calhoun's direction and crossed his arms. "You think this is funny, Calhoun? I would have thought better of you than to be involved in a wild goose chase. Entering a man's premises without a warrant? I should throw the book at you." He glared at DeLong again. "Actually, I should throw the book at both of you."

He sighed and leaned back in his chair, uncrossing his arms and linking his hands behind his head. He continued to glare between the two men.

"All right," he said after minutes passed. "DeLong, I've known you long enough to know that ninety times out of a hundred, your instincts are sound. You want to search for the man, then fine." He held both palms in the air, then slowly lowered them flat on the desk and leaned forward. "But do not, I repeat do not, do anything that would require a warrant until you have probable cause to actually *get* a warrant. Keep me posted. I'll give you two days to either find Grimes or hard evidence that he is actually missing. Two days. That is all."

"Yes, sir. Thank you, Captain," DeLong said with a satisfied nod.

"Yes, thank you," Calhoun echoed.

"I have to run out for a little while," the captain said with a sigh. He rose, straightening his shirt uniform. "Try not to waste too much of my time. Or yours."

"Yes, sir," DeLong acknowledged as he left the office.

"Where do you want to start?" Calhoun wondered, trailing after him.

"I suppose we should go back to the schoolyard," DeLong said, halfway out the door. "Maybe between the two of us, we'll find something I overlooked when I first looked around." Outside, DeLong blew into his hands to warm them. "Honestly, I just wanted to get out of the station a little bit. But I didn't want to go home. Sam has me sleeping on the couch these days. Anyway, I wasn't really

55

sure what I was looking for. The body wasn't there. The snow we had would have destroyed most, if not all, the evidence."

At the truck, they slid inside. DeLong adjusted the heat as Calhoun set the gear in motion. "I just want to be sure we've covered all our bases. Then let's go back to the Walkers'. I want to know more about Jonathan Walker's friendship with Manny Grimes."

Chapter 11

DeLong remained quiet. He wasn't sure what they'd find, if anything. He knew chances of finding valid evidence would be extremely slim.

There was not a body to be found. If there was once any blood, the snow would have soaked it up.

DeLong and Calhoun trailed around the schoolyard. The side door to the school was locked.

"There're a number of possible reasons why Grimes can't be found." Calhoun broke into DeLong's thoughts. "Maybe he had to rush out of town. Maybe something happened to one of his kids and he had to go to them."

They found themselves back at the swing set.

DeLong began pacing, rubbing his hand on the nape of his neck.

"There's something missing. Something we aren't seeing. They claimed to have seen someone standing over the body."

"It was very foggy. Hard to see. Maybe they saw a couple of dogs."

"Let's think," DeLong said, ignoring the statement. He turned to look at Calhoun's flushed face. "Let's just go with that the boys did see somebody. They saw a person standing over something."

As he spoke, he stepped in front of the swings, motioning with his hands.

"This person sees three people in the distance heading his way. It's dark and foggy, so he doesn't know it's only kids. Either way—."

"He runs," Calhoun finished, tracking along.

"The kids are naturally curious," DeLong continued. "After all, why would anyone be out that late at night with the weather being the way it's been? So they come over to see what's going on. They see a dead man on the ground. But no one else is around. The other guy had already gone with the wind."

"So they do the right thing and get help. When you come to investigate, there isn't anything out of the ordinary."

"Right." DeLong looked around, his mind reeling.

"What I'd like to know is why Grimes and his killer were on the school playground in the first place?" Calhoun said. "What purpose would that serve? Was Grimes into something illegal? Was he killed here? Just moments before the perp received company?"

In the distance, DeLong saw work vehicles pull to the front of the school and a few workers in hardhats climbed out. To assess the damage, he surmised. A woman wearing a pantsuit and a posture of authority stepped out of her car. Maybe the principal.

DeLong pulled out the paper Walker had given him with the list of names connected to Grimes.

The first was Principal Janice Cook.

"Let's go ask her," DeLong pointed.

Together, they made their way to the front of the building.

"Principal Cook," DeLong called out.

The principal, hearing her name, glanced over and then met them halfway.

"Yes?" She looked slightly annoyed at the interruption.

"I'm Lieutenant Jim DeLong. This is Russell Calhoun. We're investigating a possible disappearance. Your assistant principal, Manny Grimes."

"Mr. Grimes?" Principal Cook repeated.

"Yes, ma'am, when's the last time you heard from him?"

"Uh," Cook looked to the sky as though she would find the

The Murder of Manny Grimes

answer written in the clouds. "About a week ago, I think. Mr. Grimes wanted to let me know he was going to use the opportunity to get work done. I told him to worry about it when we return. But he was insistent." The principal shrugged. "He likes to keep busy. I don't think he enjoys being all alone in that house of his, so he works a lot."

"And he didn't mention going away? Maybe to see his sons?"

Principal Cook shook her head. "He talks about his sons all the time. I know he misses them. He was excited about them and his ex-wife coming for a visit during the break. But Mr. Grimes never said anything to me about going to see them."

DeLong found a business card and handed it to the principal.

"If there is anything you remember will you give me a call? And if you hear from Mr. Grimes, have him call us."

"Of course," Cook replied with a smile. "I'm sorry to rush, but I need to go see where all the damage is and what we'll need to do to fix it."

"Thank you for taking the time," DeLong told her.

When she walked away, Calhoun said, "Whatever the reason was that made them come to the school, they had to want to dispose of Grimes."

DeLong nodded, then lifted a hand toward the other end of the schoolyard. "Over there. The trash. If I was going to come back to rid of the body, I might take him over to the dumpsters and toss him."

Calhoun nodded in agreement. "Guess we'll go digging in the trash."

When they arrived at the set of dumpsters, DeLong claimed one while Calhoun took the other. After long minutes crawled by, they were satisfied there wasn't a body hidden among the trash.

As he climbed out, DeLong's stomach growled.

"Think I'll check to see what Sam has in mind for lunch," he said as Calhoun slid the door of the second dumpster shut. "You hungry?"

"Nah, I'll go catch up with some buddies at the station house. See what's new."

They left the school to drop DeLong off at home. After they

arrived, DeLong climbed out with a soft moan, a ghost of a reminder of his pain.

Tell Sam I said I'll see her 'round," Calhoun said.

"Sure thing, man," DeLong replied, patting the hood. He watched Calhoun pull away and then made his way up the drive.

He found Samantha curled up on the couch with two blankets tucked around her body, watching some kind of soap opera.

"Hey," he said softly. He leaned against the doorway, staring at her.

Her hair was wrapped in a loose bun and she had slipped into his old Harvard sweatshirt, two sizes too large for her. It had always been her favorite thing to wear on a lazy day.

"Hey," she replied with a yawn. "How'd it go with Captain Stewart?"

"He gave us two days to find Grimes."

"Good for you," she muttered sleepily.

"Have you had lunch, yet?"

She glanced at the clock above the fireplace.

"No. I didn't realize time had gone by so fast. Chicken soup good?"

DeLong nodded.

Samantha let out another yawn and rose.

He changed the channel to a movie as she fixed them lunch, and when she called out to him, he wrapped one of the blankets around his body and stepped into the kitchen.

They fell into an awkward silence as they ate until Samantha decided to break it.

"Any leads?"

"Not yet," he said, absentmindedly blowing on the broth. "According to the principal, it was possible Grimes showed up at the school to do some work. Russ and I looked around the trash bins in case Grimes was dumped in there. We didn't find anything though."

"I was wondering what that horrific smell was."

DeLong smiled at Samantha's smirk. "Sorry. Guess I better shower before I leave again."

"And then shower a few more times."

DeLong took another slurp of his soup, thankful to have a

moment of normality with his wife. However, they soon slipped into another awkward silence.

"We're going back to the Walkers' after lunch."

"Okay," Samantha replied.

"So, what are your plans for the rest of the day?" he asked, determined to keep the conversation going.

She shrugged. "I don't know. Probably stay home. I need to go shopping, but but I'd rather stay close to home. I might go next door and borrow some bread to fix with the roast tonight."

He nodded. "You should go visit a friend or something. I'll be in and out more than likely, but Russ and I are going to be busy trying to find Grimes. The two days will go by fast—"

"You don't need to explain anything, Jim," she put in, placing her spoon back in the bowl. She rose with her dishes in hand and dumped them in the sink.

"What's going on, Sam?" he asked.

"Nothing," she answered. "Why?"

"Because—never mind," he replied. He rose. "I'm going to go take a hot shower."

He departed up the stairs before Samantha had a chance to respond.

DeLong figured a nice, hot shower might just be the medicine he needed to soothe his achy body and to clear his head.

Chapter 12

Balancing three boxes of donuts, Calhoun opened the door and stepped into the sheriff's department. He acknowledged Nancy behind her station and made his way through the hall.

He found the break room and set the boxes on the table where sugar-deprived officers started picking through the treats.

"Come here, I'll introduce you."

Calhoun turned, hearing Captain Stewart's voice.

"Nice to see a familiar face, Calhoun," Stewart said.

Calhoun extended his hand to shake the captain's. "Good to see you again, 'Chief.'"

"This man was famous for his treats while we were in the service together. I see today is no exception," Stewart acknowledged to his companion, flipping open each box and inspecting the contents before choosing.

"Calhoun, this is Max Greene. He's an old friend of mine from back in the day."

Greene wore a beige overcoat and a fedora, reminding Calhoun a little of Dick Tracy. They shook hands.

"Navy?"

"You called it," Greene replied in an accent from somewhere

northwest. "You served as well, huh?"

As he removed his coat, Calhoun tilted his head toward the captain.

"For a time. I was stationed in Charleston right alongside this man, way back when he was Master Chief Petty Officer and I was a special agent in the criminal investigative service."

"Well, what do you know?" Greene chuckled. "That's very impressive, I dare say. Well, Mike. I suppose I'll go ahead and take off. I'll meet with you again later." He shook his head toward Calhoun. "A pleasure to meet you. I hope we'll will again someday soon."

They shook hands and Greene exited the room.

"So," Stewart said in between bites of his cream-filled treat. "We've got a bit of catching up to do. Still a ladies' man, Calhoun? Or have you thought about settling down these days?"

"Well," Calhoun began. He padded over to the coffee maker. "I thought about it briefly." Calhoun filled his cup. "But then I decided that as a bachelor, I could be in the company of more than just one woman. The idea of settling down can be amusing, but eventually, it loses its charm. I like having choices."

Stewart chuckled. "I know how that is. Used to be that way when I was younger. Then I got married."

"How is Anna doing? She still head chef at that French restaurant up in Charleston?"

"She owns it now," Stewart said. "As far as how she's doing, I can't really say. We're divorced. And it hasn't exactly been cordial. Hence my retirement down here. Heard the position opened up, had the desire to start a new life. And met up with some old acquaintances, too. Felt like home."

"I'm sorry to hear about the divorce, man," Calhoun replied.

"Never easy being a cop's wife. Just ask your pal, DeLong."

Stewart finished his donut and went to snatch another one. "Working on a man's supposed disappearance doesn't seem like you've been enjoying your own retirement too much."

"Well, it's been nice, Chief," Calhoun said. "But I do miss bein' on the job." He laughed lightly as he inspected the remaining two donuts. He decided to go with the lemon crème.

Stewart took a bite, and followed the raspberry donut with a swig of his coffee. He motioned for Calhoun to follow him to his office. "Any thoughts on coming out of retirement on an official basis?"

"Actually, yeah," Calhoun admitted. "I didn't realize how much I missed investigative work until recently."

"Well, don't count this Grimes guy as part of investigative work," Stewart said, making himself comfortable in his chair behind the messy desk. He picked up paperwork as though he were tidying up. "Let me know if you want to come back, Calhoun. I'd love to have you on my team. We need a good investigator on board."

"I'll keep that in mind," Calhoun replied with a broad smile, hanging his coat on the back of the chair.

"What are your thoughts, anyway?" Stewart asked. "About this guy? Think he really is missing? Or that he skipped town?"

"I dunno," Calhoun admitted, his mouth full. "At first glance, I'd say something happened to him. And DeLong, you know, he has the best instincts I've ever known a person to have. He really believes something happened. And remember, he was attacked while in Grimes' house."

"I know," Stewart said. "Could have been Grimes himself. But, either way, that's part of the reason I'm allowing DeLong to look into this." He glimpsed at the clock hanging on the wall to the left. "Wow, time's flying like the wind today. I don't mean to push you out, but I've got work to do," he told Calhoun, pointing to the stack of files he had just straightened, "and I suppose so do you."

Calhoun rose and shook the captain's hand firmly. "Yeah, well, guess I'll be seeing you around, possibly more than we may think."

"We ought to get a cold one now and then," Stewart offered.

"It's a date." Calhoun agreed. He grabbed his coat off the chair and stepped out of the office, shutting the door behind him. Slipping his arms through the sleeves of his coat, he nodded to the officers, slapped a few on the shoulder, and headed for the door.

Chapter 13

The hot shower DeLong took hit the spot. He was warm, muscles were relaxed, pain dormant.

For the time being.

He combed back his hair, shaved his five o'clock shadow and splashed on aftershave.

Tuning into Samantha humming as she folded laundry in the adjoining room, DeLong picked up his black and gray striped dress shirt and stood in the doorway watching her as he dressed.

"Can we talk?" DeLong asked.

"About what?" Samantha said distantly.

DeLong leaned against the doorframe. "Us. You and me." He fidgeted with his shirt button so he wouldn't have to look at his wife. He had decided as he took his shower that if they were going to try to fix their marriage, then everything needed to be brought out into the open. And he decided he needed to be the one to begin talking. Find out what kept her closed off from him.

He forced himself to look at her. "We need to talk about what's been happening between us."

Samantha lifted her eyes to gaze at him for a second, then carefully folded Bella's shirt on top of another shirt.

DeLong went to her, grasped her shoulders so he could turn her to face him. He looked gazed into her sad eyes, wondering what she had hidden behind them. His heart weighed heavy in his chest. He felt a pang of guilt but didn't know why.

"We really need to talk about this, Sam," DeLong pleaded. "I need to know."

"Know what?" she asked with a weak laugh, a hint of tears beginning to fill her eyes. She stared at the floor past him.

What are you hiding? he thought. "Tell me," he said. "I know you. There's something you need to talk to me about. I had the feeling you wanted to talk so many times. I just need you to talk to me. For the sake of our marriage."

"I don't know what you're talking about, Jim. I really don't know."

She regarded him, managing to put on a straight face, albeit too late to hide her sorrow.

"Don't you?" he asked matter-of-factly. "I think you do."

Samantha's eyes flashed with hot anger, and she groaned, slapping her forehead with frustration. When she spoke, her voice raised a pitch.

"What do you want me to say to make you happy, Jim? That I'm having an affair?"

Her eyes skirted around the room, looking at anything but him. She pushed past him to sit at the foot of the bed.

"Are you?" he inquired, a lump forming in his throat. He asked himself if he really wanted to know. He told himself it wasn't too late.

That he could get back to work and keep the skeletons locked up.

Her silence was all he needed. She put her hands over her face, beginning to sob quietly. Her thin frame shook and, as DeLong watched, he began to feel dizzy.

An affair, he thought. He held onto the wall so he could keep his balance. *I can't believe she'd do this to me.* Closing his eyes, he felt a single, hot tear threatening to come loose. *It'll be fine, Jim. She still loves you. Just ask her what you can do to make things right.*

Before he wanted to find out what they could do to fix their marriage, he needed to find out who it was. He wanted to know, but at the same time, he didn't. He felt conflicted about asking her the question.

"Who is he?" he asked, trying to control his hurt and anger. The question tasted bitter in his mouth. For a second, he thought he'd be sick. "Tell me who you wanted to be with more than your own husband." The last statement slipped out before he could stop.

Anger rising.

Hurt falling.

And vice versa. So many feelings.

"Oh, Jim," Samantha sobbed. "Please forgive me!"

"Do I know this guy? Did you get picked up somewhere? Or did *you* pick him up? Where did you meet him? A bar? The hospital? Is that why you quit?"

"I loved you, I still do," she forced out. "Jim, with all my heart, I do. We never wanted to hurt you."

"Who is 'we,' Samantha?" DeLong demanded, his voice rising. "I don't want to play this game anymore, Sam! We never used to have secrets. Now we're strangers. You have to tell me. Tell me!"

After a tense-filled moment of silence, she released a shaky breath. "It was...it was Russ Calhoun." She whispered his name.

DeLong felt as if she had shot him through the heart. The room spun faster, and his knees buckled. He needed to get out of the room, get out of the house. But, where would he go? To the office where his good friend Russ Calhoun was?

He drew in a breath.

Samantha reached for his hand, but he quickly withdrew it, backing away toward the exit.

In case he needed a quick getaway.

He closed his eyes tightly, pressing his fingers against the lids. It made so much sense, he wondered why he never realized it.

"It wasn't mine, was it?" he demanded, amazed his voice could sound so strong, so deep.

"Jim," she whispered. "Don't do this. Please."

"Stop stalling, Samantha!"

"I don't know," Samantha whispered. "I didn't want to know."

"Are you still sleeping with him?"

She shook her head fervently. "No, we called it off months ago. I couldn't bear the thought of hurting you."

Her voice was nearly inaudible, and all DeLong could think about was his wife in his bed with his best friend. He stared at her, trying his best to wrap his mind around the betrayal. He realized his fists were bunched tight; blood could not continue to pass through the veins in his hands. He unfurled his fingers and shook them until feeling returned.

Calhoun.

Samantha.

Together.

So many feelings.

He closed his eyes, shaking his head, trying to erase the image. But he knew it would always remain embedded in his mind.

"I'm so sorry, Jim." Her trembling voice filled the room. "I hate myself for what I did. But we can make things the way they were. I promise we can."

"How can we?" he demanded, pacing angrily, forgetting to calm himself. He felt the heat within his body boil, ready to erupt. "If it were anyone else—you betrayed me! Both of you did! My wife. My best friend! And then you lied about it for months!"

The anger he felt, the hurt, the pain all ran together, and nothing else mattered.

DeLong's ribs throbbed, but even that didn't faze him.

Hatred swam inside his soul. He glared at her. Samantha covered her head with her hands as her body shook.

"You know..." he began as he paced the room some more to keep from looking at her. Then he cut himself off with a shake of his head. He wasn't quite sure what he wanted to say.

"Mommy."

DeLong looked toward the doorway at the sound of the tiny voice.

"Daddy woke me up."

DeLong's heart took another dive, and he went over to her. "I'm sorry, baby. I didn't mean to." Kneeling, he gave her a hug. "Let's get you back in bed."

She nodded and took his hand in hers. She guided him to her

bedroom and crawled into bed.

"The monster's out of the closet," she whispered tiredly.

"Monster? I don't see any monster." DeLong looked around the room.

To appease her, he looked under her bed, inside her closet. "Nope. No monster. I think he left."

Bella yawned. "Good."

He stayed with her as she drifted off to sleep.

"I do love you, little girl," he whispered, planting a kiss on her forehead.

He stepped out of the room, past Samantha who had been watching by the door.

"Jim," she said. The word caught in her throat.

"I can't do this right now. I-I just can't."

With no other word, he stalked out of the room, out of the monstrous haze that continued to grow inside him.

Before he did something he'd later regret.

Chapter 14

DeLong drove around, unsure of where to go. Augusta was finally alive and vibrant again as though nothing out of the ordinary had happened.

The stores and restaurants were opening, people were on the road, children out playing.

His car moved as if on autopilot, heading wherever the wheels would take him. Should he go to the station? Should he confront his old friend? Or should he wait until everything cooled down?

Soon, he found himself at the bar of Philadelphia Jack's. For the first time in over a week, the bar was open. Only two vehicles were parked at the normally busy watering hole. As he sat in the truck, he longed to pull in and park his truck next to the others. Just long enough to down five glasses of whiskeys. It had been years since he had a real drink. His throat burned for the taste. His heart begged for something to deaden the pain or numb his brain long enough not to remember.

And his old friend, Jameson, had always been there for him. The whiskey would take away everything...for a while.

He gripped the wheel.

Stared at the "open" sign.

DeLong inched his way to the parking lot.

He stopped, let the engine idle. Slowly, he lifted his foot off the pedal to get the truck rolling again.

Then the police radio came alive with static.

He stared at the radio, dumbfounded. The static sounded as if it were whispering.

Help me.

DeLong grabbed his radio. "This is Lieutenant Jim DeLong, do you copy?"

Help me.

"State your name, please."

Silence.

DeLong began to pass it off as his imagination.

Help me.

The static made it hard to discern whether he was imagining things.

DeLong rubbed his tired eyes. Was this a dream? With everything that had happened, could it all be nothing more than a dream?

On the other hand, could this be his mind's way of telling him something? He thought about the voice he heard as he was leaving Grimes'. Could these incidents be related? Or was DeLong finally going mad after all these years on the force?

Why was he imagining these things, hearing them?

He began driving, trying to put as much distance as he could from the bar. He looked back and forth at the radio until he found himself steering toward Manny Grimes' house. He hadn't planned on going back so soon, but he felt as though something was pulling him back there.

DeLong looked toward the attic window. It was as still as night.

The world around him was silent.

No birds.

No whispers.

Nothing.

A light illuminated the attic window, dancing in the shadows.

"What is that?"

Then the light was gone.

He blinked a few times to get his mind straight. When the light flicked on again, he got out of his truck. He stood in the cold, staring, watching as the light illuminated the frosted window. He found himself walking into the house and up to the attic.

Peering inside, he saw everything was left the same way he found it the last time. DeLong explored the house, listening to any sound. He searched for the journal in the office, and when he found it, began skimming through. After a few minutes of consideration, he decided enough time had passed since the boys made the report. Under the law, Manny Grimes was missing.

That gave him the authority to remove the journal.

DeLong slipped it into his jacket pocket and left the office to enter the billiard room. The pool cues still leaned against the table and the balls were scattered.

He shook his head. Something felt wrong...he could feel it deep down.

The house was dead silent.

DeLong's breath was shallow as he listened to the stillness of the house. He couldn't even hear the soft blowing of the winter wind, or the bristling of tree branches.

Cold air passed through his right shoulder, but it felt almost solid.

DeLong slowly and stiffly turned around and faced the empty space.

"Grimes?" he called out hoarsely. "Are you there?"

Only the silence answered, and he began to feel juvenile.

"Get a grip on yourself, Lieutenant," he grumbled, allowing a weak laugh to loosen the tension in his body.

His cell phone broke the stillness, disquieting him.

After he calmed his nerves, he answered the caller.

"Hey, kid," Calhoun said.

"Yeah?" DeLong muttered, his eyes skirting the billiard.

"Ready to head over to the Walkers'?" Calhoun asked.

Slowly, as he exited the room, DeLong returned to his world.

"Uh, no," DeLong replied. "Actually, I don't need you with me. So I'll be going alone."

"Is something up, Jim?" Calhoun asked. Concern laced his

The Murder of Manny Grimes

words.

"I just don't want to deal with you right now, Russ. I-I just can't deal with you right now. Get it?"

"No, I don't get—."

"I know about you and Sam," DeLong interrupted. Slowly, but surely, he felt his blood once again boil. "And I want you to stay away from me and my family."

There was a harsh silence that fell on the line.

"Look, man," Calhoun stammered, finally. "I can explain. What happened with me and Sam—."

DeLong abruptly ended the call and turned to leave. All he cared about now was finding out what happened to Manny Grimes—he would deal with Calhoun later.

As he considered what he knew and didn't know about Grimes, he left the house and climbed into his truck.

DeLong drove, reflecting on the note Calhoun found: *MC at Columbia Dec. 2, 9:00 p.m.*

Was MC a name? Or was it a place? He couldn't think of restaurants or stores with the initials MC.

It was reasonable, DeLong mused, that 'Columbia' was the Columbia County Elementary School.

But why meet there? That was the question continually echoing in his mind.

He turned the last corner into the neighborhood of the Walker family's house and stopped at the curb in front of his destination.

DeLong took in a deep breath, held it, then let it go. Before climbing out, he called the number. DeLong cursed himself as he did so, all the while praying that he could get through this investigation as a professional.

Only a few hours ago he had called upon an old friend for help with the investigation because he trusted him. Because his friend was one of the best investigators DeLong knew. Because everything he learned over the years on the force, he learned from his friend.

His mentor.

And as far as DeLong was concerned that part hadn't changed.

"Yeah?" Calhoun's voice, for the first time since DeLong had known him, sounded old and tired.

"Meet me at the Walkers."

"Already on the way."

DeLong was slipping the phone back into the pocket of his jeans before Calhoun finished speaking. When he climbed out of the truck, he began cursing at the unbearable cold weather.

"You can do this," DeLong muttered underneath his breath. "Just keep cool. Keep it professional."

He drew in a deep breath and walked to the door which instantaneously opened.

"Lieutenant," Walker acknowledged. "Have you found him yet?"

"No, sir," DeLong told him. "My partner will be arriving shortly."

He hoped Walker hadn't noticed the cringe in his expression after saying the word "partner."

"I'd like to apologize for disrupting your life again, but I would appreciate it if you could spare a few more minutes of your time."

Walker opened the door wide enough for DeLong to step through.

"Where are Mrs. Walker and the boys?"

"They went to get some groceries. We weren't fully prepared for the storm. They'll be back shortly if you wanted to speak to them."

"No, actually, I wanted to speak with *you*."

Walker nodded slightly. "Very well. Have a seat. What can I do for you?"

DeLong obliged as he said, "Your sister-in-law informed me that you and Grimes had a falling out. Care to elaborate?"

"It was just a misunderstanding," Walker stated.

"What was the misunderstanding?"

Walker paused as if contemplating whether to answer. "He thought my wife was having an affair with my brother, Alan."

"But she wasn't?"

"I asked her, and she denied it. She told me she and Alan had met for lunch a couple times which wasn't uncommon. The three of us and Grimes, we were friends."

"Close friends?" DeLong pressed as he heard a car door slam

shut.

"Since sophomore year at college. That is until Manny started insisting my wife and brother were being unfaithful."

"He killed her before committing suicide, didn't he?"

Walker nodded.

"At a motel, right? Do you know why they were meeting there?"

"I haven't the faintest idea, Lieutenant," Walker replied uneasily. "It's a question I've asked myself over and over. But I'm afraid I knew the answer all along. I just didn't want to admit it. All I know for sure is that Alan had been very distant for a while. Then my wife started acting strange. And I ended up having to identify my brother and wife because police said he killed her, then himself and wrote a suicide note."

"Your wife began acting strange?" DeLong repeated, "How?"

Walker wavered his head from side to side to let him know he couldn't say.

At the knock on the door. DeLong called for Calhoun to enter.

"Right. Okay, let's discuss the note found at the scene. Do you remember what it said?"

Walker paused in thought as Calhoun entered the living room. "He said something about being sorry for what he did. That he needed to atone for his mistakes."

"Did you know what he meant? What mistakes he needed to atone?"

"Another mystery," Walker replied.

"You told me you haven't seen Grimes in the past few weeks, correct?"

Walker nodded as Calhoun appeared in the room.

DeLong cleared his throat. "This is my partner, Russell Calhoun. He's consulting with me while I'm trying to find Mr. Grimes. After searching Grimes' home for me, Calhoun found this check made out to Cash and signed by you. The date on the check was only a week ago."

DeLong found the photo of the check Calhoun sent him in a message a little while ago and held the cell phone out for Walker to see.

"I had mailed it to him," he explained, looking directly into DeLong's eyes.

"What was it for?" Calhoun asked.

"I borrowed money, and I repaid it," Walker responded. "I'm sorry, but I don't see why this has anything to do with him disappearing."

"Just covering our bases," DeLong informed him.

"Why did you make it out to Cash?" Calhoun questioned.

Walker shrugged. "He wanted it that way. I didn't question his motives. At the time, he was doing me a big favor. When I got the money to repay him, I sent him the check. I just wanted to be completely done with him."

"What was it for?" DeLong repeated Calhoun's question.

"It was between Grimes and me," Walker replied, becoming irritated. "I'm sorry, am I a suspect? Should I be calling my lawyer?"

"No, we're just following up," Calhoun replied. "The more information we have, the better chance we have of finding your friend."

Walker considered the statement, then crossed his arms over his chest with a frown. "Well, some things I'm willing to share. Others, I'm not."

DeLong nodded, exchanging glances with Calhoun. "Very well. Thank you again for your time."

Calhoun followed DeLong toward the door and stepped outside.

"Don't leave town," he instructed Walker.

Walker stared past them at the white earth.

"Exactly where would I go?"

"Thank you for your time," DeLong reiterated as Walker shut the door behind them.

DeLong forced himself to mutter a thank you to his friend as he walked down the driveway.

Calhoun stood outside his truck, arms tightly across his jacket, fighting to get warm. He appeared to be contemplating something.

"Get in the car where it's warmer, idiot," DeLong snapped, opening his own door and sliding behind the wheel.

"Look, Jim," Calhoun said softly, stepping to the driver's door. "About Sam..."

The Murder of Manny Grimes

DeLong narrowed his eyes, sucking in a breath full of cold air.

"Forget it, Calhoun. I don't want to talk about it. I need your professional help during this investigation, and afterward, maybe we'll talk. But I wouldn't hold on to that."

He slammed the door and drove away as quickly as the slick roads would allow him.

Chapter 15

DeLong spent several hours at the station in his office going through the paperwork piled on his desk and making phone calls to Grimes' coworkers. Most of them claimed Grimes had planned on spending a majority of the time catching up on work at the school because when his sons came to visit, he wanted to spend as much time as possible with them. He never mentioned going out of town. One man had told him ever since the Walker suicide, Grimes had been acting dejected.

Witnesses noted that Grimes was keeping himself busy with work but also began to act paranoid. DeLong didn't know any other details.

He also managed to get a hold of Grimes' ex-wife, who said she hadn't heard from him for the past few days. Before hanging up, she assured him that if she did hear from him, she would have Grimes contact him. As he spoke to her, she had concern etched in her voice. When questioned about it, she insisted as far as she knew, there was nothing to worry about.

When his eyes began to blur and tire, DeLong decided it was time to put the case to rest for the day.

It was almost eight o'clock when he pulled up to his house.

DeLong sat in his truck with the heater running, daring himself

The Murder of Manny Grimes

to take the steps toward the front door.

He felt a lump form in his throat as he placed his hand on the door handle for the third time, only to let it fall to his lap. DeLong closed his eyes as a headache slowly began to form.

What was she doing right now? Was she resting? Or waiting up for him? Did she even expect him to show up tonight?

He reminisced arriving home late at night during the last year, covering Samantha with a blanket, leaving a kiss on her cheek. At first, she would wait up for him but kept falling asleep in her rocking chair, then on the couch. Finally, she threw his pillow and a blanket down the steps, leaving a note saying, *tonight, you sleep down here. Don't bother coming up.*

In the beginning, DeLong had slept on the couch without any fuss.

After all, he had been staying out late. Mostly working, often talking to his buddies. Slowly, he began to realize something was seriously wrong.

Eventually, they became two strangers sharing a house and a child.

Sometimes he would walk up to their room, turn the knob, only to find it locked. He had heard quiet whimpering; he'd softly called her name, but she would say nothing. DeLong would return to the living room and fall asleep on the couch. From then on, that was where he found himself, never understanding why, and never being told why.

Now he understood her actions.

Guilt.

Guilt made even the sanest people act out of character.

Now, from the truck, he looked toward the master bedroom and spotted Samantha pulling the window curtains apart to gaze down at him.

He turned off the ignition.

Tried to contain his anxiety.

He stepped out of the truck.

The snippy wind bit through his jacket.

He wanted to wave and send her a kiss through the air, but he couldn't bring himself to do so. Instead, he stood in the cold, staring up.

The moon was nearly full and lit the sky.

His heart heavy, DeLong locked his truck, hearing the two *beeps* of the horn, and walked up to the door. He hesitated, looking around his yard, remembering the peace he once felt when he went up the walkway. Would he ever feel that way again?

Samantha opened the door for him.

Tears stained her cheeks and her eyes were blotchy.

"I'm so sorry, Jim," she whispered. Her voice was so low and shaky, it was almost inaudible. "I do love you so much."

"Why?" he whispered. He looked around his neighborhood, finding himself unable to gaze into her eyes. "Why would you do this to me? To us?"

A group of children was outside, having snowball fights or building a snowman. Both rare in this part of the south. None of them knew the pain of growing up.

"I felt lonely," was Samantha's response.

Her face filled with more tears. He wanted to grab her for a long hug but resisted. He was still angry, still unforgiving. Amidst the outrage he felt for her, for Calhoun, and for himself, he couldn't deny what he still felt.

"I love you more than anything," he finally managed to say. He tried to keep his voice strong, but to his ears, he failed. The children laughed in the distance. "I hope you know that. Whatever problems we have to face, we'll work it out. If that's what you want."

"What about the counseling?" she said, her voice quivering, full of hope.

DeLong nodded. "We can do that."

In response, she stood on her toes and kissed his lips softly. DeLong wrapped his arms around her waist and brought her close to him. He held onto her body, wanting desperately to rewind the past, fix whatever went wrong in their marriage.

He heard her stifle a sob. She sighed weakly as her arms tightened around him.

"Is Bella asleep?" he asked, speaking into her hair.

"Yes," she whispered into his shoulder. "She wanted to wait for you, but she fell asleep not too long ago."

The Murder of Manny Grimes

DeLong pulled away so he could place his hands on either side of her face. With his thumbs, he wiped away tears.

Samantha gave him a half-smile. Her eyes showed signs of regret. He grasped her hands, led her to the couch.

"Let's sit," he suggested.

When she sat, she leaned forward so her elbows rested on her knees and her hands covered her face. She tried to stop the tears from coming, but some managed to fall down the corner of her eye.

"Look, Sam," he began. "Nothing will ever stop me from loving you. I will always love you. We'll find a way through this. Okay?"

Samantha took a chance and turned to face him.

"I'm so sorry about this. I want to fix this, Jim. I want our marriage to work and I don't know how to fix it. I...I don't know how!" The sobs came pouring forth.

He didn't know how either. He wasn't even sure if there was a way to undo the damage done.

"Just like we fix most anything. One day at a time."

"I'm so sorry," she said again. "You have no idea. You were gone so much. Staying out so late. I know it's no excuse. I know I shouldn't have been feeling the way I felt, but..." Her words trailed off.

"I know," he admitted. "It has always been hard to be married to a cop. I should have focused more on you than I was. We can't fix what happened in the past, but we can find a way to fix what will happen in the future. And I think marriage counseling is a good place to start."

"Okay," she said with a nod. "We'll work it out." The final words were full of calm assurance.

They sat in uncomfortable silence for a few minutes.

Then DeLong heard a knock.

"Who's that?" he asked, glancing at the clock above the television. It was almost nine o'clock.

"What?" she stared at him curiously.

"At the door," DeLong said. "The knock."

"I didn't hear anything," she told him. "It's probably nothing."

He heard the banging again and jumped off the couch, groaning as he jarred the pain still haunting his body.

"I'm going to find out who's at the door," he replied. "Might be important."

"I didn't hear anything," she repeated, watching him.

He unlocked the door and swung it open.

He felt the color rush out of his face.

Manny Grimes stood in the frame, his face as pale as snow, but very much alive.

"Grimes!" he exclaimed, his voice unleashing the shock of seeing the man he'd been searching for. "You're alive! We've been looking—."

"Help me," Grimes said, his voice hushed, hoarse. "MC. Go to MC."

"Who is it?" Samantha called from the living room.

DeLong turned to the direction of his wife, his eyes wide. She still sat on the couch, stretching her neck to peek around the corner at him. "It's Manny Grimes," he told her.

He turned back toward the door.

Empty space.

He had disappeared.

DeLong stepped outside and looked around the neighborhood as far as his eyes could see, but there was no trace of Grimes near his house. He stood, unable to move, not noticing the bitter wind enveloping his body.

"What just happened here?" he muttered under his breath. DeLong rubbed his eyes hard, blinked, and stared where Grimes once stood.

The entire residential neighborhood seemed quiet. The children had gone inside. Most people were home, snuggled under thick, warm blankets and Lieutenant Jim DeLong stayed in the unusual arctic weather of the south, unable to move after Manny Grimes disappeared right in front of his eyes.

He finally realized what the missing man had said.

Go to MC.

What was Grimes trying to tell him?

DeLong stepped farther out into the yard, desperately looking around, trying to find any trace of Manny Grimes and where he could have run off.

There was no movement except a stray cat scouring the neighbor's trash. DeLong was ready to deem himself mentally unstable.

DeLong turned slowly and stepped into his house. He leaned against the door, his eyes closed. He put his fingers to his eyelids, pressed hard, then reopened.

"What's wrong?" Samantha asked, her voice deep with concern.

He didn't answer.

"Tell me what's going on," she begged.

He still couldn't form words, but he saw the worry in her eyes.

DeLong shook his head as he headed for the stairs. He'd often been too close to an investigation, but nothing like this. He wasn't the type to see and hear things that weren't there. What was wrong with him? DeLong stopped in front of the large rectangle mirror by the stairs to gaze at his reflection.

The man staring back at him, he didn't recognize. It looked like DeLong, but it was a pale-faced stranger with dull eyes staring back.

"I need to get some sleep," he muttered. "I don't think I've been getting enough sleep on the couch. It's catching up with me."

Samantha said nothing, only watched as her husband moved past the mirror and ascended the stairs.

Chapter 16

The sun peaked above the horizon, quickly climbing to present the new day.

All night long, Calhoun had lain awake, thinking about DeLong. About Sam.

About himself and Sam.

Every time he met with her, every time he touched her, he was torn with guilt. But he had convinced himself it was DeLong's problem and, if he really loved Samantha, he would spend more time with her.

It took time, but he had managed to shut off the little voice in his head telling him what they were doing was wrong.

Deep down, he realized there was no good excuse for his actions, no matter what he thought. He had betrayed a good friend.

This morning, he'd been driving around the city, trying to clear his head. Trying to make sense of what he'd done.

Finally, Calhoun laughed at himself, realizing how foolish he'd been.

He saw the hurt when his and DeLong's eyes met at the Walkers', and he saw the pain in Sam's eyes every time they were in the same room together during and after the affair.

The Murder of Manny Grimes

He shook his head as if to shake his thoughts loose before realizing he had pulled into DeLong's driveway. Calhoun considered leaving, but made no move when he saw the curtains move aside in the living room window, and Samantha gazing out. He absentmindedly exited the truck and walked to the door.

When she opened it, his heart skipped a beat.

Her black hair was disheveled, and she wore no makeup. Her eyes were puffy from crying and she looked tired.

He stood before her, at a loss for words. After recent events, what could he say? He wanted to make it better. He wanted to rewind the past.

What would the future bring now, he wondered? Would he be able to fix things? Fix his friendship with DeLong? The haziness of the days to come only told him one thing: he deserved no mercy.

"Hey," he said finally, speaking in a low voice.

She opened her mouth to speak and immediately closed it. A few more seconds of chilly silence ticked by and she opened the door wider for him. The house wasn't much warmer than outside, and as he stepped inside, he considered leaving. Before he could change his mind, Samantha brushed by him, forcing his heart to dive into the pit of his stomach.

"Jim's asleep," she said softly. "He's asleep."

The repetition of the sentence seemed more of a warning.

"Actually, I'm here to talk to you."

She backed against the wall as though he had moved toward her without realizing.

When he remained still, she went for a seat.

"How are you holding up?" Calhoun asked.

"Good. We talked about counseling. It sounds promising." She paused for a few seconds. She looked at the fire roaring away, giving off what heat it could, then back at Calhoun. "But we hurt him, Russ."

"I know. I know. I hate it. I hope we can rise out of this. It's such a mess. I don't even know how it all started."

"You have always been there when I needed a shoulder. For that, I will always be thankful."

Calhoun nodded. "And I will always be. I want you to know

that. I hope after the storm clears we will be able to go back to what we used to be."

Samantha gave him a small smile. "I hope so too, Russ. You have no idea."

"Tell Jim to give me a call when he wakes," he told her. "We need to talk about how we'll proceed in this Grimes thing."

Chapter 17

DeLong woke from a dream. One after another, he dreamt of Manny Grimes. He had tossed and turned relentlessly throughout the night until he finally opened his eyes.

Bypassing a shower, DeLong threw clothes on for the day, then retrieved the journal.

He skimmed the contents with careful eyes, looking for anything that might seem important.

The majority of the contents were about how much he missed his ex-wife, Sarah, and their sons. In the middle of the journal, Grimes wrote that he was renovating the house to comfortable living conditions. It had once been his ex-wife's childhood dream home. Grimes was hopeful that he and his ex might reconcile.

When DeLong neared the last entries, he began to read more slowly.

Nov. 24
When I met with Alan, I could tell something was up. I knew he

needed to talk to someone. I never knew that much fear could be seen in a man's eyes. After begging for him to talk to me, Alan told me he did something horrible. He made me so nervous with his pacing. I felt my heart climbing into my throat every second he was quiet. He said over and over that 'it happened a long time ago.' He wouldn't explain what he meant. I wish he'd trust me.

Nov. 26
Alan's dead. They say he killed Christy and then himself, leaving a suicide note. But I know there's something deeper at play here. The police won't listen to me. As far as they're concerned, it's all cut and dry. I need to figure out what Alan meant by what he said the other day.

Dec. 1
I know the truth now. I know the secret he carried with him all these years.

DeLong placed the book on the table. It was the last entry Grimes wrote. Why didn't he write more to it? Was he afraid someone would find and read his journal?

"What did you find out, Grimes?" DeLong muttered. "What did you get yourself into? What was Alan's secret?" He stared at the final entry as though everything would start to reveal itself.

DeLong's ears perked when he heard a door open and then close. He tore his eyes away from the cryptic pages of Grimes' journal, hearing faint voices on the floor beneath him. Walking to the foot of the stairs, he saw it was Calhoun who had arrived and was now standing in the living room.

DeLong strained his ears to listen to what was being said, but when he got close enough, he heard only silence. He slowly crept down the steps, peeking around the corner.

He saw Calhoun standing over his wife while she sat on the couch. He saw him smile slightly, but couldn't see Samantha's face.

He heard Samantha tell him that Calhoun had always there for her and that she would always be thankful. And then they agreed they wanted things to go back the way they "used to be."

The Murder of Manny Grimes

DeLong's fists were bunched tightly, his ears burning. He watched Calhoun turn to leave, and he desperately wanted to chase after him and put his tightly clutched fists through his chest and rip out his heart.

Seriously?

After everything that had happened. After Samantha wanting to go for counseling. They were still hoping to end up together.

When DeLong heard the door shut, he watched his wife slowly rise from the couch. She turned to see her husband standing on the stairs.

Watching everything.

"Jim."

DeLong's throat felt hoarse.

She looked toward the door, then back at him, eyes wide.

"It's not what it looks like, Jim," she told him. "It's over, I promise! Please don't be upset. He was just..." She bit her lower lip and pushed back a strand of black hair. She muttered incoherently.

DeLong padded over and watched as she tried to control her tears. He wasn't sure what to do with his arms, so he jammed his hands in the pockets of his jeans.

"I love you, Sam. I always have, and it will not go away so easily. You've *got* to know that."

"I do know," she whispered. "I love you, too."

"I hope you understand what I'm about to do is just something I've got to do."

"What?" she asked nervously.

"I'm going to leave for a few days."

"What? No," Samantha begged. "Please don't."

"I have no choice, Sam. I can't be around here. I need space, you know? I think you do too. We just need to figure out what we want. I can't do this. I-I just can't deal with this right now. We'll set up a time with the therapist, okay? It may help get our priorities out in the open."

She sniffled and nodded.

"I guess I'll talk to you soon." He closed his eyes, rubbing his lids. "Tell Bella I'll talk to her tomorrow."

Yearning to grasp her arms and pull her into a kiss, he hurried out the door, not taking the chance to look back.

DeLong didn't know where he wanted to go from there. He thought about Philadelphia Jack's, how tempting it was.

So tempting.

The thirst in his throat continued to burn.

He tried to ignore it, but it wasn't easy.

DeLong allowed his mind to drift. He had been away from Samantha before, but never in anger. They used to have a pact that, if they should ever have a major argument of any kind, then they would work it out before the night was over.

But that obviously flew out the window ages ago.

He longed to keep the pact and turn around.

Forget about finding a motel.

He beat the steering wheel as he turned onto the next street. No matter what his wife had done to him, he was still in love with her. They had their problems in the past, he reminded himself, as he turned again. But they had always worked it out.

Her affair, he decided, wasn't much different.

He shook his head to clear his thoughts.

As he continued to drive, a vague memory of his dreams began to guide him, but DeLong wasn't sure of what it was.

Or where he was going.

He drove until he stopped and turned off his truck.

Nothing was here, he reminded himself. He had looked twice. But, yet, DeLong had driven on autopilot back to the Columbia County Elementary School.

He stepped out of the truck and headed across the snow and ice to where the boys first claimed to have seen Manny Grimes.

Near the front of the school were the principal and several construction workers, working on the damage the storm caused.

As he neared, he saw a man standing by the swing sets. The sun illuminated the school grounds, and he knew immediately who stood there.

"Grimes!" he called out.

Grimes turned and headed toward the building, followed by DeLong, all the time wondering if he was going insane.

He was hearing voices and seeing things.

The Murder of Manny Grimes

He had to be losing touch with reality.

Or was he?

At this point, DeLong didn't know.

Grimes stopped at the back door of the school. It was still locked, and DeLong pulled at the door with frustration.

It was then a sparkle in the bushes caught his eye. He leaned close and saw it was a key. Dark red spots splattered the edges.

DeLong retrieved it, inspecting the key.

On a hunch, he slipped it into the lock. The door opened with ease, and DeLong followed Grimes inside, who waited at some distance away.

Finally, Grimes led the way down a dark stairwell.

"What's going on, Grimes?" DeLong asked. He found himself feeling inane. Was it real? Was anything real anymore?

All he heard were whispers, which seemed to echo in the blowing wind.

Grimes finally stopped, and DeLong stared at the floor of the basement for the longest time.

"Sweet Moses," he whispered.

DeLong continued to stare down, taking in every inch of dried blood resting on the frozen body of Manny Grimes.

Chapter 18

DeLong dialed the number directly to the main office. It was the desk sergeant who diligently answered.

"Columbia County Sheriff's Office, how might I direct yer call?"

"DeLong here, Nancy," he said. "Notify Captain Stewart that I found something which may be of interest to him."

"What's that?" Nancy asked. He heard the scuffle of a chair indicating Nancy had rolled from her desk, then the shuffling of paper.

"The body of Manny Grimes," DeLong replied, unable to take his eyes off the frozen corpse. He made no reaction when he heard a gasp on the other side of the line.

"Ya mean the fella th' kids were—."

"Yes, this is the same man." He heard her chair rolling again, then a soft thump as though she bumped into something. "Have him meet me in the back basement of the elementary school."

"I'm tellin' the captain now," she acknowledged.

The Murder of Manny Grimes

When she cut the call, DeLong used the time to kneel and stare at the body. The spirit—or image—or hallucination—or whatever it was that took the form of Manny Grimes was gone. He found it hard to believe Grimes' ghost had led him to his body. Which was why DeLong decided to keep that part of the story to himself and drum up another to make it more believable of how he came to his discovery.

DeLong placed his fingers over a bruise on the man's face. The skin was icy to the touch. He took notice of Grimes' broken glasses, laying approximately three feet away from the body. His legs were curled up underneath his body, old sheets strewn over him in a way that suggested he was tossed into the basement.

He sent a mass text to his CSI team, requesting their immediate presence, then another one to Calhoun.

He took a look around the room to see if any weapon was lying around that the killer may have left behind. But all he found in the darkened basement was nothing more than janitorial items and old school books.

There had been no attempt to hide the body or to cover it up.

DeLong mused that perhaps the killer had originally planned to recover the body and do away with him, but, thanks to the Walker boys, his plans were ruined.

He began to ascend the stairs.

DeLong saw Principal Cook pacing by the front entrance, huddling against her cloak, unaware of what happened to her assistant principal.

She was speaking on her phone as construction workers drug large debris from the site.

In the distance, two cars, one with its lights flashing blue, the other a pickup, parked next to DeLong's truck. Calhoun stepped out of his pickup. The captain and Officer Harrison John exited the squad car.

DeLong waited until they neared the building before he started out to greet them.

"What do we have, Jim?" Captain Stewart asked, his cold breath slowly disappearing into the air.

"Grimes' body," DeLong answered. "He's in the basement."

The captain sighed and lit his cigarette. "What made you think to look in the basement? Did Grimes come to you in a dream?" Stewart chuckled at his own humor.

"You're not too far off," DeLong mumbled underneath his breath.

"What's that?" Stewart asked as they entered the building.

"Instinct," DeLong replied with a shrug. "I couldn't imagine where else the body might have been. Considering the truth of what the boys told me, I figured given the short time frame, it left little for the boys to have seen the body by the swings, walk to the station, and for me to arrive. Russ and I didn't find his body earlier in the dumpsters. So, there was one place we didn't look."

"Inside the school," Stewart replied.

"Inside the school," DeLong echoed. "The perp probably wanted to wait until he felt it safe to return for body disposal, or even leave it in the basement as a dump site."

He held the key by the edge for all to see.

"Door was locked, but I found the key thrown in the bushes."

The group dispersed around the basement, taking in the scene. The captain and Calhoun knelt by the body, the former investigator holding a mag light to illuminate.

DeLong remained standing behind him.

"Whoever did this to Grimes hated him," Stewart murmured. "And they did a good job of it, too."

Calhoun grunted in response.

The captain looked back at DeLong. "One of these days I'll learn to fully trust that gut intuition of yours, Lieutenant."

"Well, I never was good at letting things go," DeLong admitted as he heard the sound of footsteps above them.

Jeffrey Newman, a young man in his mid-thirties, appeared, followed by a fairly new member of the crime scene investigation team. A quick search of his mind, DeLong recalled her name: Taryn Elliott.

DeLong nodded in acknowledgment. In quick commentary, he told his people what was so far known.

Once satisfied his team was prepared to take care of the crime scene, DeLong turned the key over to Newman, who bagged it as evidence, then followed Stewart and Calhoun outside, leaving Officer John behind as a precaution. Before he left, he told John to notify Principal Cook and have her cease reconstruction of the demolished section of the building until further notice. If she had questions, she could get in touch with DeLong.

As DeLong made his way for his truck, the captain and Calhoun trailed after him.

"Seems like summer will never get here, don't it?" Calhoun said conversationally.

DeLong huffed. He took out a cigarette, lit it.

"Could I bum a smoke?"

DeLong silently passed his pack to Calhoun.

When he saw Calhoun searching his pockets, DeLong sighed, removing his lighter. After Calhoun's cigarette came to life, DeLong shoved it into his pocket.

At his truck, DeLong slipped inside, noting John was returning to the crime scene to block it off with police tape.

Stewart and Calhoun lingered by DeLong's window.

He cracked the glass enough to talk, but to keep most of the cold air out and warm air in.

Calhoun rested his arm on the hood and leaned over. "What do you say we go get a bite to eat? Haven't had breakfast yet. You could tell us how you found the body."

As DeLong's stomach grumbled at the thought of food, he shook his head. "I've got things to do." He placed his hand on the gearshift, taking one last glance at his old friend. "Like check into a motel."

The statement warranted an eyebrow raise from the captain, but he only nodded and looked the other way, knowing it wasn't his place to impose.

Calhoun's face fell, which gave DeLong a sense of satisfaction.

"You left Sam?" Calhoun asked with unmistaken surprise. He took a step back as if he planned to make a quick getaway to his own truck.

DeLong searched Calhoun's face. It seemed as though he attempted to recover his fallen looks, but failed. Calhoun opened his mouth as if he was going to say something else, but closed it. He could tell Calhoun was genuinely apologetic. However, DeLong wasn't even close to forgiving his friend. Instead, he moved his gearshift into reverse.

"Not to worry, my friend," DeLong said coldly. "I'm quite sure everything will turn out just fine. In the meantime, I suggest we both put our personal drama aside and focus on catching Grimes' killer."

Before anyone could respond, DeLong pulled out of the parking lot.

In the rearview, he saw Captain Stewart was speaking to Calhoun, then nodded in the direction of the departing truck.

Chapter 19

As Officer John taped off the crime scene, Elliott and Newman went to work, wearing white latex gloves and plastic shoe covers.

"Footprints," Elliott stated. She knelt, snapped a picture and made the casting. "They look fairly recent, probably no more than a few days ago."

"Might be DeLong's," Newman muttered. "His shoes weren't covered when he found Grimes."

"No, they look bigger than DeLong's," Elliott replied. "It seems to be close to a size eleven, maybe eleven and a half. DeLong looks like he wears, what? Nine?"

"Think the print may be from a male?" Newman asked.

"Most likely. Though I've known some females with big feet."

"Someone's been smoking here," Newman said, kneeling by the stairs. He snapped a picture before retrieving the used cigarette butt with his tweezers. He inspected it before placing it safely in a plastic bag.

"Looks to be a Marlboro," he declared as Officer John stepped down the stairs. "I used to smoke this brand."

"Well, now that we know the brand, we need to know who smoked it," Elliott muttered, eyeing the partial footprints. Deciding an attempt to make a casting of the other prints would be a waste of her time, she stepped over to the sheets and carefully dusted it for prints. She found several partials, which didn't surprise her. She carefully folded the two sheets and slipped them into two separate bags.

"I have something here. Looks like blood." Newman glanced over to where Officer John stood. He went to swab the red dropping, squeezed a small amount of Luminol and watched as it turned pink.

He slid the swab into a container and placed it in a bag. "Good eye. You'll make yourself a fine CSI someday."

"Do you really think so?" John wondered eagerly. "I've always considered it."

Standing, Elliott let out a cough. "I think we've done all we can here," she stated, looking around.

As if on cue, two men from the coroner's office appeared at the top of the stairs.

"Okay if we come now for the body?"

"Yeah," Elliott replied with another cough. She looked over at Newman. "C'mon. Let's go find Grimes' office. I need to get out of this dust."

Chapter 20

DeLong pulled into the Fisherman Motel's parking lot, which, in his opinion, would have been more aptly named the Bates Motel. Only one pale red light illuminated the overstretched building, at the door where he would check in, while each of the fifty or so rooms left him with an eerie feeling.

He sat in his car for a few minutes re-thinking his decision to stay. He almost decided he would be much better off going back to his wife until he remembered he needed some space to work things out. After all, he wouldn't be staying at the motel too long. It would only be for a couple of days.

Even as a police officer, the feeling he felt about the motel was too strong and made him proceed with caution.

If he felt like this one would make him too wary, he would leave. But he took his Smith and Wesson from his holster, made sure it was loaded and packed it tightly in his pants. He opened the car door and was greeted by the cold air and strong wind. DeLong made his way to the front office and grunted as he forced open the door, sweeping snow to the side.

No one sat behind the desk. Paperwork was strewn on top in no particular order. He noticed a pegboard on the wall behind the desk with keys on almost all the hooks. He counted the keys. Four rooms were occupied. *That could be good and bad*, DeLong mused. *Maybe I should raise my standards and go somewhere else.* As he turned to leave, he heard a voice call out in the back room, where he noticed the door was ajar.

"Yeah," a bored voice replied.

"Uh, what are your rates?" DeLong asked.

"Depends. What you lookin' for?"

"A place to stay for a few nights."

"What's a 'few' nights?"

DeLong sighed heavily. He noticed the bell on the lower part of the desk and reached his hand to ring it repeatedly. "I find it kind of odd talking to a door. Come out so I can see your face."

"A'ight, A'ight." A second later, a skinny white man with thinning hair appeared in the doorway. His clothing left something to be desired: a ratty brown shirt and torn, faded blue jeans. He didn't smile, making his annoyance evident. "You're interruptin' my show. Now, what can I do for ya?"

"I told you. I need a room," DeLong said, matching the other man's tone.

"How long?" asked the clerk, rolling his eyes.

"Can I pay by the night?" DeLong asked. "I'm not sure how long I want to stay."

"Yeah," the clerk told him. "Just so you know, you'd probably get your money's worth if you buy a packet."

The clerk continued to look behind him toward the sound of the television in his office.

"Look. I'm a very busy man," DeLong snapped. He snatched his badge from his belt and slammed it onto the counter. "I have an ongoing murder investigation to deal with and I cannot do it if I have to stand here and listen to your bulls—."

"A'ight," the man said, holding his hands up. He had a distinctive scar down the middle of his right palm. "Why didn't you tell me you a cop to begin with? Coulda gave you a fair rate. Now,

The Murder of Manny Grimes

how 'bout one single bedroom, thirty pop a night? Cop special."

Now DeLong understood what brought him to this rat-infested motel.

Cheap and pure insanity.

"Seems fair," he said, reaching for his wallet and pulling out a twenty and two fives.

"You will be in room twenty." The clerk reached behind him and removed the key from the hook.

"Thank you," DeLong muttered. He turned to leave.

"What murder?"

DeLong considered telling the man he would not discuss the case, but decided that by lunchtime tomorrow, the whole state would know.

"A man named Manny Grimes," he answered. "Know him by chance?"

The clerk shook his head thoughtlessly. "Nope."

DeLong had already turned his back on the man after he shook his head.

"Well, have a good night," the clerk called after him.

DeLong walked to his motel room and found it was as he expected: dirty. He grimaced at the stains on the wall, the poorly made bed, and the hair in the sink. He sighed aloud.

Only for a little while, he promised himself.

He threw his bag on the bed and watched as dust flew, dissolving in the air. *It won't be too long.*

DeLong retrieved Sarah Benson's phone number and called her.

"I'm afraid I have some news for you," DeLong told her when she answered.

A pause.

"You found him." It wasn't a question.

"I'm afraid so, a little while ago. Will you be able to come to Augusta and identify the..." He paused, somehow unable to say the words. It never came easily when discussing the news of a loved one's death. "We'll need someone to identify him."

For a long time, Sarah didn't respond. He knew she was still on the line by the soft sniffling sounds. DeLong waited patiently, using the time to inspect his temporary home.

"Yes," Sarah finally replied. "I'll be in town this afternoon."

"Thank you, Ms. Benson," DeLong told her. "And I'm truly sorry for your loss."

"Me too," was the reply before she ended the call.

He sat still until he heard loud noises on the other side of the wall.

Curious, he walked to the wall and placed his ear against it to listen.

Tuning in to the noise, he heard a mixture of gasping, moaning, and screaming. Something sounded as though it was trying to burst through.

He sat on the hard mattress and lowered himself to the bed. Yes, this would be quite the adventure.

Chapter 21

Newman and Elliott carefully stepped through the debris in the front of the school building, looking for anything pertinent to the investigation.

Elliott knelt by the desk and picked up a container. Looking at it carefully, she inspected the stale potatoes. On the floor were the remaining potatoes and a mixture of dust and roast beef.

"So, he was eating dinner here," Elliott stated.

"Computer's barely working," Newman muttered as he narrowed his eyes at the flickering monitor. "It looks like he may have been in the process of ordering supplies."

Elliott rose and looked around what was once an office.

"Such a mess. It'll be hard to find anything with these limbs and snow. But—." She stopped speaking and looked past the overturned chair.

"Newman, give me a swab."

When Newman complied, she carefully rubbed the cotton against the snow that had fallen through the open roof. Her partner knelt by her side.

He handed her the Luminol.

She sprayed the swab, and the substance turned pink, indicating blood.

Elliott put the cover on the specimen and gave Newman a sidelong glance.

"So, Grimes probably began here," she said, "then somehow ended up by the swings where those kids first found him."

Newman nodded in agreement. "So, maybe he came into work, then was interrupted by the assailant. They struggle, he tries to get away. He runs out of the building, away from the attacker." He paused. "But where's the car? He had to have had transportation."

"The killer must have stashed it someplace."

"I'll get Officer John to look into the vehicle's whereabouts. In the meantime, let's check the halls. Try to find the route he took to escape."

After leaving the office, they walked through the hallway and glanced down three long passages.

Newman tapped Elliott's shoulder.

When she glanced over at him, she followed to where he was pointing. A sporadic blood trail was lining the hallway. They followed the trail quietly, walking the halls almost zigzagged. Classroom doors were all locked. When they arrived at the exit door, they noticed larger patches of blood.

Newman pushed the door and a gush of cold wind blew into Elliott's lungs.

"Blood trail ended at the door," Newman announced. "The snow must have covered our evidence."

Still, they walked toward the swings, keeping an eye out for anything else that had been left behind. They found nothing.

Elliott sighed in disappointment as she glanced at her watch.

"Our killer got lucky. All he had to do was stash the body, and Mother Nature would take care of the rest. Let's text DeLong what we know so far."

Newman nodded as he retrieved his phone. "I'll do that. You call the coroner to see if he's finished with the autopsy."

* * *

The Murder of Manny Grimes

DeLong read the text from Newman, letting him know he and Elliott were finished at the school. They found the point of origin, but nothing to help find the killer. A few minutes after the first, a second text came through saying the autopsy was still underway and the coroner would call once it was completed.

DeLong replied to the texts to let them know he had things to take care of, and they should meet Calhoun at Grimes' house. He added he would catch up with them as soon as he could. He also told them Sarah Benson would be driving in town from Alabama to identify the body and would arrive later this afternoon.

Before getting to work, DeLong wanted to swing by his house and pack a few clothes and necessities. He wished he had grabbed what he wanted before he left earlier. But then again, he wasn't aware he was actually going to leave.

He stepped out of his motel room, took in a sharp breath and pressed his fingers to his eyelids. He didn't realize until now how weary he had become. His body was stiff and still ached from his fall at Manny Grimes' house the other day. His eyes were worn, and all he wanted was to shut them for a few hours.

With another breath, DeLong reopened his eyes and gazed at the cloudless sky. Then he realized he wasn't doing anything except deferring what he knew needed to be done. DeLong hadn't felt this nervous since his first official date with Samantha. It had ended up okay back then, so it had to end up okay now, he thought to himself. Then he let out a wary chuckle because he knew the two situations were as different as day and night.

Peace and chaos.

Next door, a couple walked out, hand in hand. The woman smiled warmly at DeLong as she leaned in close to her companion, who gave him a cold, hard stare. Nodding in greeting, DeLong set off to his truck.

Behind the wheel, he turned the ignition, which stalled at the first two tries. As if it would torture the vehicle to do what he wanted, he hit the steering wheel with an irritated groan. After trying once more, the truck rumbled, then roared to life.

With satisfaction, DeLong turned on the radio to Perry Como singing "I'll Be Home for Christmas." Before the first verse finished,

DeLong turned the radio off to continue the drive in silence.

On the way to the house, DeLong began to contemplate about why he left. He was still hurt and angry by the betrayal. He knew if he returned home to his wife, the aura of her unfaithfulness would always surround them, and he would not be able to handle living with her.

Or could he?

Was he capable of that ounce of forgiveness?

What was it the Bible said about forgiving others?

DeLong hadn't been inside a church in so long, he felt a complete stranger to the whole thing.

DeLong turned the corner.

Maybe one day soon he'd try the church scene again.

Maybe it would help him find peace. If it was to ever be found.

DeLong made the final turn, and after he drove through the neighborhood, a groan escaped when he saw the SUV still in the driveway.

He hadn't considered Samantha would still be at home.

Parking two houses away, he considered leaving and returning later. With a shake of his head, he had to remind himself there was little time for foolishness. He just needed to find the courage to walk into his own house, grab what he needed and walk out. He had work to do and needed to be sure he had fresh clothes for the next few days.

Simple as that.

That thought in mind, he inched the truck forward.

Then stopped.

Bella skipped out of the house, toward the SUV. She opened the back door and climbed in as Samantha locked the house. She was oblivious to DeLong's truck sitting nearby.

Waiting with half-satisfaction and half-disappointment, he watched as his wife leaned in the back, made sure Bella had buckled herself in properly, then climbed behind the wheel. The car roared to life, with the brake lights illuminating in the snow. She backed out of the driveway, then drove in the opposite direction. DeLong took the chance and inched up the driveway. He hurried to the door, unlocked it with his key, and slipped inside.

The Murder of Manny Grimes

Standing at the door, he took in the harsh silence.

DeLong felt as though he were an intruder. That he didn't belong.

The home he had come to know the past few years felt unfamiliar. The furniture and decorum sent an unwelcome sensation, which made him hurry up the stairs to the master bedroom. He needed to get out of there.

What if she forgot something and returned?

He shook his head at the thought as he entered the bedroom. It was his house, after all. Why should he feel like a stranger?

Forcing the thought from his mind, DeLong opened the closet and snatched a black gym bag from the top shelf.

When his cell phone disturbed the silence, he flinched. Putting his hand over his racing heart, he answered.

"DeLong."

"Lieutenant," said a familiar, calm voice. "This is Claire Walker. I need to talk with you."

"Uh, okay," he said, attempting to clear his mind of his personal issues. He grabbed dress shirts and pants and stuffed them into the bag, then went into the bathroom. "What can I do for you, Mrs. Walker?"

"I think I might have important information about your case." She sounded nervous.

"I see," DeLong muttered. "What's up?"

"In person," she replied. "I can't risk him hearing me. Can you meet me at the Evans Diner in thirty minutes?"

DeLong glanced at his watch.

"Yes, sure," he told her. "I'll be there."

"Thanks, dear." She hung up.

DeLong took another look around to be sure he had everything.

Grabbing a picture of Samantha and Bella from the table by the door, he locked up behind him.

Chapter 22

Newman was dusting for fingerprints in Grimes' billiard room when he heard Elliott's irritated tone carry down the hall.

"You're a scoundrel," she piped.

"Really?" Calhoun sneered, his words laced with amusement. "You seem the type to like scoundrels."

Elliott's protests grew louder as they neared the room.

Newman had come to know her well, and could guess at the expression on her face: agitation amidst fury.

"Getting to know one another?" Newman asked as they entered the room. If he had met Elliott a few hours ago, the look she shot his way would have melted him to the ground. But, knowing her for almost a year, he only smiled bigger.

"Screw you, Newman," she demanded, one hand on her hip.

"How do you do it, man?" Calhoun muttered in his ear. "What's your secret?"

"In the beginning, I wore earplugs," Newman replied, his grin stretching ear to ear. He tilted his head toward Elliott, then said in a whisper, "Be careful, man. She ain't your type."

"Types have no meaning to me, friend," Calhoun responded in kind. "I've been with women who hated me and women who loved me. Either way, I come out satisfied."

Newman glanced in Elliott's direction. She was scanning the tall bookshelves, inspecting it as though expecting to find a switch.

"I'm just warning you. Be careful with her."

"You don't gotta crush on her, do ya?"

Newman held up his ring finger, revealing the white gold band. "That answer your question? I just know her pretty well. That's all."

"Hmm," Calhoun replied. Newman scrutinized him, realizing Calhoun hadn't been listening. "How about a bet? I'll be undressing her in two weeks."

Newman shook his head disapprovingly. "No bet. And she's right. You're a scoundrel."

Calhoun only snickered.

"Are you girls finished gossiping?" Elliott interrupted. She turned to face Newman. "Or have you finished down here?"

"Yeah," he replied, ignoring the icy tone. He motioned to the pool cues by his evidence bag. "Looks like our vic got into a fight or something. Found blood."

"Interesting," she said as she stepped over to the cues.

"Also found a good majority of fingerprints. Most were partials. I grabbed the laptop from the office. We'll see if anything relevant is on it."

"There's nothing more to be found in the attic," Calhoun said, "or in the rest of the house for that matter."

Calhoun's cell rang. He answered, and after hearing the bits of the one-sided conversation, Newman decided it was the coroner's office. After the call ended, the veteran investigator pocketed the cell.

"The autopsy's complete."

"I'll text DeLong," Elliott replied as she grabbed her own cell and headed out of the room. "We'll go see what the coroner came up with, then analyze what we found."

"She's only been here a year and thinks she's runnin' the show,"

Newman muttered.

Calhoun let out a chuckle as he stared off to where she exited.

"I heard that!" Elliott exclaimed.

Newman shrugged, allowing his lips to curl in a slight smile before they followed behind.

* * *

While they waited for the coroner to arrive, Calhoun's mind drifted to DeLong. He couldn't help but wonder if it was a good idea to be working together. Their conflict had been snaking its way through his thoughts since his old friend found out the truth about him and Samantha. He was sure he would be able to handle the situation professionally. It was DeLong, however, who worried him. They'd known one another for so long, Calhoun knew how short DeLong's temper could be, especially when pressed.

There had been several times over the many years they'd been friends that he and DeLong shared fists.

Part of him wished DeLong would take a punch at him.

At least then he'd get his anger out.

Then maybe they could work on getting through this.

He shook the thought out of his head.

That hadn't happened in years. Yes, he and DeLong fought one another, and most of the time, DeLong was the initiator, but those were trying times, and DeLong had worked hard to change his whole persona since.

And now, they both had jobs to do, and he was positive his friend knew his. Calhoun just had to keep the mindset to focus on the case.

And he knew no matter how angry Jim DeLong was, work always came first.

Of course, Calhoun mused, that was part of the problem with his young friend's marriage.

Regardless, if push came to shove, Calhoun decided he would back off the investigation.

Simple as that.

After all, he wasn't officially a part of the department. He was merely a consultant.

The Murder of Manny Grimes

Calhoun forced his mind to his present surrounding. The coroner's room was small and void of color. One slab sat in the middle of the room with Manny Grimes' body, a sheet covering everything except the head, resting for eternity. An adjacent room had a shelf full of jars and buckets preserving body parts.

Calhoun was accompanied by DeLong's CSIs. He'd known Jeffery Newman for a couple of years, and he debated on how well he wanted to know Taryn Elliott.

She glared at him, shooting ice pellets, as he skimmed the perfect curve of her figure until his eyes rested on her moist, pinkish lips.

She huffed, then turned from him to study Grimes' face.

Out of the corner of his eyes, Calhoun saw Newman consistently glancing at his watch.

"Got a hot date with the wife, Jeff?" Calhoun asked.

"Just wondering when the doc's going to get here," Newman responded. "We've been here for some time."

Calhoun diverted his attention to his friend with a smile. "He'll be here soon, I'm sure."

"Did Lieutenant DeLong know Grimes?" Elliott wondered. She brushed back a strand of her blonde hair, which escaped from the tight bun she wore.

Calhoun shrugged. "He hasn't said anything to me."

"Well," Elliott said, "rumor has it DeLong's been obsessed with finding Grimes."

Calhoun didn't reply.

Elliott looked over at Newman. "Of course, if I had problems at home, then I'm pretty sure I would've been obsessed too."

"What makes you think DeLong's having problems at home?"

Elliott glanced back at Calhoun. "Another rumor."

"Well," Calhoun retorted. "The lieutenant's personal life's none of your business. That said, I suggest you don't go around makin' assumptions. Soon as you do, you're liable to get into sticky water."

Elliott opened her mouth to respond, just as Dr. Chris Harmon walked in with his clipboard.

"I'm sorry I'm late, fellas," he began, "went to get a quick bite, then the car wouldn't start." He stopped, noticing Elliott. "I apologize, Miss...I didn't realize I was in mixed company."

"There is nothing *mixed* about your company, Doctor," Elliott insisted hotly. "Now, I'm sure we'd all appreciate it if you would just give us the time of death and the cause."

"Yes ma'am," the doctor answered, glancing at Calhoun, raising an intrigued eyebrow.

Calhoun lifted the corner of his lips in a smile, then changed his expression to what he hoped to be a business one when he noticed the young investigator glaring at him. He moved his eyes toward the body, waiting for the doctor to educate the group on the death of Manny Grimes.

"Well," Dr. Harmon began as he slipped on his rectangle glasses.

"Your vic put up quite a fight. I already took skin samples from his nails and sent it to the lab. He was beaten pretty badly. Three broken ribs." The doctor turned the head to reveal a bloody gash. "Blunt force trauma to the back of his head, and asphyxiation due to strangulation. See the bruises on his neck?" He turned the head to its starting point.

"He was strangled by bare hands," Newman said to himself, staring at the finger marks on either side of his neck.

"Suggests killer was a male," Calhoun muttered.

"Are you saying a woman couldn't strangle a man?" snapped Elliott, glaring once more with icy eyes.

"Why, could *you*?" he challenged, his lips curved into a mischievous smile.

"I could," she insisted, her head held high.

"Maybe one day you can prove it," he replied.

"Maybe I'll prove it now," she countered, taking a few steps toward Calhoun.

"And finally," the doctor interrupted. His eyes skirted to Newman, who lifted his lips in an amused smile.

Elliott gave Calhoun one last glare and returned to her spot by the cadaver table.

"He was shot once in the leg." He lifted the white sheet to reveal the left leg and a bullet hole in the shin. The doctor rolled Grimes to his side to show the bullet holes within two centimeters from each other. "And twice in the back. The COD is a gunshot to his head. I took the pleasure of extracting the bullets for you." He handed Newman the metal pan.

"Looks to be a .38 Special," Newman concluded.

"As for the time of death, I would say sometimes three nights ago, by nine thirty at the latest."

"The boys had originally claimed to have seen the body around nine twenty," Calhoun announced.

"Fits the time frame," Elliott said with a nod.

"Could they have seen the murder?" Newman asked.

"They said they saw someone run from the body," Calhoun stated.

"So, reflecting on the evidence we have so far, Grimes met someone named MC at the school. A fight broke out in his office. He managed to escape outside where he died. But the boys showed up so there wasn't any time to figure out what to do with the body."

"So, they stashed him where he wouldn't be found immediately," Elliott concluded. "Gave him time to get away."

"The man had a heck of a fight in him," Newman commented.

"I can't imagine," Elliott muttered. "A horrible death. For anyone."

They stood in silence as they observed the body, which, despite the pain he endured, looked peaceful.

Chapter 23

DeLong stepped into the Evans Diner. It was quiet except for the sound of the television set. The news recounted the last few weeks of the winter storm, including bits and pieces of the murder.

He looked around the small diner and immediately found Claire Walker sitting in the corner, sipping coffee. When she caught his eye, she gave him a warm smile and waved him over.

"Thank you for meeting me." She proceeded to rise and greet him, but DeLong motioned for her to remain seated. "How are you?"

"I'm fine, Mrs. Walker," DeLong answered. He slid into the booth opposite her. The waitress sashayed over and DeLong ordered coffee. He felt hungry but didn't think he should eat with Claire Walker.

"When I heard you found Manny, I just couldn't believe it. I knew I needed to see you."

He nodded. "What's on your mind, Mrs. Walker?"

"I hate this so much," Claire said, tearing up. She began twirling her hair as she glanced at the small TV hanging on the corner wall.

"I can understand how you feel," DeLong replied. "Knowing

your family was friends with him."

When DeLong received his coffee, he dumped in a sugar packet and stirred.

"It's not that. I wish it were, I really do." Claire began looking around nervously. "I'm sorry, Lieutenant DeLong. Maybe I shouldn't say anything. Thank—thank you for your time. I'm sorry I wasted it."

She began to rise. DeLong did the same, blocking her path.

"Mrs. Walker, I understand you've gone through a lot the past few weeks. Please, if there's something you need to tell me, something related to Grimes, I have to know."

"I don't know, Lieutenant. It's probably nothing."

"In investigations like this," DeLong pressed, "everything's important. Everything matters."

A tear escaped, and she swiped at it. She bit her bottom lip and twirled her hair as her eyes moved to the white outdoors. She closed her eyes tight and released a soft sigh.

"It's Jonathan," she began.

She sat back down, DeLong hesitantly following suit.

"They used to be such good friends," she continued. "But lately, every time they were in the same room together, they'd fight. It was so awful. It had Jonathan so upset. Manny, um, called him a few days ago."

"He did? Are you sure? Because Walker told me he hadn't seen or spoken to Grimes for a week or more."

"Manny just wanted to make it right, I think. I convinced Jonathan to go talk to him. I told him we were all family. That we all loved Alan and Christy. Because of everything Alan did to us, we needed to stick together."

"So, Walker agreed to go see him," DeLong finished.

Claire nodded.

"Afterward, when Jonathan came back home, he was angry. He said he knew he shouldn't have gone. I've never seen him like that. He said he was so mad he could kill him."

"And you think he might have?"

"Well, at the time, I thought nothing about it. He was just upset. Jonathan gets angry. He tends to lose his temper. Although that was the angriest I've ever seen him, I just brushed it off as Jonathan being Jonathan. I even forgot it ever happened. Jonathan tried calling him after you first came by. But then, I saw the news. That he was dead. Everything Jonathan said that day came back. I don't know what to think. Please tell me it's nothing. That I'm just going crazy. I mean, I already lost my husband. I can't bear the thought of losing Jonathan too!"

"I promise you, I'll find out what happened to Grimes. And for all your sakes, I truly hope your brother-in-law didn't do anything wrong. I understand your family has been through a lot this month."

She dabbed the corner of her eyes with her napkin.

"Mrs. Walker, do you think it's possible your husband was having an affair?"

Claire blinked.

"I don't know. I want to say of course not. But it was all too..." She trailed off and broke his gaze. "He just changed one day. Then he and my sister-in-law were found dead in some hotel room. Can't really wrap my head around what's true, you know? Jonathan fought Manny for so long. He was so sure nothing was going on. Even now he is. At least that's what he says."

She took a sip of her coffee, then wiped the remaining tear stains from beneath her eyes. Setting her mug on the table, she fished through her handbag and pulled out a mirror. She stared at her reflection, trying to erase the mascara, which had run from her lashes.

When she looked back up, she smiled sadly.

DeLong thought about the journal entries he read and his previous conversation with Walker.

"Grimes had a journal," DeLong said. "One of his entries stated that your husband did something terrible a long time ago. Did Grimes or your husband ever mention anything like that to you?"

Claire curiously narrowed her eyes.

"No. But like I said, Alan had changed. The man they say killed my sister-in-law, then himself, was not the man I married."

The conversation trailed off, and DeLong decided to let her sit on the thought for a while. Maybe later, something would arise. After DeLong drank the last bit of coffee, he removed his wallet.

The Murder of Manny Grimes

"Thank you," he told her. "We'll follow up and I'll keep you informed."

"Thank you," she echoed.

"I assure you, I take complete pride in my team."

"I'm sure you do," Claire told him as they slid out of their booths.

Claire reached up, placing her cool, moist lips to his cheek. "I'll see you soon and thank you again."

Claire walked out of the diner, leaving DeLong with his stomach curled up in knots.

Chapter 24

DeLong removed his jacket when he entered the break room at the sheriff's department. He grabbed a cookie from the table and attempted to fill a Styrofoam cup with more coffee. Realizing the canister was empty, he turned to Nancy. Out of the corner of his eye, he watched Calhoun and the CSIs head in his direction.

He let out a curse and snapped. "Nancy, why is there no coffee?"

Nancy, in a conversation with her peers, widened her round eyes.

Calhoun froze. Newman paused behind Calhoun, cleared his throat, peeling off his jacket. Elliott's eyes narrowed; her brow furrowing, attempting to make sense of what was happening.

Nancy's white face quickly colored as she patted her hair unnecessarily. She stammered.

"I'm sorry, Nancy," DeLong apologized. "I'm just a little tired. And I hadn't had anything to eat today."

He turned around, closed his eyes. After he counted to five, he set his unused cup on the table and turned back to face his team.

"Jim," Calhoun acknowledged with the usual nod of his head.

If he can act like everything is peachy, so can I, DeLong decided. He extended his hand toward Calhoun's.

"Hey man," he said cheerfully. He hoped it didn't appear too forced. "How's it goin'?"

Calhoun immediately took the hint and smiled, gripping his hand tightly. "Good, Jim, good. We just got back from Doc Harmon."

Newman and Elliott, though not before exchanging curious glances, seemed satisfied everything was okay as they gathered around the coffee stand.

"So, what do you have so far?" DeLong asked. He led the way into a conference room so they could sit comfortably, then listened as the group reiterated what they found, which was not much, except for the blood on the pool cues.

DeLong listened to the information, then mentioned his meeting with Claire Walker. He went on to share what he read in Grimes' journal.

"So, Walker lied. Again," Calhoun stated. "Why am I not surprised?"

"I think we should start digging deeper into the history between the Walkers and Manny Grimes. To cover more ground, we should split up. Newman and I will go have another talk with Walker. We'll also talk to the boys again." He nodded toward Calhoun. "You and Elliott can review Alan Walker's suicide. I wasn't a part of that investigation, so once we familiarize ourselves with it, we may learn more about the family and their friendship with our vic. We may also find a way to link it to Grimes' murder. Every little detail counts. So, let's make it count."

* * *

Since DeLong had already formed a bond with the boys, he thought they would be more comfortable re-telling the story to him.

Walker stood by the fireplace, his arm resting on the mantle. His fingers softly drummed against the polished wood, clearly in a state of agitation. DeLong informed him that it was now an official case, so they needed more official statements for their records. Walker only grunted in response.

DeLong leaned forward in his chair to look at each of the boys. His eyes landed on the oldest. "I understand this can be difficult for you. The reason we want to talk to you again is that sometimes a new memory might pop up. Like the other day when you remembered seeing another person by the swings. Why don't you tell us again from the beginning what happened? Begin from the time you left home."

"We climbed out my window," Tommy said.

"At what time?" DeLong asked.

"Around eight, I think," Bobby put in. He was sitting next to Tommy, his back crouched against the sofa.

"How can you be sure of that?" Newman wondered.

"Seven is our bedtime," Tommy answered. "We wanted to stay up and watch a movie, but Uncle Jonathan wouldn't let us. We were already late going to bed." He paused to look at the ceiling as he began to remember.

"So, we went upstairs. After we shut our door, we climbed out the window. It was my idea," he admitted with a shrug. "I wasn't tired or nothin'. We haven't really been outside much. Mom won't let us stay out too long. I was just bored. We don't live too far from school, so we thought it'd be easy to walk there."

"It took a while to get there because the weather was so cold and windy," Bobby grumbled. He sat on the floor, frog-style as he played with his matchbox cars. "I wanted to go home."

"No one said you had to come." Tommy kicked his brother.

"Tommy," Walker snapped. His eyes narrowed. "Just answer the questions." Walker knelt to toss more wood in the dying fire, then prodded at the lumber. The fire sparked and slowly began to dance.

Since he sat in the chair near the fireplace, DeLong felt the warmth of the flames beat against his leg.

"Then what?" DeLong continued as he jotted in his pad.

"We just got there and saw two people. One was on the ground and the other was standing over him," George said.

"The one standing must have seen us or somethin' 'cause he

bolted," Tommy continued.

"Did you notice anything special about him? Was he male or female? Tall, short?"

They shook their heads.

"So, you went over to the swing sets," DeLong pressed.

"Yes, sir," George put in.

"And saw the body—um, Mr. Grimes," DeLong said.

"Yeah, and after that, we went to the police station to find you," Tommy concluded.

"And that was about nine thirty-five," DeLong stated.

"I think so," Tommy told him. "And then you went to go find him. You didn't stay too long though." The last part sounded accusatory, but DeLong let it slide.

"Do you remember *anything* else?" he asked instead.

They pondered the question, but all shook their heads.

"Okay, boys, I guess that's it for now," DeLong told them. "You can run along." They paused, then one-by-one shrugged and exited the living room. Bobby was the last to leave.

"Did we help this time?"

"Yes, Bobby, you were a great help," DeLong assured him. "More than you know."

As Bobby left the room, DeLong turned to Walker. "Mind if we ask you more questions?"

"I really have nothing more to say," he insisted. "I told you all I know."

"I know," DeLong muttered, rising. "I just have one more question for you. Just to clear something up." He cleared his throat. "You told us you haven't seen Grimes for a week or so."

"That's right."

"However, we learned you paid him a visit a couple days ago. Do you remember that?"

Walker's eyes flashed. He crossed his arms over his chest and looked away. He muttered something incoherently.

"If you'd rather," DeLong suggested, "we can finish this conversation at the station."

"Yeah," he said softly after a few minutes passed. "I did."

"Why did you lie?"

"Because I wanted to forget about it. It wasn't a good visit. I wouldn't have gone over there if my sister-in-law hadn't insisted. But I went because a part of me wanted to clear the air with him."

"We found blood on the pool cues," Newman told him. "Would you happen to know how it got there?"

Walker let out a heavy sigh.

He slowly moved to take Tommy's spot on the couch. DeLong sat again in his chair.

"Grimes, for a while, has been telling me my wife and brother were having an affair. I didn't believe it. But he never would let up, so I finally ended our friendship. But, when I went to see him, I thought maybe enough time went by and he'd drop the whole thing."

"But he didn't," DeLong interjected.

"No. He told me he went to confront Alan about the affair. I didn't let him finish what he was saying. I hit him with my cue. I hit him a few times before I left. Told Manny to never contact me again."

"What about the check?" DeLong asked. "Are you ready to tell us how that came about? Because we can and will get a warrant. It would be easier on us all if you gave us the information."

Walker sighed.

"Fine. You win. But it happened more than a year ago. It shouldn't even matter. I've paid my dues and got help for it. I'm done with it."

Walker paused as though he were hoping DeLong would let him slide.

But the lieutenant waited.

"I owed a gambling debt," Walker reluctantly answered. "I only had four grand on hand, but I owed them nine. I didn't have it. I knew Manny had money put away, so I asked him for help."

"And he just gave you the money?" Newman asked. "Five grand?"

"Not exactly," Walker said. "In the beginning, when I asked, he said no. He told me he's learned the hard way to never lend friends money. But, shortly after I asked, I was at a bar. When I left, these guys were waiting for me. They beat me up pretty badly. Told me it was only a taste of what they would do to me if I didn't have the money by the end of the week. Manny witnessed the whole thing. He gave the money right away."

"When was this?" Newman wondered.

"A little more than a year ago. I don't know the exact date. Might have been sometime in March."

"All right," DeLong said. "These guys you owed money to, do you know their names?'"

"Brett Barker and Randy Whitmore."

"Where can we find them?"

"They're usually downtown at the Dance All Night strip club. Barker often emcees there, so it's kind of their hangout."

DeLong was scribbling the information in his notes, but looked up.

"Barker is an emcee at the club?"

Walker shrugged. "Thursday nights the club votes on the best lady dancer."

DeLong glanced toward Newman, who raised his eyebrow.

"Interesting."

"Well, Barker and Whitmore have a reputation for their crude sense of humor."

"The reason that intrigues us, Mr. Walker, is we have reasons to believe Manny Grimes planned on meeting someone with the initials MC on the day he was murdered."

Walker's eyebrow rose in curiosity.

"Manny didn't frequent the club that often. Usually he'd only go because I dragged him along."

"So, you don't know about Grimes' relationship to either Barker or Whitmore?"

Walker's shoulder rose and fell. "Like I told you before: Manny and I haven't had much to do with each other for a while. So, it's not like he'd call me and tell me he was doing business with them."

DeLong made a quick note in his pad.

"In Grimes' journal," DeLong said as he finished writing, "he said something about Alan doing some horrible thing a long time ago. Did your brother or Grimes ever mention anything like that to you?"

"No," Walker said, narrowing his eyes with curiosity. "Why?

Do you think my brother's suicide had something to do with Manny's death?"

"We're just following every possible lead," DeLong replied.

"My brother's affair with my wife pretty much destroyed all of us. So, I can't say anything other than I have no clue."

"Okay, Mr. Walker," DeLong said. "I think that'll be it for now. Thank you. Again. And if there's anything else you can think of, anything at all..."

"I'll let you know."

Chapter 25

Calhoun and Elliott spent time reviewing the case of Alan Walker's suicide before questioning witnesses. The case notes stated he was shot with a .380 Beretta, the gun on the floor just inches from Walker's hand. His fingerprints were on the weapon, but he had no residue on him.

They agreed it was curious, but they knew not every suicide victim gets residue on them.

Photos showed Walker sitting, slumped over the table, hand hanging limply by his side. His eyes were closed, the bullet wound at his temple.

Christy Walker was found at the foot of the bed, shot once in the chest. She lay on the floor, one hand resting on her stomach. Eyes wide open.

The suicide note admitted into evidence had been written in loopy handwriting saying he couldn't live with his mistakes anymore and the secret he held was too painful.

Calhoun and Elliott studied each crime scene photo in silence as if something that didn't fit would begin to reveal itself.

They drove to the Econo Lodge where the suicide took place and asked to speak with the maid who found the bodies.

"Yes," the maid said shyly as she walked into the main office. She tucked her chin to her chest, afraid to look at her visitors.

"I'm sorry to bother you, ma'am," Calhoun told her. "We're here to follow up on Alan Walker's suicide from last month. Do you remember that? You were the one who found him?"

"Yes, sir," she said, her voice beginning to shake. Her face paled against her Hispanic complexion.

"Did you hear gunshots?" Elliott asked.

"No ma'am. I just start work. He hang no sign on door, so I go in. I see..." The memory brought tears to her eyes. "I see him on chair, dead. Then I see her on floor, dead."

"Who worked before you? Do you remember?"

"Miss Alice. Um, Miss Alice Cross."

"Can you write down an address or phone number so we can contact her?" Calhoun asked.

"Um, okay," she replied, her face turning green. "But I'm no sure how she helps."

"Why is that?" Elliott asked.

"Miss Alice deaf," the maid told them, searching the front desk for a paper to write the address on. She handed the paper to Calhoun.

"I go now, please?"

Calhoun nodded, and she took off, faster than she came.

* * *

DeLong received a call from Captain Stewart, who informed him Sarah Benson had arrived and was prepared to identify her ex-husband's body.

He and Newman met them at the coroner's office.

She was an average-height woman, shoulder-length auburn hair. She was in her early forties but looked as though she could pass for late twenties. Mascara stained underneath her eyes.

DeLong extended his hand.

"Ms. Benson, I'm Lieutenant DeLong. We spoke on the phone."

"Yes, Lieutenant." Her voice was soft, but firm. "It's nice to finally put a face to the voice."

The Murder of Manny Grimes

"You too." He hesitated. "How are you doing?"

She blinked back tears with a shake of her head. "I'm just ready to get this over with."

DeLong nodded. "I understand."

"Then let's do it," Captain Stewart suggested.

They led her into the autopsy room.

Dr. Harmon stood by the table, prepared to remove the sheet from Grimes' face.

Sarah sucked in a breath, held it, and exhaled.

"I'm ready."

Dr. Harmon folded the sheets to Grimes' shoulders and stepped a few paces back.

DeLong studied the ex-wife carefully as she regarded her husband's body.

She blinked. Tried to keep herself composed. Sarah reached her hand to the face, ready to touch the body, but lingered before jerking away. She laid a shaky hand on her chest.

A tearful moan escaped her lips.

"It's him. It's Manny."

She backed away and hurried from the room.

"I'm sorry," she told them when the others joined her in the hall.

"It's quite all right," Captain Stewart assured her. "I'm truly sorry for your lost."

"I just didn't want to believe it would be him. What am I going to tell my sons?" Tears slid down her cheeks.

"We're doing everything we can to find out who did this," Newman told her.

"Ms. Benson, we'll need to ask you a few questions," DeLong said. "Is now a good time? Or do you need time—a day or two? However, I recommend we not wait too long."

"Now," she replied. She moved to sit on a bench across from the coroner's room. "I just want this whole ordeal to be done. So I can get back home to my boys. They need me."

DeLong and Newman sat on either side of her. Captain Stewart remained by the door.

"Can you tell us when you last heard from your ex-husband?" DeLong asked.

"About two weeks ago. We talked on the phone."

"Did he say anything to you? Maybe about someone wanting to hurt him?"

"No. I don't understand who would want to do this to him. We may be divorced, Lieutenant, but I loved him. He was the father of my children."

Sarah paused as she tried to take in a deep breath.

"Wait. I do remember something. For a long while, he was worried about someone. A friend of his. He wanted to know what was going on with him."

"Alan Walker?" Newman prompted.

She nodded. "Yes. Um, Alan had wanted to tell him something, but he never got around to it. Manny was very upset over whatever was going on with Alan."

"Do you know if your ex-husband found out what was going on?" DeLong wondered.

"No. At least he never said anything to me. But Manny had always been..." she stopped as she considered a word, "dedicated."

"Can you elaborate?" DeLong asked.

"Before he was an assistant principal, he was a lawyer. And a very good one. One of the best. If there was a truth to be found, he'd find it. Manny was worried Alan had gotten himself into trouble."

"Did he say anything else to you?" Newman asked.

"No, just that..." Sarah paused, her eyes welling up with fresh tears, "just that he loved me." She swiped at the tears, her hands shaking violently. "I'm sorry."

"It's okay. Take your time," DeLong said.

"He, um," Sarah cleared a catch in her throat. "He went to a therapist." She pressed her fingertips against her eyelids. "What was his name? A-a-a Lucas Gordon, I think."

"Do you know where he works?"

Sarah shook her head. "I don't know much about it. Only that he was going to a therapist. For a while, he kept telling me how Dr. Gordon was putting things in Manny's life in perspective again. I'm sorry. That's all I know."

"It's okay," DeLong assured her. "You did great. Let us know if you think of anything else. You can call me day or night."

The Murder of Manny Grimes

Sarah nodded. "Thank you, Lieutenant DeLong."

"One more question, Ms. Benson," Newman said. "Do you know what kind of car your ex-husband drove?"

"Um, a black Mazda, maybe navy blue. I can't remember the color."

"Thank you," Newman said, as he jotted the information in his pad.

When she left, DeLong rose, Newman following suit.

"A therapist, huh?" Captain Stewart said after she was out of earshot. "People say and confess to their therapists about all kinds of things."

"Well, let's see about finding a phone number," Newman said, "I think we should go get some counseling."

Chapter 26

Riding in Elliott's car, because she stated she couldn't stand being in his "redneck truck," they pulled into the driveway of a small white house in the middle of a cul-de-sac and stopped behind a brown station wagon. The house was decorated with red and green along the roof, a lighted reindeer decor by the door. Someone had also wrapped lights around the dogwood tree in between the Cross house and the yard next to them.

The other houses in the neighborhood, except for two, were also decorated for the Christmas season.

While Alice Cross' house had its Christmas lights on, her next door neighbor didn't.

Calhoun and Elliott climbed out of the car.

"Ever talk to a deaf person?" she questioned edgily.

"You got a problem with it?" Calhoun wondered.

Elliott shrugged. "Nope. I just don't know any sign language."

"Well, we'll have to hope she has paper to write on," he replied.

Elliott scoffed and followed him to the door, hot on his heels. She pushed pass him and rang the doorbell.

"If she's deaf, then how——."

Calhoun heard her unintentionally breathing a sigh of relief when a man opened the door.

"I'm Taryn Elliott of the crime lab. This is Russell Calhoun. Does Alice Cross live here?" She showed him her badge.

"Uh, yes, officers. Is there something wrong?" he asked.

"May we speak to Mrs. Cross?" Calhoun said. "We're following up on a murder/suicide that happened at the Econo Lodge last month. I believe your wife was on duty around the time it took place, so we need to ask her a few questions."

"Come in," the man said, opening the door wider. "I'm Alice's husband, Harvey. She's in the kitchen."

Mr. Cross led the way to a small kitchen where a tall, blonde haired woman stood at the stove, basting a turkey. Cross walked behind her, put his hand on her shoulder. She looked at him, smiling warmly.

"We have company," he said, as he signed with his hands. "They're from the sheriff's office. They have questions for you."

Alice turned and gave them a big smile. "Merry Christmas," she said, signing her greeting. "Make yourselves comfortable. What can I do for you?"

"I'm Taryn Elliott," she said, speaking loudly. "And this is—"

Alice waved her hand in the air, cutting Elliott off. "You can yell all you want, Miss Elliott. But seeing as I'm deaf, I won't hear what you're saying."

Elliott cleared her throat, her cheeks turning unusually red.

"But if you speak in your normal voice, I can read lips," she said, motioning to her mouth. "Or, if you prefer, my husband can interpret."

"No need, ma'am. We're sorry if we made you feel uneasy," Calhoun replied.

Elliott narrowed her eyes at Calhoun but remained silent.

"Please," Alice said, motioning to the kitchen table. "Have a seat. Would you care for something to drink? Coke? Coffee?"

"No, thank you, ma'am," Calhoun answered, sitting. "We won't take too much of your time."

"I wouldn't be a good hostess if I didn't offer," Alice replied.

"As my partner was saying, she's Taryn Elliott, a crime scene investigator from the sheriff's office, and I'm Russ Calhoun. I'm here only as a consultant." He pulled out his notebook, flipped to an empty page and set it on the table.

Alice watched his movements closely. Her husband was at the turkey, taking over the cooking for his wife.

"You work at the Econo Lodge, correct?" Calhoun asked.

"Yes," Alice answered.

"Do you recall a murder/suicide that happened there?"

"Yes, I do. I remember I had just gotten home. An hour later, my husband saw the news."

"Mrs. Cross," Elliott began.

Alice held up her hand. "Call me Alice, please, Miss Elliott." Her smile was soft and friendly.

"If you wish," Elliott said. "Anyway, did you hear—I mean see—anything out of the ordinary? Someone who didn't belong, someone who struck you as odd, creepy..."

"It's a hotel, Miss Elliott, anybody belongs there. And a lot of creepy people show up."

"Were you to clean room 101?" Calhoun asked.

"Yes, I was. But I didn't go in the room. When I got to work, he had a 'do not disturb' sign on his doorknob. So I didn't go inside."

"Did you see anybody go in or come out of his hotel room?" Elliott asked.

"No," Alice responded. "I'm sorry, but I thought this was already solved? That he killed that lady and then himself?"

"We're investigating another murder," Calhoun explained. "It could tie into the suicide. We just need to get our facts straight."

"Oh, that is awful! I'm sorry, Mr. Calhoun and Miss Elliott. But I don't know anything that could help. I didn't go in his room, and I didn't see anyone. If I think of anything, though, I can call you."

Calhoun slid his chair away from the table and rose, extending his hand. He shook first with Alice, then her husband.

"Thank you for your time," he told them.

"I'm sorry I couldn't be much help," Alice repeated. "My husband will walk you out. I must get back to cooking him dinner." She let out a giggle.

The Murder of Manny Grimes

When they reached the car, Elliott climbed in the driver's side and groaned. "I have never seen anybody smile so much."

Calhoun chuckled, looking sideways at her. "You really are something."

"Is that yet another come on, Calhoun?" She glanced his way, her lips curving into a slight smile. Or was it a scowl? He couldn't really tell.

She set the car in reverse, backed out of the driveway and drove out of the neighborhood.

Chapter 27

When they arrived back at the crime lab, the investigators began to process the evidence they'd managed to find so far.

The computer found a ninety-eight point seven percent match on a Doc Marten shoe, size eleven. Elliott's lips had a ghost of a smile, pleased she was correct about the size. She looked around for Newman and saw him across the hall, impatiently waiting for the lab technician to finish sampling the blood Officer John had found.

He glanced over, saw she was staring back at him. Elliott tilted her head, motioning for him to come over.

"DNA from the cigarette butt isn't conclusive," Newman announced as he stepped into the room.

"Maybe we'll have better luck with the blood drop," Elliott suggested.

"Chances are, the drop from the school basement and what you found on the pool cue in the billiard room are from Grimes. But if luck's on our side, maybe it'll belong to the perp."

Newman laughed. "Doubtful. Besides, a little mystery in our life

The Murder of Manny Grimes

is just what we need, don't ya think?" He winked.

Elliott gave him a smile. "As for the print I found, it's a pair of Doc Martens, size eleven."

"So, what we're looking for is a man with nothing else to do but buy a hundred-dollar pair of shoes, then commit murder," Newman mused.

"With a .38 Special," Elliott added.

Newman's phone rang.

Elliott waited until he finished talking and hung up.

"We're in Grimes' computer. The guys recovered deleted photos of Alan and Christy Walker in the trash bin, but nothing conclusive enough to say whether they were having an affair or not. What they did find of interest was a file marked 'MC.'"

Elliott raised an eyebrow.

"Amanda will upload everything in a zip file for me. I'll text DeLong and we can set up a time for breakfast tomorrow to confer."

The lab technician stepped into the room with a sheet of paper clutched in his hand. "I didn't find anything useful from the fingernail scraping, and the blood at both scenes belonged to the victim."

"Thanks, Glynn," Newman acknowledged, accepting the print-out. He turned to Elliott, who glanced at her watch.

"You know, I'm hungry. It's been a long day."

* * *

As the investigators processed evidence, DeLong and Calhoun drove in silence to Dance All Night, a strip club downtown. When they found a parking space, they got out and bypassed a long line of men waiting impatiently to get into the small club.

"Seems like a place you'd enjoy, Russ," DeLong said.

Calhoun chuckled. "Maybe a hundred years ago."

"Sam would probably shoot me if she ever knew I came to a place like this." They pushed by a man looking more like seventeen rather than the allowed age of twenty-one.

"Well, if that happens, I'll make sure to put on your headstone 'died in the line of duty.'"

"I appreciate that." They made it to the door where two brawny men stood, bulging muscled arms crossed over their chests. DeLong showed them his badge. "We're looking for Brett Barker and Randy Whitmore."

He had to yell to be heard above the pulsing music inside.

"What's the problem?" the guy on the left asked, his voice more of a growl.

"Unless you're one of the two, we're not obligated to share that information," Calhoun answered him. "Now, why don't you let us in and point in their direction."

The bouncers hesitated, but decided to open the door. The one on the right silently led them inside and pointed to two men getting lap dances at the corner bar.

DeLong and Calhoun zigzagged between tables and people until they arrived at the bar.

"Brett Barker and Randy Whitmore?" DeLong asked.

"Who's asking?"

They continued to move their hands along the women's legs, reaching under their short skirts. It was apparent neither woman minded as they nuzzled the men's necks.

"The police." DeLong showed them his badge. "We won't take up too much of your time. We have a couple of questions concerning Jonathan Walker."

"Take a break, darlings and come back later," one of the guys said as he slapped the woman's bottom.

"Haven't seen that pea brain for a while."

"How long ago has it been?"

"I'd say about a year or so, is that right, Barker?"

"Sometime or other. He accusin' us of somethin'?"

"No," Calhoun replied. "Should he be?"

"Nope. Like Barker said: haven't seen 'im."

"Tell us about your encounter with him," DeLong said.

"He borrowed a little bit o' Benjamins and we requested it to be returned," Barker said with a shrug as if it were a common thing.

"So. You beat him up?" Calhoun pressed.

Whitmore chuckled. "Guess you can put it that way."

It was obvious these guys couldn't care less that they were speaking to the law. However, DeLong mused, they didn't have a

The Murder of Manny Grimes

reason to be afraid of them right now.

"So, Walker owed you money and you beat it out of him," DeLong summarized, "did you by any chance see what happened to him afterward?"

"Didn't pay no attention."

"Oh, there was that mouse guy, Barker. 'Member?"

"Oh, yeah," Barker said mockingly. "He came, interrupting our conversation. Told him to go find cheese."

The two men erupted in laughter at the joke.

DeLong rolled his eyes over toward Calhoun. "So, you met Manny Grimes."

"The mouse has a name?" Whitmore snorted.

DeLong gave him a fake smile. "The mouse is dead."

Both men's eyes widened at the statement.

"Have you ever spoken to him before or after the night you beat Jonathan Walker up?" Calhoun asked.

"Nope. We said all that needed to be said, so we went on our merry way. Got our dough back soon enough."

DeLong paused, then looked at the dancers, then back at Barker. "I hear you emcee?"

"Yeah, so?"

Shrugging, DeLong said, "So nothing. I just find it's interesting that you're an emcee at a strip club and Manny Grimes had a note to himself saying he was going to meet someone named MC on the day he was murdered."

He saw Barker swallow hard.

"Hey, man, come on. Am I a suspect?"

"We're gathering information," Calhoun replied. "We thought we'd bring that coincidence to your attention."

"Look, man," Barker said. He slid off the stool and stood half an inch taller than DeLong, who figured Barker could crush his skull in one hand. "I ain't no killer."

"No, you just like to beat people up until they're close to death."

Calhoun moved in closer as if he was ready to step between Barker and DeLong.

"Thank you for your time," DeLong said. "I wouldn't go too far if I were you." He pulled Calhoun away. The throbbing music was giving him a headache, and he was aching to leave.

"So, for once Walker told the truth," Calhoun replied as they went out the door.

DeLong had to strain to hear.

He nodded. "We've connected Grimes to giving Walker the money, but it seems to be a completely separate incidence to Grimes' murder. Unless Walker got fed up with Grimes accusing his brother and wife having an affair, I don't see how he's our guy."

"I agree," Calhoun said. He looked toward the door. "But I'd say Brett Barker or Randy Whitmore may look good on our suspect list."

A text came through to DeLong's phone. He glanced at it. "Newman wants breakfast in the morning. Our computer tech hacked into Grimes' computer and found deleted photos of Alan and Christy Walker and a file folder titled 'MC.'"

"That's interesting," Calhoun stated.

They returned to DeLong's truck, falling into a tense silence.

DeLong drove Calhoun to his own truck, then went on his way. Being inside the club alongside Calhoun, there was just something he had to do, and he decided he didn't want to resist it any longer.

Chapter 28

The next morning, DeLong woke early, his head feeling as if a large animal was kicking him. Even before he opened his eyes, he felt the room spin. When he did open his eyes, the light shining through the window seemed as though someone was holding a flashlight to his face.

He closed his eyes with a groan and lay back down. His body felt like jelly and he knew if he stood, he'd only end up on the floor.

He thought he would retch any second.

DeLong tried to remember what it was he needed to do today.

He opened his mouth to call for Samantha to bring him an Advil, then closed it.

No, he wasn't home. Bits and pieces of memory reminded him he had left. He was at a motel. But what motel was that?

Oh, yeah.

The Fisherman Motel.

He decided he wanted nothing more than to stay holed up in his room.

Manny Grimes.

That's what he needed to do. He needed to solve Manny Grimes' murder.

He allowed himself to remain immobile until the spinning room slowed and he could gather his bearings. Then, slowly, and hanging onto anything he could grasp, he made his way to the bathroom to take a hot shower, hoping it would burn away the alcohol that still lingered.

It didn't work, and all he could think of was the desire to stock up on some liquor.

DeLong stepped out of the shower and wrapped a towel around his waist. He checked his messages and listened to Samantha's voice telling him she had made an appointment with a couples' counselor for that afternoon if he was still willing to go.

He tore a page from an old book and scribbled *Sam, 1:00, therapy*.

Calhoun was the next voicemail informing him they were going to meet for breakfast at the Waffle House.

DeLong detested the sound of his old friend's voice. He considered skipping the breakfast meeting but decided he needed to stay in for the long haul. This was his case. His team. He pulled on a pair of jeans and buttoned his red plaid shirt, eyeing the two bottles of whiskey lying on the floor.

One empty, the other about halfway there.

He didn't remember even bringing liquor back.

No wonder he was still under the influence.

He cursed himself.

Almost seven years of sobriety and he ruined it in one night.

He ran fingers through damp hair a few times before slipping his arms into his coat, stepping out of the room.

As he made his way to his car, he walked slowly so he could maintain his balance and looked at the Bing app on his phone. He typed the name "Doctor Lucas Gordon" and hit enter. Once Dr. Gordon's office number popped up in the browser, he tapped the screen to make the call.

It was a voicemail, so DeLong left a brief message, informing the psychiatrist who he was and why he was calling. He ended by requesting for him to return the call and set up a good time to answer questions.

* * *

When he arrived at the restaurant, it was buzzing with conversation and banging dishes. One of the waitresses shouted out the order for some teenagers—a boy and girl, both with matching pink hair and mohawks, or were they faux hawks now?

The noise didn't appease the slaughter of his head.

The light still hurt his eyes and the earth continued to spin, but DeLong found his team sitting in the far left corner.

"Can I get some coffee?" he asked a young girl, standing at the register.

She looked at him as though he threatened to throw fire on her.

Slowly removing her hand from the register, she grabbed a coffee mug, all the while looking astray.

DeLong shrugged it off and reached his table.

"Hey, man, you look awful!" Calhoun stated, sipping his coffee.

"Yeah, Lieutenant," Newman replied. "Your shirt isn't buttoned correctly."

"And you look a hundred years older," Elliott added.

DeLong ran his fingers through his hair again. He had not bothered looking in the mirror as was his normal habit.

"Maybe that's why that girl looked at me like I threatened to zap her into nothingness."

"You haven't been drinking, have you?" Calhoun asked pointedly, his eyes narrowing with concern.

DeLong scoffed. He wanted to reach over and strangle the life out of his old friend, the traitor. However, he knew it was unwise at the present time to suggest there were problems brewing between them—as if the investigators didn't already know, according to the glances they tossed at each other. He drew a deep breath, counted quietly to three, then thought of a half-lie. "I had a bad night, that's all. Motel beds are different from the ones at home. Couldn't sleep."

"Maybe you should get some rest and let us handle everything today," Elliott suggested. "We *do* know how to do our job, you know."

"Taryn, leave him alone," Newman said, annoyed.

Elliott said nothing, but her expression instigated Newman to swallow hard. DeLong sat next to her as the young girl set his coffee in front of him. After he thanked her, she stood before him, staring.

DeLong continued looking at her, waiting for her to speak, but she chose to remain quiet.

"That's all for now," he said to her.

She huffed and took off behind the counter, leaving DeLong amazed at her rudeness. He shared glances between his companions and raised his shoulders.

"Guess bad mornings are contagious?" he offered.

Newman let out a light chuckle. Elliott took a bite out of her toast and Calhoun blew into his coffee to cool it.

DeLong held onto his mug, allowing the heat to burn his hands.

"What did you get from the lab?" he asked the investigators, attempting to force his mind to focus on more pressing matters.

"Not much." Newman recounted to DeLong what he and Elliott learned at the crime lab.

"Well, it isn't much, but it's something," DeLong said between sips of coffee. The liquid made the hole he imagined Sam burned within him char even more. Maybe if he drank enough coffee, his entire existence would just go away.

He laughed to himself.

No, that would be too easy.

"Were you able to get in touch with Dr. Gordon?" Calhoun jarred DeLong's attention back to Manny Grimes.

"I called on the way over and left a message."

DeLong slowly drank what remained of his quickly cooling coffee, relishing the caffeine.

"Let's hope we'll have better luck with Manny Grimes' therapist," Newman mused. "So far we have very little to go on."

"Let's go through the list of Grimes' friends and acquaintances, split it up and see if they can shed any kind of light. Something's bound to pop up," DeLong suggested. "Walker told us Grimes didn't want to lend him money because he learned the hard way not to. Maybe Grimes gave someone money in the past and it somehow caught up to him."

Calhoun nodded as he pulled the paper out of the notebook he

The Murder of Manny Grimes

had with him. Once they split the list, they sat in uncomfortable silence.

Elliott was the only one still eating, so she finished her breakfast quickly, and released a sigh as she stuffed the last bite of her heavily buttered toast in her mouth.

"I'll be back," DeLong said, looking down at his shirt. "I better fix my appearance before heading out. My suggestion to you guys is to never dress in the dark."

He let out a small laugh.

He made a beeline for the restroom, unaware Calhoun followed him until the door shut behind them.

"What's going on, Jim?"

DeLong eyed his friend as he began unbuttoning.

"What are you talking about?"

"What am I talking about?" Calhoun echoed. "I'm talking about you. You show up here, shirt buttons out of sorts, circles underneath your eyes. Your breath smells like liquor."

"I had a late night. I told you, it's not easy sleeping on a motel bed. Didn't sleep."

"If you're drinking again…" Calhoun muttered underneath his breath.

"If I'm drinking again," DeLong repeated as he finished buttoning. He fluffed his hair in the mirror and splashed cold water on his face. "Then it's your fault. But don't worry, Russ. My drinking is under control."

"*My* fault?" Calhoun scoffed. "How is it *my* fault?"

"Well, you did have an affair with my wife." DeLong shrugged and turned to face him.

"That's just like you, Jim," Calhoun snapped. "You've never been able to accept the responsibility. Why haven't you learned that by now? You're at fault that you're a drunk. Not mine, not Sam's." He closed his eyes and pressed his thumb and index finger to his eyelids. "You may not believe it, kid, but I value our friendship. Sam and I made a mistake. But we still love you. That never changed."

"You're right, Calhoun, you're right," DeLong told him with a half-hearted nod. "I don't believe it. And it's not your fault I'm an alcoholic. Just your fault I took a drink after seven years of hard-earned sobriety."

With that, he pushed past Calhoun and left the restroom.

DeLong removed his wallet and went to pay for his coffee. The blonde, still looking lost, took her time to ring him up and hand him his change. Stuffing the bills into his pocket, DeLong nodded to the girl before turning away.

"Newman, you're with me," he muttered as he hurried from the restaurant.

Chapter 29

DeLong's and Newman's first stop was a young, single mother who was assistant to Assistant Principal Grimes between her college classes.

When they arrived at the apartment, Newman knocked and a second later, a child of maybe five, opened the door. He leaned on the knob and stared wide-eyed at the two strangers.

DeLong couldn't help but see Bella in those wide, curious eyes.

"Hi there," DeLong said with a smile, kneeling to become eye-level. "What's your name?"

"Adam." His voice was soft and low. Adam's eyes danced from DeLong to Newman and back again.

"It's nice to meet you, Adam," DeLong told him. "My name is Jim DeLong, and this is my friend, Jeff. We're with the sheriff's office." He showed his badge to Adam, who inspected it with curiosity. "Is your mother available?"

"Mommy!" Adam hollered over his shoulder. "There's a man at the door!"

A second later, a girl in her early twenties appeared. She placed her hands on Adam's shoulder.

"Adam, what did I tell you about opening the door to strangers?" she scolded him. She smiled at her visitors, wiping at the flour lingering on her cheek. "Hi. Sorry about that. Can I help you?"

After DeLong made the introductions again, she introduced herself as Alana Philips and said, "Adam, your breakfast is on the table. Go eat. Mommy will be there in just a second."

Adam skipped out of sight, then Alana looked at DeLong and Newman, eyes changing tones.

"Is this about Mr. Grimes?"

"Yes ma'am," DeLong replied.

She opened the door wider to invite them inside.

"It's hard to believe someone killed him," Alana said softly.

"Were you close to him?"

"I wouldn't say close, but he's always been friendly toward me. He was friendly toward everyone."

"Can you think of anyone who would want to hurt him?" Newman questioned. "Maybe you overheard him in a heated argument?"

"Mr. Grimes rarely argued. Everyone loved him. All the kids. He'd go around the classroom and pass out candy." She paused. "I do remember there was this one time, though. I came back to the school because I left my books for one of my classes. No one else was around, that I knew of, anyway. Mr. Grimes, he never raised his voice, he just wasn't like that. But this other guy wasn't happy. Then over the last few weeks, he did start to act differently."

"Do you remember what was said?"

"No. The words were muted because I was down the hall inside a classroom. When I walked by, the door was slightly open. The man saw me standing there and stopped talking. I knocked and asked if everything was okay. Mr. Grimes seemed embarrassed. He said they were fine. Before his friend left, he did say 'if you don't drop it, you'll be sorry.' Then he stormed out."

"Did you ask Grimes about it?" DeLong wondered.

Alana nodded. "Mr. Grimes told me not to worry. He said they were just friends having a disagreement."

"Can you describe this man?"

The Murder of Manny Grimes

"He was short, about my height. Brown hair. That's all I can remember. I never heard a name."

DeLong used his cell phone to pull up a picture and showed it to Alana. "Is this the same man?"

Alana inspected the photo as she tried to remember. Finally, she nodded. "It's been a few weeks, but, yeah, I think so."

"Did he ever mention the initials, MC to you, or maybe you overheard him talk about it?"

Alana shook her head.

DeLong took a business card from his wallet. "Thank you for your time. If you can think of anything else, don't hesitate to give me a call."

"Of course," Alana replied. "I hope you catch this guy. Mr. Grimes didn't deserve to die like that. Nobody does."

"Well, we already know Walker was out of sorts with Grimes," Newman said as they left the apartment. "He even admitted it."

"Let's go visit the principal and see what else she might know."

Chapter 30

Elliott and Calhoun rang the doorbell at Blake Wright's house, which was in the same neighborhood as Jonathan Walker's. Calhoun looked around the snow-filled yard, his eyes resting on the two small snowmen standing by the road. One of the snowmen was decorated with a scarf, carrot, and something, he couldn't tell what, for the eyes. The second snowman was left unfinished with only black button for eyes.

Finally, the door opened and a man in his mid-fifties appeared in the frame, wearing a plaid bathrobe.

"Good morning, sir," Calhoun said. "We're sorry to bother you. We're from the sheriff's office. I'm Russ Calhoun and this is Taryn Elliott."

"What'd the boys do now?" the man narrowed his eyes and crossed his arms.

"Nothing, sir," Elliott replied. "We're here to ask you some questions about Manny Grimes."

"Oh," he said. "Sorry. But my boys have been giving me a headache since the day they were born. I love 'em to death, but there

The Murder of Manny Grimes

are times when enough is enough."

Calhoun released a friendly chuckle. "I can understand that. Do you have a moment?"

"I think I can spare a few, but I don't think I can be much help. I'm afraid I didn't really get the chance to know him."

"You're a janitor at the school, correct?" Elliott asked.

"Yes."

"Can you tell us if you've noticed any strange behavior with Grimes in the past few weeks?"

"Well, he did seem pretty different. Unnerved. I overheard him on the phone about, maybe a week ago. I don't know who he was talking to, but it seemed serious enough."

"What was said?" Calhoun asked.

"I can't really say. He seemed like he was begging someone. I thought it sounded like 'don't hurt them, please.' I put it down to too much crime detective shows." Wright scratched his head in thought. "Man, I didn't know Grimes was in any trouble. I really didn't. I wonder if he was talking to him." His voice trailed off, and he stared in the direction of Walker's house.

Elliott and Calhoun followed his gaze before turning back.

"You think he was talking to Jonathan Walker?" Elliott inquired.

"You know him?" Wright asked.

"His son and nephews were the ones who found the body," Calhoun replied.

"Really?" Wright said. "How convenient."

"What was their relationship like?"

Wright shrugged. "I've seen them together from time to time. I think they're friends. Must have had a falling out. According to my sons, they've been fighting quite a bit these days."

"Mind if we speak to your sons?" Calhoun asked.

"Sure. They're at the other end of the neighborhood shoveling snow. At least that's what they're supposed to be doing. If you catch them throwing snowballs, do me a favor and tell them they're grounded."

Elliott smirked. "Will do."

"Thank you for your time, Mr. Wright," Calhoun said. "Please call the sheriff's office and ask for either us or Lieutenant Jim DeLong if you remember anything else."

Wright agreed and took the business card Elliott handed him. Then they walked in silence to the car.

Pulling away from the curb, they drove through the neighborhood until they spotted two teenage boys shoveling snow away from a driveway.

Elliott pressed the button to lower the motorized window and stuck her head out.

"Excuse me. Are you Blake Wright's sons?"

The taller boy tossed his shovel to the ground and walked over. "Yeah. Something wrong?"

"No, we just wanted to ask you a few questions," Elliott told him. As she climbed out of the car, she showed the boys her ID. "I'm Taryn Elliott of the crime lab. This is Russell Calhoun. We're investigating a murder. Manny Grimes. You know of him?"

"Guess so. I think he worked with my dad. He's dead now?"

Calhoun nodded. "We have it on authority that he was friends with your neighbor, Jonathan Walker."

The younger boy let his shoulder rise and fall.

"I don't know about 'friends,'" the older brother said. "I seen him at Mr. Walker's house several times. They're always arguing."

"About what?" Elliott wondered.

The shorter boy stepped up. "We were raking their leaves one day when we heard something crash in the house. We went to see what it was. Mr. Walker threw a vase or something against the wall."

"Do you know anything about what they were talking about?"

"No," they replied in unison.

"But Mr. Walker was angry," the taller boy replied. "I mean real angry. We went back to work so Mr. Walker didn't know we'd been listening."

"Were you afraid he would have hurt you?" Elliott inquired.

The boys shrugged.

"Anything else?"

When they shook their heads, Calhoun and Elliott thanked them and climbed back into the car.

* * *

DeLong and Newman had finished with their portion of Grimes' coworkers and friends. They said the same things: Grimes was friendly and kept to himself. He did begin acting frightened of something over the past few weeks but didn't let anyone in on the secret. No one could think of anyone who hated him enough to kill him.

Dr. Lucas Gordon had returned DeLong's call and agreed to help if he could, however, the only time he'd be free was 1:00, his lunch hour. DeLong had a therapy session with his wife, so he told Newman he'd be otherwise occupied, but they could reconvene at the office afterward.

Officer John had also called Newman and informed him they found a black Mazda matching the description of Grimes' car parked behind a building next to the school. They searched the car, but it had been wiped clean. A tow truck would retrieve it and take it to the impound lot.

In the meantime, Newman sat with DeLong at Mellow Mushroom, waiting for Elliott and Calhoun to arrive for lunch.

Newman spotted them coming in and leaned across the table to DeLong. "It looks as though they're arguing again."

DeLong twisted to see, and sure enough, Elliott was flapping her arms in annoyance as they bustled to the table.

"You really need to work on your people skills, Elliott."

"Oh, please. That idiot little boy ran into me."

"I think you may have scared a few years off his life. He was, what, six?"

They slid into their seats as the waitress came over to take their order of drinks and a large pepperoni pizza.

"What's going on?" DeLong wondered.

"Some kid ran into her," Calhoun shrugged. Then he lifted the corner of his lips to a smile. "As fate would have it, she fell right into my arms. I have suspicions it was planned."

"Oh, please," Elliott scoffed. "I'd rather gouge my eyes out."

But as she waved the topic off Newman saw the redness in her cheeks. He chose to not point it out and was glad the waitress interrupted them momentarily to place their drinks in front of them. She informed them the pizza would be out shortly.

Alone again, Elliott focused her attention on DeLong. "How can you ever have been friends with this idiot?"

"Because I was one too," DeLong said simply, as he sipped his Coke.

He ignored the glare from Calhoun.

Calhoun appeared to want to respond, but he thought better of it.

Instead, he changed the subject to Christmas shopping.

As Newman waited for his pizza and joined the conversation, he felt the tension growing in the team. He tried to ignore it, but had the sickly feeling something was going to blow up in all their faces. He hoped he was wrong.

DeLong, however, for the rest of lunch, avoided looking in Calhoun's direction.

Chapter 31

"If you don't mind," Dr. Lucas Gordon said as he unwrapped his sandwich, "I'll eat lunch while you ask your questions. Today's sessions have been off the charts."

"Go right ahead," Newman agreed. "We know you're a busy man. We'll try to keep your time to a minimum."

"I was truly shocked to hear about Manny," Dr. Gordon began as he squirted mustard on his turkey. "He was a good man. More than a patient. I considered him a friend."

"Did Grimes say anything to you about who may have had a grudge against him?" Calhoun asked.

Dr. Gordon chewed his sandwich slowly. "Not to my recollection. Our sessions are recorded, so I may be able to skim through and see if there's anything on there." He swallowed and took a sip of his drink.

"Why did Grimes need therapy?"

"Ever since he got divorced, Manny's been coming to see me. He wanted to reconcile with his wife. That was the majority of our sessions."

"What was the cause of his divorce? Did he say?" Elliott wondered.

"I'm afraid that falls under doctor-patient confidentiality. You'll have to ask his ex-wife."

He picked up his sandwich, but off a piece, then set it down. "I do remember a few weeks ago, all he wanted to talk about was a friend of his."

"Alan Walker?" Newman inquired.

The doctor shrugged. "I think that was the name from the news. Manny never really said. But supposedly his friend was having an affair with his brother's wife. The brother wouldn't believe Manny. I think the fight had been going on for quite a while. Then, in one of our sessions, Manny started talking about that friend of his. He became obsessed with uncovering some deep secret. Especially after his friend killed himself and another woman."

"Did he find anything?"

Dr. Gordon ate slowly as he thought back.

"I'm not sure, to tell you the truth. I do remember he had missed a session. I ran into him at the library. His face was white. Like he saw a ghost. When I stopped him to find out why he skipped our session, he just kept saying, 'It's not possible. It's not possible.' He continued to mumble something before he said he needed to 'take care of it.'"

Dr. Gordon folded the uneaten portion of his sandwich in its plastic and tossed the remains into the wastebasket by his desk. "Manny wasn't making any sense. I couldn't get what it was he was trying to tell me. I tried calling him later, but couldn't reach him."

Dr. Gordon leaned back in his chair.

"Wait." The doctor leaned forward, linking his hands together against the desk. "Something about a man called McCoy." Dr. Gordon shook his head. "He just kept muttering the name McCoy."

"How long ago was this?" Calhoun asked.

"Last week. I never saw him again. But he called me a few days after. He said he was in Birmingham and he wanted to see his kids. I don't think he let his boys know he was there. He just wanted to watch them. Then, just before he hung up, he told me he had proof. He supposedly hid it at his ex-wife's house."

"Did he say what it was?" Elliott asked.

"No, I don't think so. I just wanted to calm him down. I wanted to help him, but he was too nervous to listen to what I was saying."

"Did he say exactly where he hid this proof?" Newman asked.

Dr. Gordon squinted his eyes, trying to remember.

"I don't know exactly. But he said that 'it'll always be under the boys.' I don't know what he meant by that. Manny was a wreck. He hung up, and that was the last I heard of him. Until now."

"Thank you for your time, Doctor," Calhoun said, his mind buzzing. "You were a big help."

"I hope so. I truly hope so."

* * *

DeLong sat uncomfortably in his own therapist's office. He crossed his legs, only to uncross them.

"Are you okay, Lieutenant?" Dr. Davis asked. He wrote something on his pad.

"What? Oh, I'm fine," DeLong told him.

Apparently unconvinced, Dr. Davis let it slide.

"How do you feel about Samantha's loneliness?"

Her loneliness?

What about her betrayal?

DeLong cleared his throat before answering.

"Well, I hate it," he claimed matter-of-factly. "I just wished she said something a long time ago."

Before you decided to sleep with my best friend.

"I did!" Samantha jerked her head in the direction of her husband.

Dr. Davis held his hand up. "Let's let Jim elaborate his answer. Jim?"

"It's not easy being a cop," DeLong explained. "I work literally all hours of the day. I try to balance my work life with home life. But it's not always easy. It's not like I want to be away from her. But she shuts me out. And after so much of that, she...get this..." DeLong leaned forward to empathize. "She tells me she has an affair with my best friend. And she uses her so-called loneliness as an excuse." He leaned back, throwing his hands in the air. "And I'm the bad guy!"

"Yes, let's talk about this—"

"Yes, let's do," Samantha interrupted. She positioned herself on the couch to see her husband better. "Russ was a good friend. He was always there for me, especially when you weren't."

"Then you screwed him. For over a year. Even got yourself pregnant." He laughed mockingly. "Congratulations, by the way. A little late, but better than never."

"You know what?" Samantha shouted. "No one can blame me. I got sick of people coming to me, asking me, 'Sam, why is Jim with his friends more than you?' 'Sam, is Jim drinking again?' 'Sam, why are you so sad?' So, I found a way to not be sad. You know what, Jim? I'm glad I did it."

With that, she snatched her handbag from the floor and stalked out of the office, leaving the therapist and her husband staring after her.

"Let me ask you this," Dr. Davis said softly after a short, harsh pause. "Do you want to save your marriage?"

DeLong swallowed hard. That didn't go as he had hoped. *Nice one, Jim*, he thought bitterly. Then he realized his therapist was still waiting for an answer.

He rubbed the nape of his neck. "Yeah. I do."

"Then my suggestion today is to stop accusing and start listening. That's where real healing begins. And I'm not telling just you. I'll tell your wife the same thing."

He waited until his words sank in, then picked up his pen.

"Why don't you go and I'll bill you for half a session. Have a conversation with her, then come back next week, same day, same time."

Chapter 32

DeLong paced outside the sheriff's office trying to calm his nerves. He knew he couldn't enter the building where Calhoun was waiting to co-solve a murder with him. Not when his own investigators were working closely with them, watching their every move. He knew if he saw Calhoun right now, he'd snap.

But of course, he also knew he had a job to do. He reminded himself that he was a professional. He just needed to get through this investigation, then he could—.

Could what?

What would be waiting for him in the future?

He didn't know.

He didn't *want* to know.

The motto of his AA meetings was "to take life one day at a time."

Well, he figured he could throw that out the window. His years of sobriety were over. And did he care?

After he had enough of the cold, he finally decided he was calm enough. He closed his eyes and sighed a deep sigh before jogging through the empty streets and up the steps.

"Hey, Jim," Calhoun Calle out kindly when the lieutenant stepped in the office. Calhoun was peeling his coat off his shoulders. Newman and Elliott were chatting with another officer by the coffee canister.

"Hey," DeLong echoed with a nod.

He decided not to let any awkward moment have a chance to weasel its way in, so he jumped to business.

"What did our doctor have to say?"

He listened carefully, focusing on the case at hand.

"Have you asked Sarah Benson about her knowledge of this evidence?"

"We called and left a message for her to call back," Elliott replied as she replenished her coffee. "Still waiting to hear from her."

"Let's go over what we have so far," DeLong suggested. He went to his office, the others following. "The Walker children see the victim at the swings. We know they saw someone run from the body," DeLong said. "But, they couldn't see them clearly enough to get a description, whether it's man or woman, tall or short."

DeLong grabbed a pen from his desk, twirling it between his fingers.

"When you investigate, you don't see Grimes," Calhoun added. "But later you find him in the basement. So, our missing person becomes a murder."

"Whoever the killer is, killed Grimes with a .38 Special, and most likely wears a Doc Marten, size eleven and smokes Marlboros," Newman added.

"Not many people around here wears Doc Martins, and plenty smoke Marlboros," Calhoun muttered. "I haven't seen any of our persons of interests wearing Docs."

"What about the Alan Walker lead?" DeLong wondered. "Can we link it somehow to Grimes' murder?"

"Not yet," Elliott replied. "So far we only know our vic accused Alan of having an affair with Christy Walker. Jonathan Walker says he didn't want to believe it, but then again admitted he probably didn't have much of a choice but to believe. Maybe he did believe it.

He could have followed his brother and wife to the hotel room, killed her, then killed him to make it look like a murder/suicide."

"We're grasping at straws," DeLong muttered. "Grimes found something out. Something that seemed to frighten him." He leaned forward and linked his hands together. "In Grimes' journal, Alan had supposedly told Grimes he had done something horrible in the past. When he killed himself, he left an unsigned note saying he needed to come clean."

"But what did he need to come clean about?" Elliott wondered

"That's what we need to find out. We need to dig deeper and find out if he was murdered, and if that's the case, then who killed him. And once we find out who killed Alan, we may very well find out who killed Grimes *and* whatever horrible secret he's been carrying around. Calhoun and Elliott, interview Alan Walker's co-workers. Maybe they overheard him having a conversation with his killer. Or maybe they saw something out of the ordinary lying around."

DeLong rose to fill a Styrofoam cup with hot coffee. He dumped in a sugar packet and stirred, deep in thought. "I have a feeling Grimes knew something about the suicide and that something is what killed him. I don't know how yet, but it's all connected. And we just need to fit the puzzle pieces together."

DeLong waited until the instructions sank in and the hot coffee finished sliding down his throat.

"Newman and I will continue trying to find Sarah Benson to see if she knows what Grimes meant by 'it'll always be under the boys.' And let's go to the library to see if anyone remembered seeing him or what he was doing. Maybe we'll get lucky. According to Dr. Gordon, something Grimes found at the library was upsetting."

DeLong paused, absentmindedly stirring his coffee. His mind buzzed so loudly, his head began to pound.

So many things.

So many issues at once.

"Right now, I'm going to give Captain Stewart an update, then I'll meet Newman at the library."

Chapter 33

There were few people browsing the bookshelves of the local library, some sitting at tables reading or speaking in hush tones amongst each other.

Anyone they came across had only recognized Grimes from the news. They began to lose hope before finding an older lady wearing half-moon glasses engrossed in a book at a corner table. She had a travel mug of coffee before her and a sweater wrapped tightly around her frame. The air breezed through DeLong's body, resulting in a slight quiver. He resisted the urge of hugging his own jacket.

As they padded closer to the woman, DeLong saw her eyes skirt across the pages of a book written by Steven James: *The Queen*. Her eyes widened, as her mouth moved, silently and intensely reading to herself.

"Excuse us, ma'am," DeLong said. He kept his voice low to keep from disturbing others.

The woman made no move to reply.

DeLong placed a hand on her shoulder. "Ma'am?"

Startled, she swung her face upward to see the two men standing before her. She let out a soft, hearty laugh.

"Goodness," she breathed, her hand over her chest. "You gave me a fright."

"My apologies, ma'am," DeLong told her.

"Ah, no matter, young man. If my heart stopped, at least I'll be doing what I loved." She smiled. "Is there something I can do for you?"

"My name is Lieutenant Jim DeLong. This is my investigator, Jeff Newman. We wanted to know if you've seen this man here before?"

Newman placed a recent photo of Manny Grimes on the table and she studied it.

"Why, yes. That's the young man who's been on the news." She looked up. "Right?"

DeLong sat in the chair across from her.

"Yes, ma'am. We're investigating his death. A lead told us he was here not too long ago. About a week ago, in fact."

The elderly woman looked down again, her eyes skimming each line of Grimes' face, as though she was doing a search in her memory.

They waited until she looked up again.

"Yes, now that I think about it, I have seen him. It was Tuesday."

"Do you remember what he was doing?"

She pointed toward the small circle of computers.

"He came in, got on the computer and about an hour and a half later, he ran out. He seemed agitated, poor fellow."

"In what way?" Newman pressed.

"He was in a hurry, face pale. I was over there, I think. Yes, I was."

She pointed to a row of books.

"Do you remember anything else? Did he speak to anyone?"

"No—why, yes! I remember now. At my age, memory is fleeting, you know."

"Who did he talk to? Can you describe them?" DeLong urged.

"Of course not. He was on the phone. I can't tell you who he spoke to. But he left in a hurry. Then someone did stop him. It was someone he knew, I think. The poor fellow was flustered. He ran up the stairs."

"Do you remember anything else?" DeLong asked.

She shook her head. "I just went back to my browsing."

"Thank you for your time," DeLong told her. "You were a big help."

"Oh, I'm glad. I sure hope you can get justice for the poor fellow."

"We do too," DeLong said, earnestly, "we do too."

When they left her to resume her reading, DeLong and Newman headed for the computer. He tapped a button, and it requested him to input a password.

"Excuse me," DeLong said to the young girl behind the desk. She irritably glanced from her paperwork. "What's the password?"

"Have to have a library card," the girl said tautly.

"I have a police department badge," DeLong retorted. "Does that help?"

She rolled her eyes and came over to type the information in. The screen revealed a website containing newspaper articles.

"I don't suppose you have a record of who looked up what," DeLong inquired.

"Nope." The girl stalked away and went back to her work.

"Okay," DeLong began. "We know Grimes came here to look something up. I'll do a search on Alan Walker. Whatever's going on has to be centered on him."

After he hit search, they skimmed the results. The only ones they found told the story of Alan and Christy Walker's murder/suicide. Even so, they scanned the articles until satisfied there was nothing they didn't already know about the two deaths.

"Grimes had to have found something," Newman muttered.

"In his journal entry, he said Alan did something bad a long time ago. The suicide was more recent. In Jonathan Walker's house, there was a picture of Alan Walker with his sons. He was wearing a Navy uniform."

DeLong began typing again, including 'Navy' in the search.

One result popped on the screen.

Newman jabbed his finger against the monitor. "There. In the description, it says something about McCoy."

Clicking on the link, DeLong read the headline:

NAVAL OFFICER IS PERSON OF INTEREST IN MURDER
By Kelly Partain

Sunday night, Ensign Lawrence McCoy was murdered by fellow officers. So far, only Chief Petty Officer Alan Walker has been identified as McCoy's killer. Conditions to this crime are unknown at this point. It is unclear whether CPO Walker was acting alone, or with a partner. Fleet Admiral Ozzy Matheson has no comment at this time.

"This is getting weirder," Newman muttered as DeLong printed the article.

"So, Alan Walker supposedly kills this McCoy guy, and years later commits suicide because he can't handle it?" Newman shook his head in disbelief. "I don't believe it."

"Me neither," DeLong agreed. "It's too circumstantial. Let's get a hold of this Fleet Admiral Matheson. See if he'll be willing to talk to us. I'm not satisfied with this one little article."

DeLong and Newman returned to the sheriff's office, and after a search, they found a contact number for Fleet Admiral Matheson. DeLong called, putting it on the speaker phone so Newman could hear, and it was answered on the first ring.

After DeLong informed him of who he was and why he was calling, Admiral Matheson remained quiet. For a second, DeLong thought the call had ended.

He glanced at Newman with inquiring eyes.

"Yes, I heard about Walker when it happened," Matheson finally said. "I, along with a few of his other shipmates back then, was saddened to hear the news."

Matheson didn't offer any other response.

"I found an article," DeLong continued, "but it didn't divulge much information. Just that Alan Walker was accused of murdering an ensign. Can you elaborate?"

"Yes, I remember that. There was a reporter back then. She wanted to impress her boss or something—she was new—so she started claiming that an ensign by the name of McCoy was murdered. There was no evidence of that happening. As far as we knew, McCoy went AWOL."

"But the article—." DeLong began.

"The article was recanted the next day," the admiral interrupted. "It never should have gone to print in the first place."

"Did you at least investigate?"

"We did, but quietly. Do you want the simple truth?" Matheson asked him. "I neither wanted, nor needed, a scandal or the extra attention. And, anyway, we couldn't find anything beyond circumstantial evidence. It would have been a headache of a case."

DeLong found his heart aching for this McCoy guy. And he ached all the more knowing there was nothing he could do about it. The more he tried to wrap his mind around the two cases that seemed to intertwine with one another, it all became jumbled.

Somehow, the murder of Manny Grimes was connected to Alan Walker's death. That much he knew for sure. But was it connected to Ensign McCoy's disappearance? Or were they opening a bunch of cans of worms that didn't need to be opened?

"You know what a headache is, Admiral?" DeLong spat out angrily. "A headache is trying to find out who killed one man who had been friends with another man, who reportedly killed himself and a woman, only to learn he may or may not have been involved in a murder while serving the Navy, which as you say, 'would have been a headache of a case.'"

DeLong closed his eyes and sucked in a breath, but he wasn't near finished.

"Now I need you to stop hiding whatever it is you're hiding, or protecting whoever you're protecting, do your job, and just tell me the truth. Who killed Ensign Lawrence McCoy? Was it Alan Walker?"

"Like I told you, Lieutenant," Matheson said in a cool, collected tone, which only resulted in more anger, "we could not find any evidence of any wrongdoing."

DeLong shook his head in disgust.

"Couldn't, or is your simple truth that you didn't want to?" DeLong challenged.

The Murder of Manny Grimes

"I'm afraid this conversation is over," Matheson said. "If you want to continue our conversation, I suggest you speak with Bryan Beasley. My lawyer. Have a wonderful day."

DeLong listened as the dial tone buzzed.

Irritated, he jammed his finger on the button to turn off the speaker, leaned back and closed his eyes.

"That didn't go well," Newman said after a few minutes ticked by.

"No," DeLong replied irritably, "Suicide by cop doesn't go well. That phone call went horribly." He pushed back his chair, stepped over to the coffee machine and filled a cup.

But he didn't drink it.

He stared at the liquid, deep in thought.

Who did the guy think he was?

And who was he protecting?

The dull ache in his body returned once again. DeLong put his hand on his side where he was injured the night he had gone to Manny Grimes' house. Was it connected?

If so, how?

DeLong tossed the cup in the wastebasket and turned to Newman.

"Let's call it a night." DeLong grabbed his jacket from the chair, told Newman he'd see him tomorrow, and left the building.

* * *

After speaking with the police officer from Augusta, Admiral Matheson replaced the landline in the cradle. He leaned back in his chair and shut his eyes.

A heavy sigh escaped his lips. He realized his heart was drumming against his rib cage.

As he rose, he let out a round of curses.

This couldn't be happening. It just couldn't be.

He stared out the window, watching the leaves on the trees sway against the cold wind.

He spent fifteen years letting go of the past. How could it all unravel because of one man?

No, he told himself. It wasn't because of one man.

They'd made a mistake that would get them all discharged. They'd made a mistake that would send them to prison for life, possibly even put them on death row. It was a rookie mistake that should have been corrected. But then Alan Walker decided to grow a conscience.

It was supposed to stop with him. But, no, Manny Grimes had to stick his nose in where it didn't belong. So, of course, they had to get rid of him. But where did it stop? With Grimes? With the lieutenant who just called him only a few minutes ago? When would the past just stay in the past?

Matheson returned to his desk and used the key to unlock the bottom drawer. Inside, he kept a bottle of Johnnie Walker Scotch Whiskey. Retrieving the scotch and a rock glass, he poured himself a double shot and downed it with one swallow.

He wondered how far they would go to keep that day fifteen years ago with McCoy buried.

Matheson set the glass on his desk, sat in his comfortable chair and made a call.

Chapter 34

DeLong's ears were ringing with the buzz from the crowd at Philadelphia Jack's. He sat at the corner of the bar so he could lean against the wall. He didn't care the old paneling was filthy and laden with germs.

He was tired and ready to allow his anger to show its face. This entire day had been a waste as far as he was concerned. The more involved in Manny Grimes' murder he became, the more questions he had about the mystery.

Why couldn't one thing go right for him?

Just one thing.

Was that too much to ask?

The frustration was eating him inside and out.

He needed some release.

Much to Philadelphia's dismay, DeLong ordered Jameson on the rocks.

As he slowly drank, he cursed everyone that entered his life.

Admiral Matheson.

Calhoun.

His wife and the therapist.

DeLong closed his eyes tightly, trying to drown out the racket from the bar. The sham therapy was just that: a sham.

Whiskey usually hit the spot just right, but for whatever reason, it wasn't helping this time. He kept picturing Samantha, then Calhoun, then the two of them together, right under his nose. He sipped his bottomless glass of whiskey slowly. His attention span weaved in and out of conversations, much like his vision weaved around the four walls of the place.

DeLong noticed Philadelphia Jack at the end of the bar. He placed a cocktail napkin in front of a newcomer and set a small glass on top. Once he poured the liquid into the cup, he nodded at his customer. She smiled warmly, brushing her red hair out of her eyes.

The bartender walked over to DeLong when he finished the last drop.

"It's quite a surprise to return from my not-so-much-of-a-vacay and find that Lieutenant Jim DeLong is having a drink. Everything okay?" Philadelphia asked, wiping the bar.

"It's great," DeLong muttered above the loud music. He pushed his glass toward the bartender. "Just great. Hit me with another, Phil."

"Don't you think you've had enough?" the bartender asked. His brow furrowed in concern. "I don't want you to overdo it." Though he seemed to protest, he poured his customer another glass.

DeLong took a sip and sighed. "I don't think anything will be enough right now."

"Job or wife?" Philadelphia asked.

DeLong took another sip and then slammed the glass on the bar. "It just happens to be both." He let out a groan. "I'm just going around in circles with this case I'm working. The closer I get, the further away I'm pushed. And today the wife claims she was lonely 'cause I never was around. She's the one who wanted to quit nursing. Someone has to be the breadwinner, don't you agree?"

"Well, that's why I ain't married. Them women will drive ya nuts. Especially if you're working a job. They say they ain't made just to sit around and clean all day," Philadelphia grumbled with a slight smile. "Then when you're home, they don't want nuthin' to do with ya."

"I hear that," DeLong said, raising his glass as if to toast the statement. "I come home and find my wife all riled up 'cause I'm late." He took a big swallow, emptying the contents, handing it to Philadelphia for another. "And I just now find out, for over a year, she's been banging my so-called friend and partner."

"That's women, man. Marriage ain't all it's cracked up to be."

"Says you," DeLong replied with a weak smile.

The room had already begun to spin. Now it was a whirlwind.

He heard his own voice slurring, but it sounded so far away, along with every other sound. DeLong felt as though he was out of his body, watching himself succumb deeper to drunkenness. "Easy to say when you're free to roam about and close this place, then go home with two broads hangin' all over you."

"Sometimes I don't even get home." Philadelphia's lips curved into a smile.

"I wound up leaving her when all I wanted was to squeeze her freaking neck until she turned blue." For the first time since he found out the truth, DeLong's anger began to reach the surface. He felt the fire burn every nerve ending in his body. He wanted to laugh. He wanted to scream. He wanted to throw his glass against the mirror behind Philadelphia.

Most of all, he wanted to just not feel.

The bartender topped off his whiskey, then went over to wipe a spill an overly drunk customer made. Distantly, DeLong heard the drunk man throw Philadelphia every cuss word in the book.

"Get out of here!" the bartender shouted as the man knocked over two stools, stumbling to gain composure.

"Hey, Phil!" shouted a man in the corner. His friends burst out laughing. A short woman with crewcut hair wrapped her arms around the speaker, nibbling his neck. "How 'bout a round of drinks for all my friends here at the bar!"

The bar erupted in excitement.

The bartender obliged, going around, refilling drinks.

DeLong looked over at the redhead to see her looking his way. She gave him a bright smile, grabbed her drink, and hopped off her stool. A second later, she was by his side, hand on his shoulders.

She leaned into him. "Hi!"

DeLong squinted his eyes, trying to gain control of his vision. Her face was blurred. He felt his arms go limp.

He muttered some type of greeting. He wasn't sure which one.

"I'm Leslie!" She shouted to be heard over the chatter.

"I'm Jim!"

"You know, I'm new in town. Don't know a soul," Leslie told him.

"Yeah? Where you from?" DeLong asked.

"Boston. Born and raised."

"What brings you to Augusta?"

"A new life," she told him taking a sip of her drink.

The loud rock music changed to a slow tune. Leslie swayed her shoulders back and forth, her eyes closed. She had a peaceful smile on her face. Opening her eyes, she looked over at him.

"This used to be my favorite song." Leslie hopped off the barstool. "Dance with me!"

Before he could protest, she grabbed his hand and pulled him close to her. She wrapped her arms around his neck and buried her face in his chest. He smelled sunflowers in her hair. The scent made him feel dizzy, or maybe it was the drinks he had. He wasn't sure.

DeLong held onto her until the song ended and she pulled away.

He just wanted to sit.

He wanted to lie down.

He glanced around the bar, watching the blurred images fly by.

Where would he lie?

"Thanks," she said, her voice drowned out by the continuation of the loud music. "I love to dance! I miss it."

Her voice brought him a quarter of a way back to consciousness.

Her smile was flirty. She licked her lips slightly. Leslie leaned into his ears to whisper something, he wasn't sure what.

DeLong began to feel uneasy. Despite the alcohol buzzing in his head, something was sending him red alerts. He wanted to leave, but couldn't find the door.

The room wobbled as he stepped backward, knocking into an empty chair. All sounds began to fade away, still his head beat in tune with the background music.

DeLong gripped the edge of the counter, trying to control the dizziness. In the mirror, his eyes were dull, and his cheeks were pale yellow. He began to turn away to face Leslie, but something made him turn back.

In the mirror, he saw Manny Grimes standing behind him. He reached out as though he was trying to grab him.

Help me.

Grimes' voice was garbled.

Blood began trickling down his face.

The boys. Under the boys.

The image in the mirror began to change, but DeLong couldn't see straight. He couldn't tell what Grimes was telling him, if anything. The room continued to spin faster, faster. He closed his eyes and shook his head. When he opened them again, he saw only his pale, yellow face staring back. Leslie swayed her hips to the loud music, her eyes closed.

He turned to face her.

"I should go," DeLong said, still holding the edge of the bar.

He walked to the bar and paid his tab, as well as hers. Ignoring what the bartender was saying to him, he left Leslie behind and staggered outside toward his truck. He knew he wasn't in any condition to drive.

He decided to close his eyes for just a few minutes, then he'd go home.

After he fell into his truck, he blinked once, and drifted out of existence.

Chapter 35

DeLong woke with the sun blinding him. He groaned and rubbed his eyes.

A headache once again returned. DeLong waited a few minutes before sitting up. When he did, he looked around his unfamiliar surroundings.

He found himself in a small room on a couch. The walls were dirty and plain except for a Bob Marley poster. The door was slightly ajar; he could hear soft talking on the other side.

Memory was a haze.

The last thing he remembered clearly was investigating inside the basement at the Columbia County Elementary School. Struggling to clear his head, he slowly rose.

DeLong stumbled back onto the couch, beating his head against the wall.

Flashes of light exploded in his eyes. He couldn't see past the stars circling his pupils. DeLong laid himself back on the sofa, deciding he shouldn't move just yet.

The noise had someone stepping into the room. When the door opened, DeLong opened his eyes slightly and saw the background of the bar, and Philadelphia Jack in the doorframe. The two-hundred-pound man leaned against the entranceway, arms crossed.

"I'm glad you're up," Philadelphia said with a frown. "I'll be having more customers and don't need Augusta's finest passed out on my couch."

"What?" DeLong grumbled. "What time is it?"

"Seven," Philadelphia told him.

DeLong massaged his throbbing temple.

He tried to remember the night before, but couldn't. It had been years since he blacked out completely. Then again, it had been years since he even touched alcohol.

Samantha's going to kill me, he thought groggily.

"How'd I end up back here?" he asked, probing for possible answers to explain his state of mind.

"Found you passed out in your car. You know, it's nearly two degrees out there, man. Do that again, I might just let ya freeze to death," Philadelphia said, passing his towel back and forth in his hand. "I couldn't just let you stay out there, so I brought you in here."

He looked intently at DeLong for a few minutes, pure concern imprinted in his facial lines. DeLong rolled to a sitting position and leaned his head toward his knees, trying his best to defeat the hangover. "You know, I had a feeling I shouldn't have served you those drinks. You have a problem?"

DeLong looked at the bartender, a million thoughts racing through his mind. He tried to weed them out but failed.

"Listen, why don't you go on home?" Philadelphia suggested. "I would have taken you last night, but didn't know what motel you're staying at."

"Motel?" DeLong grumbled.

"Yeah, you told me last night you left your wife," the bartender reminded him. "Remember? You were staying at some 'dump motel,' I think was your phrase."

"Vaguely." DeLong lifted himself from the couch and stumbled toward the open door.

"Whoa, there," Philadelphia said, putting both hands on DeLong's shoulders. "Maybe you should have some coffee. That'll wake you up."

"As long as it's Irish," DeLong mumbled.

"Can't do it, man," Philadelphia told him. "Had I realized you had a problem, I wouldn't have served you alcohol in the first place. I just thought you were trying to drown out your sorrows."

DeLong snorted. "Isn't that what drunks do?"

Philadelphia helped DeLong to a barstool and poured him a cup of coffee. "How long has it been?"

DeLong hesitated, letting his eyes slowly come into focus as Philadelphia wiped the bar, waiting for an answer.

"I've been sober for seven years," he said, blowing into the coffee.

"All that time you come in here, I wondered why you always only ordered a Coke. But I figured you just didn't drink. Imagine my surprise when you did last night."

"Yeah, well," DeLong said, lifting the mug to his lips. "Sam's going to kill me."

The bartender shrugged. "Don't tell her. She'll never know if you don't tell her. Just go to your motel and rest a bit. Then, once you're fully alert, you can pretend it never happened."

DeLong snickered. "She'll know. She always knows."

"How long have you been married?"

"Five years...tomorrow," DeLong realized.

"I guess it's not happy anniversary," Philadelphia said. "Sorry, man. I really feel for you."

"Yeah," DeLong scoffed. "So do I."

He finished his coffee, paid, though Philadelphia tried to wave it off, then rose unsteadily to his feet, looking at his watch, his vision still out of focus.

What he needed and wanted was a good night's rest.

After assuring the bartender he was lucid, he walked to his truck.

DeLong looked in his rearview mirror as the parking lot began to crowd with more early morning drinkers. Something took hold of his chest, squeezing the air out of him. He sat in the truck for a few minutes, trying to regain momentum.

It seemed everything was spiraling out of control. One thing would lead him one way and another would lead him a different way. He knew he was losing perspective, but didn't know how to handle it. For a man who was always direct, he felt the pieces of his life fall apart.

He felt like this one time before. Only that time, he had something—some*one* to live for.

This time, all he wanted was another drink. Nothing else mattered.

DeLong shook the thought out of his head.

No.

He was wrong.

Bella mattered.

Even if nothing else did, his daughter *mattered*.

He removed his wallet from his back pocket and stared at a photo of Samantha, himself and their daughter. The radiant ocean rose in the background. Sam's long black hair was damp and disheveled, a warm smile on her face. He stood next to her, arm draped across her shoulders.

He was staring into Sam's arms where their newborn daughter rested. Too young to be enjoying beach life.

DeLong ran a finger over the photo, his heart aching. He didn't want to lose the happiness found in the picture.

With a newfound devotion, he set the photo on his dashboard and jammed his key in the ignition. The truck roared to life. He found his phone and called Newman, watching in the rearview mirror as Philadelphia Jack's faded into the fog.

Chapter 36

When DeLong stepped into the office, the first thing he saw was Samantha.

At first, he thought she might be waiting for him. DeLong swallowed, then prepared to go to her, to apologize for what happened at the therapy session.

He took a step.

Then stopped.

Calhoun had approached, handing her a Styrofoam cup. She accepted with a small smile.

DeLong furled and unfurled his fist.

He continued in their direction.

"Hey, Jim," Calhoun began. "I—."

The fist DeLong connected with his jaw blocked off anything else Calhoun might have planned to say.

Retaliating, Calhoun made a speedy recovery, diving toward DeLong's body, knocking him backward, hitting the ground hard. A crowd gathered around, unnoticed as the two men fought, rolled, and tumbled on the ground.

The Murder of Manny Grimes

DeLong felt someone take hold of his arms, jerking him back.

Calhoun was held back by Newman while Captain Stewart had DeLong in an arm lock.

Elliott stood nearby, mouth agape.

DeLong spat out blood and wiped his bloody lip.

Both men's shoulders heaved as they took in quick breaths.

They stared into each other's eyes, both burning with rage. DeLong broke away from the heated glare and looked over at Samantha. She mouthed something in disgust and crossed her arms, infuriated.

"Nothing more for you to see, people!" Stewart bellowed. "Get back to work!" The crowd hesitantly began to thin out. Directing his attention to DeLong and Calhoun, he said, "In my office, now!"

Without waiting for an answer, he stormed away.

"What was that about?" Newman asked.

"Ask Calhoun," DeLong demanded. He resisted the urge to throw another punch.

"How am I supposed to know!" Calhoun spat out, his hands resting on his knees. "All I know is I saw your fist coming at me!"

"You're still going after my wife!" DeLong shouted.

"So that's how you like to handle things?" Calhoun replied heatedly. "Kill first, ask questions later?" He waved his hand in the air. "I told you it was over. We both told you it was over. And we *meant* it."

DeLong watched as he stalked toward the captain's office.

After seconds of silence, Elliott moved on, followed by Newman.

Then it was only Samantha and DeLong.

"How dare you," she spat out.

"How dare I?" DeLong snapped. "This is my place of employment, Samantha. You don't have the decency to keep your affairs at home? You have to come to where I work? To shove it in my face?"

"Is that really what you think? That I'm going to be all over Russ. After I assured you that it was over, you think I'm going to be all over him just to make you hurt? Is it? Or maybe that's what the whiskey I smell on your breath is telling you. You are ruining your life, Jim. The sad thing is, though, it's not only your life you're ruining. It's mine, it's Russ's. It's your *daughter's*! You need help."

DeLong sucked in a breath. He put his fist through the wall, then rested his forehead against the structure.

"I know," DeLong whispered. "I know."

"Well, you should get help. However, I'm not sure if Bella and I will be around waiting for you to be healed. Not this time."

She walked away, letting her words cut into him.

He saw his captain impatiently standing outside, waiting.

Finally, DeLong walked to the office, prepared to face his captain's wrath.

"Just what were the two of you doing out there?" Stewart demanded. His words seemed to vibrate against the walls. He paced behind his desk as if he were addressing several men in a platoon. Stewart glared from Calhoun to DeLong.

Stewart's eyes glowed with fury and his chest rose and fell in quick movements.

He let out a round of angry curses.

"Captain, I—."

Stewart slapped a hand on the desk with enough force, the items on top shook.

"Zip it, Lieutenant! I don't want to hear a word out of either one of you!" He slapped his hand on his desk and glared at DeLong. "I don't know what your problem is with Calhoun, Lieutenant, but if you want to continue working as part of *my* task force, you *will* put your personal baggage behind you, starting *right* now. If you felt the need to go hand-to-hand, the least you could have done is wait 'til you were out of *my* building!"

He shifted his glare from DeLong to Calhoun.

"And you. I expected more out of you. Could you not have provoked him? Haven't you learned to walk away from a stupid, *senseless* fight?"

In exasperation, the captain swiped his arm across his desk, knocking two stacks of paperwork and a pencil holder on the floor.

DeLong and Calhoun exchanged glances. They mirrored each other, both with blackening eyes, bruised cheeks and bloody lips. DeLong's arms were scraped, and his rib cage throbbed. The pain of the fractured ribs returned with a vengeance. The worst injury Calhoun seemed to have succumbed was his left eye swelling shut.

Stewart cupped his hands over his mouth, shaking his head, then turned to stare out the window, across the parking lot. "I'm gonna tell you what I'm gonna do. DeLong, you're suspended for a month. Without pay. Calhoun, I'm letting you off with a warning since you don't even technically work for me. Get back to work."

"Yes, sir," Calhoun obliged. He left the office, leaving DeLong alone with the captain.

"Captain, I—," DeLong started again. He stopped short, unsure of what he could say to rectify the mess he instigated. Running a hand through his tangled hair, he exhaled, realizing the best course of action would be silence. "Am I dismissed as well?"

Stewart turned from the window to frown at him. "That's the smartest thing I've heard you say. I was quite sure you were going to fight me on the decision I made. But that would have been a bad move on your part, wouldn't it?"

"Yes, sir."

"Do you think I should have given you a warning?" Stewart wondered. "Since I gave Calhoun a warning?"

"No, sir," DeLong said, clearing his throat.

"Hmm. Why not?"

"I threw the first punch, not Calhoun."

"Are you normally a violent person?" The captain had his hands face down on his desk, body hovering to glare into DeLong's eyes.

He wasn't quite sure if Stewart had meant this to be a rhetorical question. But DeLong figured he should answer just to be on the safe side.

"No, sir," DeLong said. "I think a month off-duty will suffice."

"I sure hope so. Give me your badge and weapon. Dismissed." The captain turned to face the window again. Setting the items down, DeLong left the office, shutting the door behind him.

Chapter 37

After DeLong left, he sat in his truck without moving. His first thought was to drive to the nearest liquor store and buy them out.

He started the truck.

Set it in reverse.

When he put the car in motion, he headed for the store.

At the red light, he turned the knob of his heater to lower the setting. The light seemed to take forever to turn green. Anxious to get to the store, DeLong drummed his fingers on the steering wheel, looking around outside. He spotted a church-like building. A sign by the street held the familiar symbol of a triangle within a circle containing two connecting A's.

Underneath the symbol read: *Unity, Service, Recovery.*

Finally, the light changed colors and DeLong began driving. Rather than heading to the store, he parked in the lot of the building.

With hesitation, DeLong switched off the ignition and climbed out.

He slipped inside and saw four rows of chairs with eleven people scattered across the room.

A young man stood at the podium telling his story.

At the sound of the door opening and shutting, the small crowd turned briefly, then faced the front.

DeLong sat in the last row.

He tapped his foot lightly as he listened to a few stories of being clean for however long, or how they hit bottom.

He shook his head.

This wasn't for him.

He knew it.

He wasn't like these people. Hadn't been for seven years.

DeLong rose to leave.

He snuck out quietly and began walking toward his truck.

"Jim!"

DeLong froze and turned to the familiar voice.

"Harry," he acknowledged, groaning inwardly. The last thing he wanted was to talk about his past. "How're you doing?"

"Great, man," Harry replied proudly when he reached DeLong. "Couldn't be better. I'm a sponsor now. I reached my ten-year anniversary a month ago."

"That's great, man," DeLong said.

"How about you?" Harry inquired.

Yeah, I'm doing just great, DeLong thought bitterly. Marriage falling apart, job falling apart, and all he cared about was getting another drink.

"It's good to see you," Harry told him softly after he saw the hesitancy. He said nothing more, however, DeLong saw the undeniable concern in his eyes.

"Wish I could say the same," DeLong muttered.

He had always liked Harry.

He knew Harry had begun drinking heavily when he was sixteen years old after coming home from a friend's house to his slaughtered family. It wasn't until he had to be cut out of his own car when he was twenty-five, he realized it was either die or live. He chose the latter.

"I'm really glad to have you in my group," Harry told him.

"Yeah, me too, I guess," DeLong mumbled.

"See you next week?" he asked.

"Yeah, maybe," DeLong said simply. Then he shrugged. "I probably don't have much of a choice."

Harry gave him an understanding smile. "Well, Jim, I've always believed, in order to actually be helped, you not only *want* to help yourself for *you*, but you should stop looking at it as something you *have* to do. Until you admit to yourself you are an alcoholic, you'll never beat this disease."

"I made peace with it a long time ago," DeLong said defensively.

"Oh, that's great. When's the last time you had a drink?"

DeLong was sure his eyes flashed with anger at the obvious sarcasm, however, he managed to compose himself and chose instead to tell the truth. "Last night."

"Then you haven't made peace," Harry said.

"Well, Harry, maybe I have," DeLong cornered. "And I just don't care anymore."

"If that were true, why are we talking in front of an AA meeting?" Harry asked.

DeLong tried to think of a smart comeback but came up empty.

"Look," he said instead. "This isn't new to me. It's going to be—."

"Hard?" Harry finished. "Of course, it's going to be hard. It doesn't matter if this is your first time or your fifth time or even your hundred and fifth time. It's going to be hard. You have to *want* to turn your life around. It's the only way to get through this. And, Jim, as long as you *try,* we will all be there with you every step of the way."

He handed DeLong his card. "Call me anytime, day or night. If you feel like you need a drink, I'll help you through it. I'll sit with you all night if need be."

DeLong took the card without a reply. He watched as Harry turned and headed back into the building.

* * *

Because Newman's wife had a doctor's appointment, and he wanted to take her out for lunch afterward, Calhoun had coaxed Elliott into having lunch with him. How he managed it, she didn't have a clue. Either way, she agreed for him to stop by her apartment.

When the knock at the door came, she was only wearing a thick white robe. Elliott opened the door for him.

Calhoun smirked. "You didn't have to not get dressed just for me."

Elliott glared at him. "Shut up or leave."

He held up the McDonald's bag.

"But I bought lunch." A mock frown fell on his face.

She couldn't help but lift the corner of her mouth into a smile.

"Well, I guess you can come on in," she sighed.

As he stepped past her, he paused and took in a long breath, smelling lilac in her damp hair.

"Looks like I'm a little late," he said softly. "And here I thought I was early."

She sucked in a breath.

"Let's eat," he suggested before she made good on her threat to make him leave. He set the bag on the counter.

Calhoun glanced around the near perfection of Elliott's living quarters. He curiously walked over to pick up the pink bra she left on her bathroom doorknob with his index finger, looking at the cup size.

"You wish," he snickered. He regarded Elliott and seemed to enjoy her glare.

Elliott shut the door hard and snatched the lingerie from his hand, disappearing into her bedroom. "I will be right back. Try not to make yourself too much at home."

When she finished dressing in a thick green sweater and corduroys, Elliott found him settled on the brown fold-out couch in the middle of the living room.

He rubbed his index finger along the edge of a stain she had tried to hide with her flowered pillow.

"Soda may get this out," he announced.

She marched into the kitchen as she pulled her wet hair in a ponytail.

"I did not invite you in here to give out cleaning advice, Calhoun."

The side of Calhoun's mouth went up in a crooked, intrigued smile.

"What do you want to drink?" Elliott asked, retrieving two

glasses from the cupboard.

"Coke if you have it," he replied.

A second later, she set two glasses of sodas on the coffee table. The couch was the only furniture in the living room, so she decided to sit on the floor.

They began to eat in silence.

She could feel Calhoun's gaze on her.

"I can't believe DeLong did that today," she said softly, trying to come up with a conversation to keep the silence from filling the room. "Right there in front of all of us. What was he thinking?"

Calhoun didn't reply.

"So, tell me." Elliott directed her gaze to Calhoun. She narrowed her eyes slightly with curiosity. "Are you having an affair with DeLong's wife?"

Calhoun blinked twice, gaping at her. "Excuse me?"

"Don't feel too bad about it, Calhoun," she said. "If I were married to a domineering man like Jim DeLong, well, I'm sure I'd be having an affair too."

"You're too quick to judge," Calhoun noted. "No wonder you don't have friends."

Elliott opened her mouth to respond and decided against it. She knew her personality, at times, was crude.

She'd changed a lot over the years. Elliott used to be the quiet, reserved type. When the aftermath of the incident years ago cleared, she promised herself she would never be in that position again. No matter how much she found herself drawn to any certain man.

Elliott shook her head. She hadn't thought of those times in ages. And she didn't want to now.

"Maybe I am quick to judge," she said instead, "but experience taught me how to judge."

"I've known Jim since he was a kid," Calhoun insisted. "He's a good man."

"If you say so."

There was a short pause.

"It was a long time ago. A mistake. We're past that now."

"Obviously DeLong isn't."

She chewed slowly and looked around, avoiding Calhoun's eyes until she had no choice.

"What?" she demanded. "Why do you keep staring at me?"

Calhoun took a bite.

She watched him, waiting for an answer.

"Nothing," he told her as he chewed. "Well, I just think you look beautiful."

In an attempt to cover a smile, she rose to take her trash in the kitchen. She was well aware he was watching her every move.

"Not very good at hiding things, are you," he muttered.

He rose to take his own trash to the kitchen and dumped it in the bin by the counter.

Elliott, in an attempt to keep busy, began to wash the glasses.

He stood behind her, lightly running his finger against her arm. She felt her body tense, but something kept her feet in place. She wanted to move, at the same time, she didn't.

Calhoun brushed his lips against the side of her neck.

Elliott dropped the glass she held, melting into him.

Her heart skipped a beat as she turned to him. They gazed into each other's eyes. She saw the hunger he had for her. His lips found hers, his arms pulled her tight to his body.

She wrapped her arms tightly around his neck, moving deeper into the sweet, sweet kiss. Everything in her life seemed to vanish, and she swam deep in the passion, with Calhoun at the wheel.

Before she had a chance to realize what had happened, he pulled away, walking back into the living room. Her breath was heavy. She had to lean against the counter to support her legs. She touched a finger to her lips, which still electrified from his kiss.

Calhoun turned, shooting her a knowing smile.

Anger sprinted through her body and she stared him down, trying to regain her morals. "Don't think you're gonna make it to my bed, mister. I'd sooner kick you in the sack before you get into mine."

But she knew he knew it was a lie.

She stalked to the coat rack to grab her coat.

"Let's get going."

He followed her out of the apartment. She shut the door, then let out a curse.

"I forgot my handbag."

She reached above the doorframe, feeling along the edges until she found her spare key.

Elliott jiggled the key to her apartment door, cursing underneath her breath when it wouldn't open.

"Tough girl like you can't even get into her own apartment?" Calhoun provoked.

Elliott stopped her jiggling and glared at him, who kept his smile. She opened her mouth to respond; he looked around the small, dark hallway, whistling innocently.

She let out a heavy breath and continued to jiggle her key until it finally turned, and the door swung open.

"It's an old apartment," she explained irritably.

"You are one hard woman," Calhoun muttered under his breath as she ran inside.

Elliott returned, her handbag strap in place on her shoulder. Without looking his way, she started down the hallway.

Chapter 38

Sarah Benson finished washing the dishes she had allowed to pile up over the past few days. She hated a dirty sink, but she hadn't been in the mood to clean. Through the window, she watched her sons fiddle with the tire swing. They had been cooped in their room for days until she finally insisted they try to find something to do for fun outside. After much prodding, they obliged to go out in the backyard.

After she returned to Birmingham from identifying her ex-husband's body, the first person she'd called was her brother.

Kincaid was younger than her by five years and was passionate about stepping up and being the "older" sibling when she needed him.

Kincaid had kept consoling hands on her shoulders as Sarah sat the boys down to tell them the best way she knew how that daddy had an accident. They were ages six and seven, and she wanted to soften the news for them as much as possible.

Boyd, her oldest, tried to keep his tears at bay, though his lower lip quivered. His brother stared at the floor, face unreadable.

Sarah had gathered them in a long bear hug and held them as tightly as she could. She made sure they knew how much she loved them, and how much their dad loved them. She promised, though it would take time, they would get through it.

Now they stood around the tire swing, not really in the mood to play.

Their pain was so raw. She knew they had been looking forward to seeing their dad in a few weeks. She also knew they had hopes their parents would reconcile. Sarah loved him today as much as she had when they'd begun dating. Even she had hopes they'd reconcile. She never wanted the divorce. Manny had cost them so much money, it had ruined their relationship.

She remembered how her heart broke when he'd come clean about how he covered up a money laundering scandal for a client. He'd been such a good lawyer, always managing to get to the bottom of the truth and he lost his job, his family, his friends and millions of dollars because of a mistake that would tarnish his reputation forever.

Sarah knew he regretted the decisions he made. He'd worked so hard over the years to let her know he'd changed. That he wanted her back. He wanted his family back. Now there was no chance for reconciliation.

She had so much to do.

She needed to handle the funeral arrangements.

Call the florist. Find a pastor.

Lie down.

Sarah closed her eyes and swiped at the tear sliding down her cheek.

"Oh, Manny, why?" she whispered so low, she couldn't even tell if she thought it or spoke the words.

She opened her eyes, turned off the faucet and retrieved the phone from her handbag. She'd been in such a trance for the last few days, she hadn't bothered looking at her missed calls.

Now that she did, she realized she had one voicemail from Lieutenant DeLong, three from an investigator named Newman, and one from her brother from a few minutes ago.

She called Lieutenant DeLong first. Maybe he had something.

"DeLong," he said after the fifth ring.

"Lieutenant, this is Sarah Benson." Sarah realized how dry her voice was. She retrieved a glass from the cabinet and filled it with water.

"Yes," DeLong said. "I'm glad you called. How are you doing?"

She glanced outside and saw the boys picking up rocks and tossing them through the hole in the tire.

"It's a process, Lieutenant," Sarah replied after a sip. "But we'll be okay."

"I'm glad." The lieutenant hesitated, then let out a soft sigh. "The reason we've been trying to contact you is that we may have something."

"Oh?" Sarah sat on a stool at her nook.

"After interviewing your ex-husband's therapist, he remembered something that was said in one of their sessions. Your husband had hidden proof of something. He told his therapist it is where it will 'always be under the boys.' Do you know what that might mean?"

Sarah shook her head as she answered. "He's never mentioned anything to me. Do you think it has something to do with my sons?"

"I'm not sure, Ms. Benson," DeLong said. "Dr. Gordon didn't know much more than that. Do you know if your ex-husband was recently in Birmingham?"

Sarah closed her eyes.

"What do you mean?" she asked.

"Well, according to Dr. Gordon, your ex-husband was watching your sons right before he was killed."

"I'm sorry, I don't know that he was ever here."

"All right, Ms. Benson. If you do happen to find or remember anything, please call Jeffrey Newman from the crime lab, or Russ Calhoun. Thank you for returning my call."

"Of course. Keep me updated?"

"I sure will. Have a good day."

"You too."

When she ended the call, she stared across the kitchen. What was Manny doing in Birmingham? To see the boys? Did they see him? Did they talk to him?

She rose from the stool, grabbed a sweater and stepped out the back door. It seemed to her she needed to talk with her children.

"Hey guys," she said, hugging her sweater to shield herself from the cold.

"Hi, Mom," Boyd replied. Her heart broke a little more hearing the sadness in her son's words.

"Okay, I'm going to ask you a question, and I need you to be honest with me."

The boys looked at her, eyes shining with curiosity.

She knelt so she'd be at eye-level. After a heavy sigh, she said, "Have you seen your daddy lately? Has he come to see you and ask you not to tell me?"

They simultaneously shook their heads.

"Are you sure?" Sarah pleaded. "If you did see him, I promise I won't get mad."

"No, Mom," Boyd insisted. Tears laced his words. Next to Boyd his brother began to sniffle.

"Okay," Sarah replied, trying to bring on a reassuring smile. "It's okay. Come here." She put her arms out so the boys would come into them for a hug.

Sarah kissed the top of their heads, fighting the tears which still fell for loss of the man she'd never stop loving.

After the embrace broke, she told them to play some more.

Sarah watched as Boyd pushed his brother in the tire swing and then turned around to go into the house to return Kincaid's call.

Chapter 39

After DeLong ended the call with Sarah Benson, he dropped his cell on the bed beside him and lay back down, his eyes tightly closed.

He didn't blame his captain for relieving him of his duties. He knew he got off with a slap on his wrist. What was he thinking?

You were hungover, he reminded himself.

DeLong let out a groan.

Hungover or not, he knew he acted impulsively and there was no excuse.

At least he was smart enough to realize that. He only wished he'd thought before he acted.

DeLong grabbed his keys from the nightstand, rolled off the bed and left the room. The snow that had overcome his town had melted, leaving muddy ground in its wake, with bits and pieces of ice and slush here and there.

In his truck, DeLong drove around town. He drove past the Walkers' neighborhood, and his own neighborhood. He passed Philadelphia Jack's, though the yearning to stop was overwhelming. He wasn't even sure if the owner would allow him another drink. He wasn't sure if he'd be able to show his face in that bar again.

DeLong drove past a few other bars but didn't stop. He realized there was something he was craving, and it wasn't a drink. He wasn't sure what it was until he found himself in an almost-empty parking lot of a Catholic church.

Why here?

He'd abandoned religion many years ago.

DeLong took out a cigarette, lit it, and smoked the nicotine, staring at the large church.

Somehow it seemed inviting.

Slowly getting out of the truck, he puffed on his cigarette as he walked toward the doors. He dropped the remains, snuffed it with the toe of his shoe, and went inside.

The deafening silence screamed at him as he took a pew in the back of the building.

A few people were scattered around the building, some kneeling in prayer, lighting candles.

The confessional doors up front opened and a teenage boy stepped out. He clambered through the rows until he left the building.

Confession, DeLong thought darkly. *I've done too many wrongs to even ask for forgiveness. Too many, even God wouldn't forgive. What's the point?*

He stayed a few minutes longer and decided to leave. He couldn't stay there. He didn't belong anymore. He wasn't worthy to be near something so holy, so...perfect.

He found himself wishing he was.

Wishing he could have his mistakes erased.

When DeLong was outside, he jammed his hand into his pockets. He felt a crumpled piece of paper in his left hand. DeLong retrieved it and was about to toss it in the backseat of his truck when he saw the print: Harry Caruso.

DeLong straightened the business card and stared at the phone number.

He opted to punch it into his phone. Standing in the cold for a good few minutes, his thumb hovering over the *send* button, DeLong considered his options.

Then he found he didn't really have one.

The words Harry had said to him echoed in his mind from earlier today: in order to actually be helped, you not only need to want to help yourself, but you should stop looking at it as something you have to do.

He pressed send before he changed his mind.

Harry answered after two rings.

"It's Jim DeLong."

"Jim! I was just thinking of you. It was so great seeing you again after so long."

"Yeah, you too." He closed his eyes and shook his head slowly. "Listen, have you eaten? I know it's late for lunch, but I was wondering if we could talk."

"Of course!" Harry exclaimed. "I did eat, but we could definitely meet at Evan's Diner for coffee."

"Yeah, sounds good. See you in a few."

DeLong ended the call, tossing the phone on the passenger seat.

DeLong didn't know if what he did was the right thing or not, but he knew he had to do what he could in order to ignore the burning desire he felt in his heart.

A few minutes later, DeLong found himself sitting at a table in the diner, Harry in front of him, spilling everything that had been going on in his life. Harry had always been an easy friend to talk to; he proved it hadn't changed as he sipped his coffee, staring intently as he listened.

When DeLong finished, Harry set his cup down and propped his chin in his hand.

"Have you talked to your wife since the fight?"

DeLong shook his head solemnly. "She wants nothing to do with me."

"Oh," Harry said, slipping his index finger through the handle of his cup. "Did she tell you that?"

"No," DeLong admitted. "But I could see it in her eyes."

"How long have you been friends with this guy?"

"Years. Since before the academy. He helped me out of a bad situation. Russ was my mentor back then."

"Has it occurred to you she may have wanted to talk to him

about you? As a friend?"

DeLong shook his head. "Why would she? She has other friends."

"But no other friends, I'm sure, that are in the same situation." Harry paused and took a sip of coffee before continuing. "Jim, you have always been quick to act. I knew that about you from the day we first met. It's a flaw. Human, but still a flaw. Now tell me, why would your wife, who wants couples counseling to fix her marriage, meet her former lover at the workplace of her husband? Her motives for that would be?"

DeLong averted his eyes and looked outside.

No, he couldn't tell him what the motives were.

Because there weren't any. DeLong took a long sip of his coffee and looked back at Harry. He was staring, unblinkingly, as though he was waiting for an answer.

"What should I do about all this?"

Harry shook his head. "Only you can tell you that. I'm only here to lend an ear. I can't tell you what to do, when or how. I'm just a voice of reason."

DeLong lifted the corner of his lip into a small smile.

"Thank you," he said.

"I'm here always. Call me anytime. And be sure you show up to meetings. They do help. Also, go to church. Talk to God."

They sat in silence, but it wasn't one of those uncomfortable ones DeLong had been accustomed to in recent days.

It felt a little...

He couldn't think of a good word for it.

Oh yeah.

Peaceful.

DeLong's mind raced as he listed the steps he needed to go through in order to get his life in order. He knew it wouldn't be easy.

But, then again, it never was.

Chapter 40

In order to familiarize themselves more with the Alan Walker suicide and the murders of Christy Walker and Ensign McCoy, Calhoun and the investigators reviewed the case files, jotting notes pertinent to the investigation.

They knew, according to Grimes' journal entry and Dr. Gordon, Alan Walker had confessed to Grimes about doing something horrible a while back. Whatever it was, there was no formal record of any wrongdoing.

Nothing except a newspaper article, which had been recanted. The team moved on the assumption Alan's big secret was that he either was unwittingly a part of a plot in Ensign McCoy's death or was the perpetrator.

Alan Walker was found with a bullet wound in his skull and a suicide note stating that he couldn't live with the secrets he held. In the police report, a handwriting expert stated it was, in fact, Alan Walker's penmanship.

Additionally, Christy Walker was found on the floor, shot to death, which the investigators at the time conveniently listed Alan as the culprit.

Because Admiral Matheson was being uncooperative with DeLong earlier, Calhoun made a side note to contact the lawyer. If he needed to, he would go to them.

He'd just as soon not.

According to Dr. Gordon, Grimes had proof hidden where it will "always be under the boys." But what did it prove? Something involving Alan Walker his involvement in Ensign McCoy's disappearance? Or was there another connection to Grimes' murder they have yet to see?

Just like the rest of this mess, they still couldn't figure out the riddle. Until they find the hiding place, their hope rested in Dr. Gordon's taped sessions.

Calhoun, eyes strained, leaned back in his chair.

Across the table, Elliott let out a loud sigh.

"The Navy did a marvelous job at covering McCoy's—whatever it was. No witnesses, no murder weapon, not even an autopsy report. I mean, who does that?"

"Unfortunately, there're plenty of corrupted people around," Newman said. He was looking over the folder, which contained contents of the file marked "MC" on Grimes' laptop.

"Take a look at this."

Newman tossed an enlarged photo between Elliott and Calhoun.

Simultaneously, they leaned over to take a look.

"That's Claire Walker," Elliott stated.

Calhoun muttered under his breath.

In the photo, she had her hands on the cheeks of a man, leaning in, planting a kiss on his lips.

"Is that Alan Walker?" Newman narrowed his eyes at the remaining contents of the folder. "There are more, but it's hard to tell."

He spread the photos across the table. They each unmistakably showed Claire Walker making intimate gestures. In a couple of the pictures, although the man wasn't visible, his bare forearm was.

Etched in his forearm was a burn scar.

"Listen to this: MC and Claire in Atlanta on January eighth to the tenth, 2016, MC and Claire at Tybee on March sixteenth to the

The Murder of Manny Grimes

seventeenth, two thousand and sixteen. He listed dates and places where he saw Claire with our suspect. The most recent date was the week of November twenty-third. She seems to have been dating this guy this whole year."

"Could Claire have been involved in her husband's death?" Elliott wondered out loud. She clucked her tongue as the room grew silent. They scanned each photo for clues that may help identify their suspect.

Nothing stuck out except for the scar on his forearm.

"Was there anything else on the laptop?" Calhoun asked Newman.

He shook his head. "The tech guys went through the entire system and searched everything for any hidden files. They also went through the recycle bin, where they found the photos of Christy and Alan. Those didn't show anything other than that they were together, in a 'hanging out' sort of way. Even recovering deleted files, they couldn't find anything related to this case. If Grimes had gotten rid of something, then he may have used a hard delete."

"We need to talk to Claire Walker," Calhoun said. "See what she says about these photos. Then we'll get in touch with Alan Walker's coworkers."

* * *

It was Jonathan Walker who opened the door.

"I've already told you people everything," he demanded.

Calhoun smelled the sweet odor of something cooking. "Actually, Mr. Walker, we're here to talk to your sister-in-law."

Walker glanced over his shoulder, then back at Calhoun.

"Claire? Why?"

"Can we come inside?"

He seemed to think about it, then must have decided it was best to allow them to enter.

"She's in the kitchen. I'll, uh, I'll get her."

They waited in the living room while Walker said a few words to his sister-in-law. When she made her appearance, she wore an apron and her hair pulled back in a loose bun.

She smiled as she reached her hand out and loosely shook theirs.

"I'm just in the middle of making dinner."

"We won't take too much of your time," Calhoun promised.

Walker leaned against the doorway in between the kitchen and the living room. Soft whispers came floating down the stairs. Walker looked up, putting his finger to his lips.

"Mrs. Walker," Newman began. "Do you know anyone with the initials MC?"

Claire's brows furrowed.

"No," she said slowly. "I don't believe so."

"Before, or after the death of your husband, have you had a relationship with another man?"

It was Elliott who spoke and now Claire directed her gaze at her. "I'm sorry, but what are you implying?"

Calhoun unfolded the photo printout and held it for her to see.

"This was in an encrypted file marked 'MC' on Manny Grimes' laptop. Can you identify him for us?"

With an exasperated sigh, Claire took the photo and looked at it, studying the image.

"Who is he?" Elliott pressed.

Finally, Claire looked up. Calhoun had a hard time reading the look behind her eyes. She blinked and handed him the photo.

"I can only assume, Mr. Calhoun, that's my husband."

"Why would Grimes have taken photos of you and your husband being intimate?" Newman asked. "What purpose would that serve?"

"I don't know," Claire insisted. "Normally I'd say ask him, but Manny is dead. And I have to say I'm insulted you would come into my home and imply I had an affair."

"Did you?" Elliott asked pointedly.

Claire stared her down. "Miss Elliott, my husband may or may not have had been sleeping with Jonathan's wife. I'd like to think not. But considering the manner in which he and Christy were found, it's hard to believe otherwise." She blinked back tears. Claire bit her lower lip and twirled her hair. "But I loved him with all my heart. I could never have done that."

Calhoun exchanged glances with his partners, and then looked back at Claire.

The Murder of Manny Grimes

"Thank you for your time. Enjoy your dinner."

When they piled inside Calhoun's truck, Elliott huffed. "I don't believe a word she said."

"Well," Calhoun replied, "until we find evidence against her story, there's not much we can do."

Chapter 41

Calhoun dropped Newman off at his car and was now driving Elliott home. She was unusually quiet, which bothered him for some reason.

He glanced over at her.

She stared out the windows at the trees breezing by.

"What's wrong?"

"Nothing."

He didn't believe her, but decided to leave her alone with her thoughts. A few seconds later, she turned in her seat to face him.

He stopped at a red light.

"Can I ask you a question?"

"Sure."

"How long have you been sleeping with DeLong's wife?"

Although the lights had turned green, Calhoun didn't press the gas pedal. He lost all feeling in his arms and legs.

His mind swirled.

Calhoun took a deep breath to grasp his bearings. He turned his head to stare at Elliott, who was studying him intently as if she was trying to dig into the deepest part of his soul.

Calhoun cleared his throat. "Not one for subtlety, are you?"

Elliott shook her head, lifting the corner of her mouth in a sly smile.

Someone behind them laid on their horn, so Calhoun turned back to the road and pressed his foot on the gas.

"Exactly how is it any of your business?" he asked her.

"It's not," she replied simply.

"We were together two separate times," he quietly answered after a long pause. "Two times too many." Might as well get it all out in the open, he surmised. "Jim was always focused on other things such as work. Or so he says."

"You don't think he was?" Elliott pressed.

"I rarely know what I think when it comes to Jim," Calhoun admitted, steering the truck left. "He's always been the secretive type. Especially when he drank."

"Want to elaborate a bit more?"

"Jim dealt through tough stuff as a kid. No one deserves to go through what he did. It led to him drinking heavily," Calhoun explained. He took a right and pulled into the parking lot of her apartment complex. "And when he and Samantha were dating, he'd go off for days at a time to drink. Almost lost his job because he'd miss work. But thanks to Samantha, he cleaned himself up and won her heart. It wasn't easy. Jim screwed up big time with her. By the time he was sober, she'd already begun dating someone else. But Sam...Sam never stopped loving him."

"Only he ended up losing her to you," Elliott grumbled.

Calhoun jerked the car gear into park and abruptly turned to face the investigator. "Listen to me, Elliott. I'm really sick of your smart remarks where Jim and me are concerned. You watch what you say from now on, or I will personally rip your tongue out of your mouth. Got it?"

Elliott nodded, letting the corner of her mouth curve back into a smile. "Fine. I'm only saying how I see things."

"Yeah, well, you're wrong!" Calhoun insisted. "It's true, Jim's wife and I had an affair, but that's long over now. End of discussion. Keep the past in the past."

"Was it your idea or hers to end it?" she asked, spitefully. Rather than waiting for an answer, she clambered out the truck, slammed the door and stalked for the entrance of the building, leaving Calhoun staring after her, seething.

Once he regained control of his temper, he slowly pulled away to go home.

Chapter 42

DeLong's cell phone vibrated on his dashboard as he drove away from his meeting with Harry. Keeping his eyes on the road, he answered, but immediately wished he looked at the caller ID.

"Hey," Calhoun said.

"Something you need?" DeLong snapped

"I don't expect you'd want to talk to me," Calhoun began. "Honestly, Jim, you have every right to hate me."

"Glad I have your approval," DeLong said with sarcasm as he turned onto a new street.

Calhoun ignored the remark. "I want you to talk to Sam. She loves you. Even after everything, it's always been you. Always will be."

DeLong said nothing as he stopped at a light.

"I hope one day you'll find it in your heart to forgive me. Even though I don't deserve it. Sam's hoping to save the marriage. I want you to know that."

DeLong still remained quiet, listening to the silence filling the phone line.

Finally, Calhoun said, "Well, I said all I needed. Guess I'll catch you later."

After ending the call, DeLong reflected on the conversation, then decided he wanted to swing by the house to talk with Samantha.

He was halfway there when he heard it again.

Help me.

Heart racing, DeLong pulled into the suicide lane and stopped the truck.

He listened intently to the silence.

He didn't hear anything except the cars moving past him.

After a Buick breezed by, he u-turned and headed in the direction of Manny Grimes' house. He wasn't sure exactly what it was, but something continued to pull him back.

When he got there, DeLong once again searched from top to bottom for anything they may have overlooked. Everything that needed to be found had already been found.

Hadn't it? So, what were they missing?

Grimes had found something out and it got him killed.

That was the only explanation for his death.

He didn't know if it was somehow connected to Alan Walker's death, or just mere coincidence. DeLong didn't believe in coincidences.

He entered the billiard room one last time, taking in the pictures of art on the wall, the pool table, the French doors leading to the lake.

Whispers filled the air, but DeLong couldn't make out what they were saying. At the corner of his eye, he saw something move. DeLong spun around just in time to see a pencil fall to the ground.

But it wasn't the pencil he took an interest in.

DeLong eyed the DaVinci painting with Mona Lisa watching his every move.

Inching closer, he cursed underneath his breath.

As obsessive-compulsive as Manny Grimes appeared to be, the picture would not be crooked.

And DeLong was positive it was straight when he first entered a few seconds ago.

DeLong felt along the edges as though he'd find some kind of

The Murder of Manny Grimes

switch leading to a hidden hideout. He removed the painting and felt the surface of the wall.

Turning the *Mona Lisa* over on its front, he set it on the pool table and inspected the back. He pressed a lump bulging in the center and something soft gave in. DeLong carefully removed the backing of the art. Taped behind Mona Lisa's photo were a folded piece of paper and the head of a small stuffed bear, with another piece of paper taped to it.

He retrieved the first note and read the handwriting: *leave it alone if you value your life.*

The second appeared more grueling, more desperate: *here's a gift to you. A taste of what I can do.*

DeLong study both notes: the color of the ink, the curves and shapes of the letters. They were, without a doubt, written by the same person. The note was unsigned, but DeLong had a hunch it was written by someone with the initials *MC*.

Someone threatened Manny Grimes. Could the stuffed bear head symbolize his children? Were they in danger still?

He used his phone to call Sarah Benson.

When she answered, he asked whether her boys were missing a stuffed bear with a white patch over his eyes.

"I don't remember them ever having one," she replied.

"Okay, Ms. Benson." Pause. "Is everyone okay?"

"As well as you can imagine. Are you getting close at all?" Her tone changed and seemed deadened, like she was beginning to give up hope.

He didn't want to tell her they weren't even close, neither did he want to give her false hope. Instead, he promised he was doing everything in his power to solve the case.

Although not completely satisfied, she seemed to be reassured.

DeLong ended the call and carefully gathered his new evidence. He would turn it over to Calhoun in the morning.

As he left, he thought of his own family in this dark world. The world where his job was to bring men he was hunting to justice.

He had something he needed to do.

Something he wanted to do.

His future was cloudy, but if the murder of Manny Grimes

taught him anything, it was that he had two people in his life who couldn't afford to be on the back burner any longer.

* * *

Before he could change his mind and turn away, DeLong lifted his fist and knocked on the door.

A few minutes later, Samantha peeked through the crack. He tried to read her face, but couldn't.

"What?" Even the tone of her voice was impassive.

"I know I'm probably the last person you want to see right now," he started, speaking quickly in case she decided to slam the door in his face.

"But I couldn't let the day end without telling you I'm sorry about the way I acted. It was impulsive, childish, and it won't happen again."

As he spoke, her eyes were narrowed, as if loading invisible bullets to shoot at him.

Then she sighed, opened the door wider. "Why, Jim?"

"When I saw the two of you together, I thought maybe—."

"No," she interrupted with a shake of her head. "Why are you drinking again?"

He lowered his head, too ashamed to look at her. He could blame it on a whole lot of things.

Stress from the job.

Anger at the affair.

The mourning of the miscarriage of a baby which may not have been his.

Anger at himself for letting his wife fall out of love with him.

But he knew none of those excuses would fly.

Because none of those excuses were the truth.

"I don't have an excuse, Sam. I really don't. I wish I could tell you why I do what I do."

"I was at the station earlier, waiting for you. Not to see Russ."

"I know." He looked at her.

"You do?" she sounded surprised.

"Well, I guessed. I had some time to think. Then Russ called, and I thought some more. I was..."

He paused, ashamed of what he was about to say.

"I was wasted." He let out a curse. "I don't know why I'm the way I am. I hate I'm not the man you thought I was. I hate I'm not the man—or father for that matter—I should be."

Samantha said nothing, so he continued. "I'm going to meetings now. I ran into an old friend. You remember Harry Caruso? He's been sober going on ten years now. I think he'll be my sponsor. He's a good guy, you know?"

"Good," Samantha told him. "I'm glad."

They stood in brief silence. DeLong bit his lips as he tried to think of something to say, but it was Samantha who spoke. He looked into her eyes, trying to get a read behind them.

"Tomorrow's our anniversary," she reminded him with a shrug. "I went to the station because I wanted to see if you would have lunch or even dinner with me."

"I'd love to have dinner with you. Or lunch. Or even breakfast. Whatever you want. Just tell me. I'll do it."

Samantha gave him a weak smile and her sigh came out in broken half-sobs.

"I'm going to need some time to process everything," she requested. "Let me think this through. After everything that's happened between us, I have to...think. Is that okay?"

DeLong's spirit fell, but he nodded, letting her know he understood.

"I'm off duty for the rest of this month. So, I'll be available whenever you want me."

"Okay," she replied. "I'll give you a call. Let you know."

"Can I see Bella before I go?"

Samantha hesitated as she considered it. Finally, she nodded her head.

"Of course," she agreed. She allowed him to step inside as she called out for Bella.

"Daddy!" she cried out when she came down the stairs.

DeLong grabbed her in a big bear hug.

"My goodness, you are growing so much," he told her. "You really need to stop that."

"When are you coming home?" Her voice was soft and sad.

DeLong felt his heart break a little. He brushed a strand of brown hair from her eyes.

"Soon, Princess," he promised. "Daddy needs to take care of some things first. Okay?"

In answer, she leaned in and hugged his neck.

"No matter what happens," he whispered in her ears, "I love you from the bottom of my heart."

"I love you too, Daddy," Bella whispered.

After they broke the embrace, DeLong stepped outside. He turned and met Samantha's eyes and they gazed at one another for a second, then she closed the door. He stared at the door before he slowly turned to return to the motel.

Chapter 43

"Can you tell us if you noticed a change in Alan Walker's attitudes in the last months before his death?"

Calhoun sat across the desk of Victoria Lovell, Alan Walker's boss.

Lovell sat ramrod straight, hands folded together on her desk. She wore her reddish-brown hair tied in a firm bun. Her black and white suit was immaculately clean and pressed.

She looked at her wall clock several times as though she had somewhere she needed to be.

"I'm sorry," she apologized in her lazy southern drawl, "forgive me for being a bit confused. But why are y'all back inquirin' about Alan? The police already closed the case." She looked at them so her eyes would peer over the rims of her glasses. "Had they not?"

"New evidence has come to light," Calhoun informed her. "We're just covering our bases."

"Is this about that gentleman who was recently found murdered?"

"Should it be?" Elliott wondered.

Lovell's laugh was silky and light. "I can't answer that, Miss Elliott. But I do remember him comin' 'round here."

"Tell us," Calhoun prodded.

She leaned into her chair. "He was arguing with Alan. Something about his affair with his sister-in-law. He denied it, but Alan's friend didn't seem to believe him."

"Was it true?" Calhoun asked.

"The man you'd want to talk to is Lewis May. He and Alan were friends. They'd go for drinks ev'ry now and then."

Calhoun marked it in his notes.

"Back to my original question," he said as he finished writing. "Did you start noticing a difference in his attitude?"

Lovell rolled her eyes to the ceiling in annoyance. "Yes, I do remember he seemed..." she hesitated, "...dazed."

"In your own opinion, do you think Alan Walker could ever commit to murdering someone?"

"He did, didn't he?" she replied simply.

"That wasn't his question, Mrs. Lovell," Elliott leaned forward. "You worked with the man on a day-to-day basis. Spoke with him. Would you have thought Alan Walker was a killer?"

Lovell paused, considering the question.

"No," she said simply. Her eyes softened a little. "I wouldn't have thought that."

"Has Alan ever shown angry temperament?" Newman wondered. "Has he ever been known to threaten, throw things...?"

"No. He's been clearly annoyed, I suppose, but not to the point of throwing things. To be utterly honest," she told them, "when the news came out he had committed murder, then suicide, well, I was astonished. That wasn't the Alan Walker I knew." She paused. "Or thought I knew, anyway. After all, I was his boss. Not his friend."

"Did he ever mention his past to you? Being in the Navy?" Calhoun asked.

"I'm afraid not. Like I said, Lewis May is who you'd want to speak with."

"Thank you for your time, Mrs. Lovell." Newman took out a card from his wallet and dropped it on her desk.

"If you think of anything else, please give us a call."

"Certainly."

Calhoun asked for the location of Lewis May's office, then they headed in that direction.

When they entered another small office setting on the other side of the building, Calhoun asked the secretary if May was available. She hesitantly picked up her phone after claiming her boss had requested to be left alone.

"I'm sorry to bother you, sir, but some investigators are here. They're asking to speak with you...yes, I told them...okay, I'll let them know."

"He'll be right with you," she replied as she placed the phone in its cradle.

Newman and Calhoun simultaneously took a seat on either side of a round table. Calhoun chose a *Sports Illustrated* magazine and began reading an article on the Green Bay Packers. Elliott leaned against the wall, drumming her fingers softly.

Minutes later, the door opened, and a young man appeared.

"Hi, sorry, uh, come on in."

"We'll try not to take too much of your time," Calhoun assured May as they gathered into the office. "We're here to ask you about Alan Walker."

"Oh," May said, his face falling. "What about him?"

"Do you recall seeing attitude changes in him before he committed suicide?"

May shook his head and shrugged. "Well, he had been acting a little weird, I guess."

"Weird, how?" Elliott wondered.

"Jittery. He'd jump at even the slightest sound. Like he was afraid of the bogeyman."

"Do you know anything about his relationship with his sister-in-law?" Calhoun asked.

"Like what?"

"Did Walker mention an affair with his sister-in-law, Christy?"

May scoffed. "That's what the news report said. And that's what his friend accused him of. But it wasn't true. Alan told me he suspected *Claire* was being unfaithful. His friend, Manny Grimes, first told him about her affair. I remember when he asked for Alan's forgiveness for accusing him of infidelity. At first, Alan didn't believe his wife was sleeping with another guy. But then he started to see the signs. Then he saw the proof."

"So, Grimes told Alan his wife was having an affair? Did he ever mention who?" Elliott pressed.

May shook his head. "I can't remember if he did. I do know Grimes was following Claire around. Took some pictures."

"I don't suppose you have these photos lying around?" Calhoun stated.

"No, why would I? She wasn't *my* wife. Alan spent several days staring at one of the pictures, though. I saw it once."

"Can you remember what he looked like?" Newman inquired.

"I just remember he had a scar on his forearm. Alan told me the guy got it when he burnt his arm. It had something to do with the boiler room, I think. But I'm not certain of specifics."

"So, Alan knew him?" Elliott said. "They served together?"

"Yes, I think so. I remember him saying something about being full of guilt. Then he tore the picture and left." May shrugged. "And no, I don't know why he felt guilty."

"When was this?" Calhoun asked.

"The day before he killed himself."

Calhoun exchanged glances with Newman and Elliott.

"What about his relationship with his brother?" Newman asked.

"They used to be close. The three of them were together all the time. Until one day it was just Alan. I guess the whole who-had-an-affair scheme really did them in. Then Manny Grimes started coming around again. It was when Alan was being all jittery."

Newman's cell began to blurt out the theme song from *CSI: NY*. He answered, spoke briefly to the person at the other end of the line. His eyes widened as he expressed his disbelief.

He thanked the caller, replaced his phone on its clip and turned to his partners.

"You'll never guess what that was about. Someone was putting away evidence and discovered a bag which had fallen behind the shelves. According to the label, it was found by the bed near Christy Walker's body. It's a single cufflink in the shape of a bird. A blue bird."

"Blue bird? I remember Jonathan Walker having blue bird cufflinks," May offered. "I only remember because Christy came by the office once to ask whether Alan thought his brother would like it."

"Thank you for your time, Mr. May." Calhoun motioned for the others to follow him.

Once they were out of May's office, Elliott said, "Why didn't we notice it before?"

"It had fallen back."

"Pretty careless if you ask me."

"Evidence has been lost before," Newman put in as they piled onto the elevator.

"*If* the cufflink belonged to Walker, then that might place him at the scene of the crime. I think it's now time to get a warrant to search his place and bring him in for questioning," Calhoun said.

They reached the bottom floor, then the door leading outside.

"What do you think about this Claire Walker affair thing?" Elliott asked thoughtfully.

"I think the Walkers are one big, messed up family," Calhoun answered.

"Agreed."

Chapter 44

After he had the search warrant in hand, Calhoun, his team, and a few other officers went up the walkway of Jonathan Walker's house.

He knocked.

When Walker answered the door, he opened his mouth to speak, then noticed the additional officers.

"What's going on?" he asked with a hint of trepidation in his voice.

"Jonathan Walker, please step outside," Calhoun requested. "We have a warrant to search the premises."

Walker snatched the warrant out of Calhoun's hands and studied it. He looked back at the party of police officers, swallowed and stepped outside.

"What are you looking for?"

The search officers crowded into the house just as Claire Walker pulled into the driveway. The boys jumped out of the Sebring, Claire hurrying after them.

"Uncle Jonathan, what's going on?" Tommy asked.

"Do you own cufflinks?" Elliott said, ignoring the boy's

question.

"Uh, sure. They're on the dresser in my room."

"What about ones that look like this?" Newman held the evidence bag so Walker could see.

Walker sputtered. "Yeah, but I don't wear them anymore."

"This was an overlooked piece of evidence, found a while back near your wife's body."

"That's impossible," Claire said, her hands covering her mouth. "You're not insinuating—."

"That's ludicrous," Walker interrupted. "I was nowhere near that hotel."

"Where do you keep this cufflink?" Newman asked.

Walker turned his attention to the investigator. "In my top drawer. Underneath the socks."

Newman spoke into his walkie, requesting someone to check the drawer. A few seconds later, a response came back.

"We found the cufflink. One's missing."

"No," Walker demanded. "That's impossible. That isn't my cufflink!"

"I think it's best if we take you in for questioning," Calhoun replied, taking hold of Walker's elbow.

"Dad!" Bobby exclaimed.

"Am I under arrest?" Walker asked.

"I'm hoping to not go that far," Calhoun said softly. "So, if you wouldn't mind..."

After a moment's hesitation, Walker allowed Calhoun to lead him to the squad car.

"Mrs. Walker," Elliott said, "it'll be best if you take the kids somewhere else and meet us at the station."

Claire didn't respond, except to run to Calhoun as he guided Walker into the back seat. She grabbed his arm.

"I don't understand," she said, tearfully. "What's going on?"

"It would help if you can meet us there for more questioning."

"Why are you doing this? To our family?"

"Because like you, we want answers. Since we can't get it straight without bringing him in, that's exactly what we're being forced to do."

After releasing himself from her grasp, he nodded to the officer driving the police car and they pulled away.

"See you there?"

Claire bit her lower lip, nodding.

Calhoun and the investigators climbed into their car and left.

* * *

"I already told you everything I know," Walker demanded for the umpteenth time. "This is becoming harassment."

Calhoun sat on the edge of the table in the interrogation room.

"Where were you the day your brother and wife were killed?"

"I was home."

"Can anybody verify?"

Walker groaned. "No. I was alone. The boys were in school, Claire went shopping at the mall, I think. What is this about? I thought you were looking into Manny Grime's murder."

"We are," Newman replied. "It just so happens we believe the two are related."

Walker furrowed his brow. "How?"

"We were hoping you'd tell us."

Walker shook his head firmly. "I already told you everything."

"How do you explain this cufflink?" Calhoun moved the evidence bag containing the item closer to Walker, who stared at it.

"I can't. Look, it's been a while since I've worn, or even seen, my cufflinks. That isn't even mine."

"Are you certain?"

"Yes," Walker said urgently.

"You know what I think?" He looked into Walker's wild, pleading eyes. "I think you thought your brother and wife were having an affair."

Calhoun pushed off the table and went to Walker's side and leaned close to him.

"I think you followed them to the hotel, shot your wife, and forced your brother to sign a confession so people would assume he was depressed. But, of course you couldn't let him leave that room alive. So you shot him to make it look like murder/suicide."

"That's absurd!" Walker exclaimed. "Despite popular belief, I loved my wife. And Alan was my brother. No matter what they did or didn't do, I loved them. Why won't you believe me? My brother killed himself and my wife. I don't know why, but he did. Instead of questioning me, you need to go out there and find out who killed Manny Grimes!"

"The thing is, ever since we've met, you've either lied or withheld the truth," Calhoun reminded him. He straightened, walked back to his chair and sat. "If you have nothing to hide, then I suggest you start talking."

"I have nothing to say!" Walker cried out. His chest heaved as he tried to control his temper. "You're fishing. I have nothing to hide. I did not kill anyone. I'm no killer."

"Everything points toward you!" Calhoun insisted. "You find out about your brother's betrayal, you kill him and your wife. Grimes had been nosy about your brother's affair. He found out you killed your wife and brother. So, you killed Grimes to silence him. Walker, this evidence," he jabbed his finger at the cufflink, "is enough to bring you in front of a jury! If you would only start talking to us, then we can help you. But if we've got to go the hard way, we can't do anything for you."

Walker shook his head. "I don't know how else to tell you this: I. Did. Not. Kill. Anyone."

With agitation, Calhoun slid his chair back and rose.

Newman sighed and leaned back.

Calhoun paced around the interrogation room.

He knew Walker was right. It was a weak case.

Did Walker do it?

Or was he as innocent as he claimed?

"I'm not saying anything else," Walker replied after a disturbing silence. "I want my lawyer."

Calhoun and Newman went out the room to where Stewart and Elliott stood behind the two-way mirror.

"What do you think?" Stewart inquired.

Through the glass, they watched as Walker put his head in his hands.

"I think I believe him," Calhoun stated after a long pause.

"What about the cufflink?" Elliott said.

"It's a cufflink. Common enough. Anybody could have lost it. And possible Walker misplaced his, and it's simply a coincidence."

"I don't believe in coincidences."

"We don't have enough on him to make anything stick."

"People went to prison for less," Newman pointed out.

"Okay. I'll bring the ADA up to speed," Stewart said. "We'll have to see what she says. In the meantime, we'll question his sister-in-law when she comes. Put Walker in a holding cell and give him his phone call."

Chapter 45

They'd kept their secret locked in the back of their minds for almost fifteen years.

He let out a round of curses as he sipped his coffee and watched the news on the muted television.

That idiot Alan Walker.

Had he not started feeling guilty over what happened, had he not threatened to come clean, no one else would have died.

He'd be alive and so would Christy Walker.

So would that nosy Manny Grimes.

He let out another curse. And none of it would have happened if McCoy hadn't come into the boiler room that day.

But unfortunately for them, it did happen. So, there was a mess once again that had to be cleaned up. This time completely.

It wasn't easy trying to come up with a way to get rid of DeLong.

From everything he knew about the man, he worried DeLong would come too close to figuring out the truth.

He was glad when DeLong had ended up getting himself kicked

off the case. He chuckled to himself, remembering the anger DeLong had blazing through his eyes when his fist connected with Russ Calhoun's jaw.

It was better than pay-per-view.

Then all he needed to do was figure out how to steer evidence so it looked like Jonathan Walker was the perpetrator. He already believed his wife and brother were having an affair, even if he didn't want to admit it.

There was motive right there. And from the way the investigation was going, it looked as though they were gearing for the murder/suicide actually being two murders with Alan and Christy Walker's killer being the killer of Manny Grimes.

So, he had to do them a favor and help them a little.

Just nudge them. That was all.

Evidence tended to get lost. So, it would be quite possible somebody would miss a small evidence bag containing a single blue bird cufflink. It was easy getting the cufflink and planting it in the evidence locker.

He felt joy snake its way through his belly and into his heart.

He forgot how the thrill of it was. The rush he felt to keep from being caught.

He was almost disappointed it was such an easy fix. Almost. A part of him still wanted the quiet life he'd led the past fifteen years.

It'd return, he knew.

Just as long as Calhoun and company continued to do their jobs and DeLong kept his nose out of his business, everything would be right in the universe.

Yes, because one man made the wrong choice, four people ended up paying for it.

And no, he didn't care.

Instead, he continued to sip his coffee and smiled at the twenty-something brunette wearing a short miniskirt entering the coffee shop.

Chapter 46

Claire Walker arrived at the police station and demanded to see her brother-in-law. Nancy led her to an interrogation room, per Calhoun's request, then called and informed him she was there.

He entered the room and took a seat.

"Thank you for coming," Calhoun replied.

"Where's Lieutenant DeLong?" she demanded, narrowing her eyes at him. "I want to speak with him."

"Unfortunately, the lieutenant is off the case."

"But...why?" Claire asked. She narrowed her eyes.

"It has nothing to do with you or why we're here," Calhoun answered simply. "The sooner you answer my questions, the better. For you and your brother-in-law."

Claire unleashed her arms with a sigh.

"Let's start at the beginning. You were friends with Manny Grimes, correct?"

"He was more friends with Alan and Jonathan, but I suppose."

"We know Grimes at some point believed your husband and sister-in-law were having an affair. Now we believe Grimes found out it wasn't your husband." Calhoun paused for emphasis. "But you."

"I never cheated on my husband."

Calhoun set the photo of Claire being intimate with the man with the scarred arm.

"Who is this man, Mrs. Walker?"

"I told you. My husband."

Calhoun could tell Claire was becoming irritable. She crossed her arms and narrowed her eyes. "Where's Jonathan?"

He ignored the question. "Do you know a Lewis May?"

"Yes. We've met a few times at Christmas parties and other functions."

"According to him, your husband believed *you* were the one having an affair." Calhoun paused, studying her facial expressions. Then, before she opened her mouth to speak, he decided on a bluff. "In fact, we have a witness saying you were hot and heavy at a baseball game this past summer." It wasn't exactly a bluff. It was written in Grimes' notes.

However, since he couldn't question Grimes, it wasn't going to be easy to prove.

Either way, the bluff worked.

"Fine," Claire breathed. "Fine. Yes, I had an affair. But not until I found out my husband was sleeping around with Christy."

"So, you know for a fact he was? You walked in on them?"

"No. I overheard Manny's many conversations with Jonathan. I confronted Alan about it, but of course, he denied it."

"Did Jonathan believe Grimes' accusation?"

"He was like me. In denial. But I think deep down he believed it. He just didn't want to. I mean, tell me who would want to believe someone who was supposed to love you was sleeping around?"

"I'm sure it made him angry," Calhoun replied matter-of-factly.

"Sure," Claire said with a shrug. "Who wouldn't be? But I don't think Jonathan would kill his wife or his own brother."

"A cufflink matching the one in his drawer was found in the room. Passion drives people to do things they never thought they could do."

Claire remained silent. She opened her mouth and closed it

again.

"I can't—I don't—." Tears streamed down her cheeks. "This is a nightmare. It's so messed up." She paused as she stared at the evidence bag holding the cufflink. "Oh, Jonathan. What did you do?" Her whispers were barely audible.

"Mrs. Walker, I'm going to ask you one more time. Could Jonathan Walker have killed Alan Walker, Christy Walker, and Manny Grimes? Do you have any evidence at all that can clear him?"

She put her head in her hands, her body trembling. After a long minute, which seemed like half an hour, she lifted her head.

"No. I feel so ashamed. I don't know anything at all."

"Okay." Calhoun softened his tone.

He wasn't quite sure if he got any closer to solving the case. He had an unsettling feeling in his stomach that had begun to arise for a while now. Calhoun couldn't help but wonder what DeLong would do if it were him in the interrogation room.

"Thank you for coming in," Calhoun said finally. "You can go now. Mr. Walker called his lawyer and he will be coming to talk to him today. In the meantime, go spend time with the boys. We'll keep you posted."

Chapter 47

Calhoun and Newman sat at a corner table at Chili's for a light lunch, an appetizer of Mozzarella sticks between them.

"Elliott comin'?" Calhoun asked as he took a bite. He chased it with his Coke.

"Nah. She's got a date."

Calhoun raised an eyebrow. "The Ice Queen dates?"

Newman chuckled as he picked up a piece of the breaded cheese.

"She dates often. But never holds on to a single guy. Usually banging the headboard and dropping 'em like fire is her objective. Keeps her satisfied while it keeps her from being burned."

Calhoun raised an eyebrow with curiosity.

"Burned?" he echoed.

"Yeah, burned," Newman said. He grabbed his water. "One reason I keep trying to steer you away from her. Guess you can say I've become protective."

"Seems to me she's capable of protecting herself," Calhoun pointed out.

"Well." He let his shoulder rise, then fall. "She's been my partner for a year. I'm responsible for her. I'm sure you remember the loyalties of the force."

"I do," Calhoun said softly. "Tell me about her."

Newman looked at him quizzically. "I'm not going to give you ammunition just so you can win a stupid bet with yourself."

"Come on, Newman. I'm not that shallow."

"Well," Newman pushed out a sigh. "All right. Before she came here, she was partnered with a guy on the force in Connecticut. They also happened to be dating very seriously. Even talked about marriage. Anyway, one night on patrol, he tried to come on to her. Being on duty, she told him to stop, but he wouldn't."

"He raped her?" Calhoun asked.

"No. Tried to. She was young and fresh on the force, vulnerable. Like a lot of women cops, she wanted to be considered one of the guys. But when he forced herself on her, she managed to get away. I can see how she's always been a resilient woman. Anyway, at the time, she didn't realize she should keep her personal and career life separate. She was eager to please. And vulnerable."

"Did she do anything about it?" Calhoun asked. He found his insides burning with hatred toward the man who had hurt her.

"She tried to tell her superiors what happened. But the guy was a highly respected and decorated police officer. Even though she reported it, they protected him. He claimed she came on to him, but because he allegedly declined, she wanted to get back at him. Elliott was ridiculed and eventually run out of the department." Newman paused to take a bite of his snack.

"She thought about becoming a special victims' detective, but a few months on the job, she became too sensitive and too personal to handle the rape victims. She once told me she almost decided to give up. But finally, she became a CSI. I think she decided it was better to deal with the victims when they were already dead."

"Glad she found her place," Calhoun mused. "I'd hate anyone to give up their careers over something like that."

"Her heart's all cop. She grew up with it. Lived it, breathed it, is it."

Newman took another sip, then finished the rest of his cheese stick. "It's not such an easy thing to run from. She just needed to find her place on the force."

"Seems to me she found it," Calhoun said.

"Good for us," Newman agreed. "She may be, as you call her, an 'Ice Queen,' but she gets the job done. And does it well. She's not very good at letting people in. I've tried to get in her good graces, but it's no easy task. When I met her, she was the same with me as she is with you. Even more so."

"I can't imagine her being more hard-headed than she is now," Calhoun muttered.

"Well, she was. Honestly, can't say I blame her. She actually didn't warm up to me until a couple months ago." Newman smiled. "You know something, Calhoun? Knowing her, and knowing you, this may get very interesting."

They ate in silence for a few minutes, listening to the murmur of the patrons in the restaurant.

"Is everything okay here?" Their waitress made her way to the table, her order pad clutched in her hand.

"Yeah," Calhoun said. "I could use another Coke soon."

Nodding, the waitress looked at Newman. "How about you?"

"I'm good for now," Newman told her.

The waitress turned to step to a nearby table.

"If you want to warm up to her, talk about cats."

Calhoun raised his eyebrow. "Cats?"

"She loves cats. I can't tell you why." Newman turned so he could face him better. "But be sure to tread carefully. She built a wall to protect herself. I've seen the wall down, and I've seen it up. Neither makes a pretty picture."

They guided their conversation to another topic, but Calhoun couldn't keep his mind from Elliott.

Chapter 48

When his phone woke him from a deep sleep, DeLong groggily glanced at the clock. It was after noon. He groaned and felt for his phone on the nightstand.

"DeLong," he muttered sleepily.

"Hey," Samantha said.

DeLong sat upright in his bed and swung his legs over the edge.

"Hey."

"I've been thinking ever since you came by last night."

Her voice was soft and drained. She sounded as though she'd been fighting a battle, and was on the brink of losing. Her soul was probably as tormented as DeLong's and he knew he was the one that caused her pain.

Somewhere along the path, he allowed her to slip away and now every time he tried to reach for her, he'd fumbled.

"Are you busy right now? I know it's late notice, but I was thinking we should have a little lunch. It is our anniversary you know?"

She hesitated, and he listened to her breathing.

"But I have to tell you, Jim," she continued, "I can't promise anything anymore. I want us to work, I really do. But I'm just so tired. I'm tired of the fighting, tired of the drinking, tired of feeling like the whole world is crashing down on me."

"I know," DeLong said. He wanted to say something more, but he couldn't. After all, what could he say? Could he ask for her forgiveness?

How many times would it take Samantha forgiving him for her to finally throw in the towel for good?

"I know you, Jim," Samantha said in an effort to fill the silence. "I know the kind of man you are. And I want you to know you're not the only one at fault. I'm as guilty as you, if not more."

He heard her let out a relieved sigh, as though she'd wanted to say these things for a while.

"So, will lunch be good for you?"

"Lunch would be great. Fatz Cafe?" He looked at the clock. "In an hour and a half?"

He imagined her smiling. Fatz Cafe was where they had their first date, where they'd had their anniversary dinners ever since.

"That sounds good. I'll see you shortly."

When the call was over, DeLong hurried for a shower, then dressed.

He left the hotel room, then ran back in to snatch the evidence he had found, making a mental note to give it to Calhoun later in the day. As he headed for his car, he sent his former mentor a quick text informing him he found some more evidence in Grimes' home.

When he pulled into Fatz Cafe's parking lot, he saw Samantha's SUV and parked a few cars away, climbed out, gripping flowers in his right hand.

DeLong went inside, scanned the restaurant and saw where she sat.

Her head was buried in the menu, hair pulled back in a ponytail. She was wearing a cream sweater with three snowmen printed on the front, reading "Have a Frosty Time."

A hostess approached, grabbed a menu, asking him how many, but he waved her off informing her he saw his wife had already arrived. She gave him an understanding smile and directed her

The Murder of Manny Grimes

attention to the group who stepped through the door behind him.

DeLong walked toward Samantha.

"Hey." He sat in the chair opposite her, handing over the flowers.

She replied with a small smile, thanked him, and set the flowers to the side. They took a few minutes of silence to decide on food. When the waiter came over, they ordered.

"This is nice," DeLong stated after they were alone again.

"It is," Samantha agreed. "I'm glad we're here."

Silence fell on them again and Samantha grabbed a powdered donut bread to gnaw.

This is how it's been for a while now, DeLong realized. Two strangers making small talk. He didn't want their marriage to end like this.

He searched his mind for an opening of things to talk about.

"Are we still going to meet at Dr. Davis's next week?" After he spoke, he mentally kicked himself.

Nice conversation starter, Jim. Remind Sam about your failing marriage. That'll get her running into your arms.

"Sure," she replied. Her eyes told him she wanted to say something else, but before she did, she looked away. DeLong waited for her to collect her thoughts. When she finally looked back at him, she said, "I wanted to apologize for running out of Dr. Davis's the way I did. I was upset and hurt and..." she trailed off.

"I know, Sam," DeLong said. "It was me. Not you."

She shook her head. "Pastor Krupps says it's never just one person. I took time to think about us, about our marriage. It wasn't just you. I admit that."

"Pastor Krupps?"

"Yeah. He's sort of been..." Samantha looked into DeLong's eyes. "He's my pastor. I've been going to church each Sunday for a year."

"Really?"

DeLong knew he shouldn't be surprised Samantha was going to church. She had always been somewhat religious, going to church every once in a while. Growing up, she went to church every Sunday because her parents were religious. Over the years, she phased from religion, although she still believed in her faith. There had been several times during the five years of their marriage when she requested he'd join her. He went sometimes. For the most part, though, he skipped.

"He's great. His sermons really speak to me, you know? And he's always willing to counsel his congregation. He could write a book on me and my own imperfections."

She stopped when the waiter came to refill their drinks and put their plates in front of them. After being assured they didn't need anything else, the waiter disappeared around the corner.

"In one of Pastor Krupps' sermons, he was talking about marriage," she went on. She tucked a strand of black hair behind her ear. "Marriages are strongest when the couple is for Christ. You know? I would love for you to come to hear a sermon with me. Would you?"

DeLong had already been thinking about giving church another chance, but he just didn't feel ready yet. He wasn't sure if he'd ever be ready. However, he saw the hope in Samantha's eyes, and he didn't want to burst it.

"Maybe," he told her. "I'll just have to see. I mean, it never did anything to me before. Why should it now?"

"Because I know God isn't giving up on us. As singles or as a couple. Jim, I love you so much it hurts." She blinked back tears. "I can't bear thinking someday Bella will be coming home after spending a weekend or even a week at your house in another neighborhood. I spent my life since college loving you. I've loved you even before I knew you."

She swallowed hard. DeLong's voice was lost to him. He took a sip of his Pepsi to wet his throat.

"Jim," she continued. She reached her hand out and placed it on his.

"Pastor Krupps says God never gives us more than we can handle. That's something I've thought about over the past few days. I believe that. And that's why I want you to come home." Her eyes became a mixture of tears and desperation. "Come home, Jim. Let's work on us."

When DeLong first came to meet her for lunch, he'd hoped it'd give him an opening to fix their marriage. He had no idea he was coming to an invitation to move back home.

Using his free hand, he covered hers with a nod. She let out a breathy laugh.

"Last night I called him to ask for counsel about us. I didn't know what to do about us. I was so tired of feeling so alone and unhappy. I didn't want to be hurting anymore. He reminded me of a passage in the Bible: first Corinthians chapter thirteen, verses four through seven."

"What does it say?"

She smiled. "He told me the same thing I'll tell you: 'look it up.'"

His phone notified him that a text came through. He looked at it and saw it was Calhoun, first scolding him for returning to Grimes' house when he was off the case, then a second text came asking him what it was he'd found.

He quickly replied he'd touch base with him later, then DeLong turned his attention back to his wife.

Chapter 49

After DeLong and Samantha parted ways, he returned to the motel to pack his things. Before he left to turn in his keys, he removed the dusty Bible from the nightstand. He stared at the ratted cover for a long time, thinking how out of place the Book was. Then he opened it to skim the slim pages until he found the verse Samantha told him about.

Love is patient, love is kind. It does not envy, it does not boast, it is not proud. It does not dishonor others, it is not self-seeking, it is not easily angered, it keeps no record of wrongs. Love does not delight in evil but rejoices with the truth. It always protects, always trusts, always hopes, always perseveres.

DeLong set the Bible in his lap and considered the words carefully.

Then he went on reading until he reached the end of the chapter and reread the final verse a few more times: *And now these three remain: faith, hope and love. But the greatest of these is love.*

Faith.

Hope.

Love.

He felt himself fighting, but he didn't know why. Or what he was fighting. If God was there, then why did He allow him to ruin his life with alcohol? It was alcohol that made him worthless. It was alcohol that forced his family to the edge of destruction. It was alcohol that was costing him his job.

DeLong shook his head, knowing it wasn't true. The alcohol never spoke to him, although there had been many times where it seemed like it did. Especially lately.

He closed his eyes with a heavy sigh, knowing he just didn't deserve any more second chances. He knew that.

So why does Samantha continue to give it to him?

She loves you.

"God, I don't know if you're there," DeLong spoke into the empty room. "Or if you are there if you would even listen to me. I haven't spoken to you since I was a kid. But if you are there, I think now would be a good time for you to help me."

He waited as if God would throw His booming voice from the Heavens in answer.

But nothing came.

Feeling somewhat foolish, DeLong gathered the rest of his things and headed for the front office to turn in his key.

Then he drove to the station to meet Calhoun and the investigators to hand over the notes and the bear head. He'd already been through the ten-minute lecture from Elliott about continuing the investigation when he'd been relieved of duty.

DeLong shrugged it off and told her he had a hunch they missed something and needed to act on it.

"Well, as long as it's not *our* heads on the line," she retorted.

"As long as we're moving forward in some way," Calhoun countered.

He inspected the stuffed head.

DeLong stretched aching muscles. "I've already called Sarah Benson to check in. She and the boys are okay. But I'm thinking we might need to send them a protection detail. Until we find out who killed Grimes, I'm not entirely comfortable knowing Sarah and the boys don't have anybody to look after them."

"Agreed," Calhoun muttered.

He studied the notes DeLong set on the table before them.

"The penmanship seems familiar to me," he thought out loud. "I don't know whose it is, though. Can't quite place it."

"I thought the same thing," DeLong told him.

"Did you ask Sarah Benson if her sons were missing a toy?" Elliott wondered.

"Not that she knew of. I described the bear and she said she didn't remember seeing one like it before."

"Maybe it wasn't a threat to Grimes' children. Maybe our suspect only sent the head as a warning about what would happen to him if he didn't give up trying to find out the truth."

"Take it to the lab," DeLong instructed them. "See if you can get anything from him. And call around town to see if any toy stores carry a bear like this."

* * *

Sarah Benson was vacuuming in the living room, trying to take her mind off her ex-husband, but the harder she tried, the more she thought of him.

Fresh tears spilled down her face. She swiped them away.

Would she ever get through this? Through this pain?

She didn't think so.

This pain lingered in her heart ever since they divorced.

There wasn't any difference now.

In divorce, he was absent.

In death, he was absent still.

Except now, there was no hope of reconciling, no chance of letting him know she'd forgiven him. She knew he wanted to be with her still. He was doing everything he could to win her back with money he had legally put together over the years. He even bought her a house.

A *house*.

He was turning it around to fit an image of a dream home she once told him she had.

Sarah chuckled.

She didn't think he'd remember.

She could have stopped by to see the house while she was in Augusta for the funeral, but she chose not to go. It wasn't because she didn't want to. She did. She wanted to see the work he had done. She wanted to feel his spirit.

At the same time, that was the very reason she couldn't go.

The heat of anger filled her blood.

Manny, you fool, she thought. Didn't you know all I needed was you?

Her mind drifted to the possibility that Manny had come to Birmingham.

When she asked Boyd and his brother about it, they promised they hadn't seen him.

It will always be under the boys.

She turned her vacuum cleaner off and went to the kitchen to make a pot of coffee. Sarah spent her nights trying to figure out what it meant. She knew her ex-husband better than anyone else. It was upsetting she couldn't decipher the cryptic message.

When he said it to his therapist, did he mean for the message to get back to her?

That she knew him so well, she'd know what he was talking about?

She wasn't sure.

When she first learned Manny had come to her house, she searched the boys' room for something, *anything,* that would indicate he'd been there.

But nothing.

She watched through the window as Boyd pushed his brother around on the tire swing.

Of course.

That's it.

Manny had come to visit one year and put up the tire swing for the boys. They loved it and were on it every day. Boyd even did his school work sitting in the swing.

That had to be it.

With new determination, she opened the door, found two digging tools in the nearby shed and marched toward the swing.

"Hey guys," she called.

"Hi, Mom!" her youngest replied.

"I have a project I'd like help with."

"What?" Boyd asked. He grabbed the bottom of the swing to stop it from sending his brother through the air.

"I'm looking for something and need your help."

"What are you looking for?"

"I don't know exactly. But I do think it may have been buried underneath your swing. Would you mind digging for it? Think of it as looking for buried treasure."

Boyd shrugged. "That'd be cool."

She handed them the tools. "Be careful. It's okay if you don't find anything, but if you do, come find me immediately."

As she walked away, she heard Boyd telling his brother to call him Captain Smith, while he could be his second mate, Pan.

When they began to work, she watched from inside for a second, then turned to finish cleaning.

Chapter 50

Light rain began turning the snow into a slushy mess. But, still, it didn't keep the children from enjoying their winter break outside. A group of teenagers was building a small snowman, even though the rainwater melted good ol' Frosty so that his middle looked lopsided.

MC sat on the bench, watching the events unfolding around him. A young woman jogging by stopped to catch her breath. Her face was flushed, beads of sweat dripped from her forehead.

"Cold," he said to her with a smile.

She chuckled and nodded her head in agreement. "Yes, it is."

She went on her way and he watched her disappear around the corner of the park.

Scratching at his forearm, MC turned his attention to the burn he'd earned fifteen years earlier. He always kept it covered because he hated looking at it, hated the reminder of how things can turn so wrong in the blink of an eye. Still, he had formed the habit of sliding his sleeve to his elbow, rubbing the rough skin as if he were erasing the past.

He hadn't always been the bad guy. There were plenty of times when he was good, caring, even loving. Then one night everything changed.

One night everything was set in motion where he'd commit his first conspiracy, burning his forearm in the process, and eventually either killed or ordered someone killed.

It was a slippery slope.

The thing about slippery slopes, MC realized as he watched a little boy toss a snowball at a little girl, was that sometimes you didn't know what'd happened until you were halfway from the top. It was then when you might be able to take back a little control, although you were still falling. It was then when you decided how you felt about it all.

And MC decided he rather enjoyed it. His heart fluttered as the faces of those lives that were lost because of one dark night flashed in his mind. For some reason, it ignited a spark in him. It was thrilling to be able to escape the clutches of those that could come after him. It was thrilling to be so close, yet he knew they were so far away.

His lips curved into a small smile.

They promised they would protect Admiral Matheson. And he was especially determined to keep that promise.

No matter the cost.

No.

Matter.

If he needed to kill, then he would kill.

MC covered the scar when a man, tall and muscular, sat on the bench next to him. His bench-mate put his elbow on the back of the bench, set his right leg across his left knee and looked around the park.

MC waited a beat until he said, "We have a problem."

His bench-mate continued to look around the park.

"Jim DeLong is still investigating. He's very resilient. We need to proceed with caution."

"What do you suggest we do about him?"

MC thought about the question before answering. They needed to be careful. He didn't care about who lived, or who died, though he had to admit the death of Manny Grimes went a little too far. It was getting messy now.

He looked around the park, considering his options.

Finally, he settled on the only answer he could come up with.

However, knowing his bench-mate, it was a risky one.

"It's our job to protect Matheson. Remember, if he goes down, we all do. Use that as motivation and proceed carefully."

"Jonathan Walker's in jail, being arraigned. There's enough evidence to conv—."

For the first time since his companion arrived, MC turned to glare at him.

"Lieutenant Jim DeLong is one of the best investigators in the police department. So is Russ Calhoun. And those CSIs DeLong brought in, they've also shown their worth. Grimes' death was one too many bodies under our belt. No one after Alan and Christy Walker were supposed to die. That's on you. I'm not going to fail Matheson and I am *not* going to jail."

His companion finally turned his head.

"Grimes found out. He was going to come forward. You know that. He had to be eliminated."

MC waited until a jogger went by before continuing the conversation, keeping his voice low as someone else approached.

"What's done is done. You started this sloppy mess. You get to clean it up. I'll protect you as well as I'm able. But when it comes to it, I will protect myself by any means necessary."

His bench-mate's eyes burned with fury. "Don't threaten me. We're all in this together."

"Just watch DeLong. Watch them all. I don't want anyone else...*eliminated*...as you say." He pushed out a breath and turned his head to look back at the park, alive with fun and games. MC looked back at his companion with a heavy sigh. Somehow, he knew he'd live to regret what he was going to say next. "But do what needs to be done. The sooner our loose ends are tied, the sooner you can return home."

The smile broadened, and the eyes were hungry for excitement. "With pleasure." His tone was more of a growl, like when a thick piece of meat is dangled in front of a lion's nose. He rose with unmistakable satisfaction, straightened his coat and blew into his hands. "Whew," he breathed. "It's getting a bit chilly, don't you think?"

Then he left MC alone with his thoughts.

Chapter 51

The ADA announced Walker would be arraigned in the morning, so Calhoun and the investigators called it a night. With much deliberation, Calhoun agreed to allow DeLong to remain in the loop—only if he promised to stay away from Grimes' house, the school and anywhere else the case touched.

DeLong didn't seem too pleased with the arrangement, although he knew it was the best he could get. Elliott made sure she'd voiced her opinion before agreeing to the deal.

Newman and DeLong went home to their wives, while Calhoun sat at a bar with a beer in hand. After he finished the first beer, he paid for it and left, deciding to swing by Elliott's apartment.

Calhoun couldn't think of another woman. He just couldn't. If he tried, Elliott would weasel her way into his thoughts. It amazed him how he was able to focus on the case.

The more he was around her, the less control he had with his thoughts. Normally, Taryn Elliott wasn't the type of woman he'd hunt. He liked the quick, easy women. Although Calhoun imagined her to be quick when she wanted to be, she certainly wasn't easy. He saw how hard she was resisting him.

She may talk the big talk, but he could tell there were plenty of times when the two of them seemed to be thinking the same thing.

Calhoun continued to heed Newman's warning. He wanted her, so he didn't want to scare her off.

Calhoun pulled into the parking lot of Elliott's apartment complex and turned off the ignition.

He saw her exiting her building.

Calhoun opened his door, then froze.

Something was wrong.

Elliott's walk was brisk, her hand swinging roughly in the air. She grabbed a fistful of hair with her hands as if to pull on it. She let go as she neared her car. Calhoun shot after her, grabbing her elbow before she climbed in.

Elliott spun around, eyes wide with surprise. "What the—Calhoun! What are you doing here?"

Her eyes at first were cold and hard, not in their usual steel-like "all business" manner. They were also red, as if she'd been crying.

When she saw him, her eyes went from angry to sad to helpless in a matter of seconds. Without another sound, she burst into tears, falling into Calhoun's arms.

Stunned at the sudden change of demeanor, he wrapped his arms around her waist, not knowing how to console her. He searched for something to say but came up empty.

After seconds passed, Elliott pulled away, eyes puffy and wet.

He wiped the tears from her face with a half-smile.

"Want to talk about it?" he asked softly.

"Why are you here?" Elliott demanded, her face hot and red.

"Well, I've been thinking," Calhoun told her. "We haven't had a chance to really know each other, you know. I was hoping to get you to have dinner or something with me. If you want."

At first, she stared at him as though considering the proposition. Then she let out a scoff.

"You know what, Calhoun? I'm not like one of those women who'll sleep with you at the drop of a hat. I actually have standards."

With that, Elliott slammed her car door, turned on her toes and headed back to her apartment before he could respond.

Not wanting to let it go, Calhoun followed her.

"I'm just trying to be a friend," he called after her.

"Do you even know how to be a friend?" she spat out as she hurried up the stairs. "You can't even be a friend to Jim DeLong. In case you didn't know, sleeping with his wife isn't very friendly."

"I don't see how any of that is your business."

He was nearly out of breath, trying to keep up with her furious rush to her apartment.

She opened her door and turned to face him.

"Listen, Calhoun. I'm really not in the mood for talking. Please leave." She swung the door shut, but he caught the edge before it could slam.

Pushing it open, he took in the view of Elliott's usual neat-as-a-pin apartment. It seemed someone had had a tantrum: clothes strewn across the floor, chairs overturned, even the television had taken a beating.

Calhoun watched in silence at Elliott.

Elliott, oblivious to the mess, turned away from him as if she were ashamed. She monotonously set the coffee to be made and began to reach into the cabinet to pull out two mugs. Calhoun placed his hand over hers.

The touch of her was electrifying.

She was shaking.

"I'll get the coffee. Why don't you sit?"

Unable to speak, Elliott nodded. She turned to straighten the apartment as best as she could until her legs buckled under her and she fell on the floor by the couch.

Calhoun poured the coffee before he sat next to her.

"Want to tell me what happened?"

Elliott shook her head firmly.

She sighed and found a spot on the floor to stare at. "Jonas is here."

"Who's Jonas?" Calhoun wondered, putting a hand on her shoulder and massaging the knot he felt.

Fresh tears spilled from her eyes and sobs of anguish and pain shot out from her lips. She sniffed as she failed to gather herself.

"He was my partner. A long time ago. We were in love," Elliott whimpered. "At least I thought we were."

He nodded, remembering the story Newman told him. It dawned on him that Jonas must be the cop who destroyed Elliott's young life. He moved closer to her so she'd rest her head on his chest.

"He's been calling me." Her voice cracked as she spoke. "I've been telling him to leave me alone. He told me he missed me. That he loved me and he was sorry." Elliott shook her head in angst. "I told him to stop calling me and I moved on."

"But he's not giving up, is he?"

Again, Elliott shook her head, pushed air out of her mouth. "He came by to see me. I guess he wanted to convince me with flowers."

Calhoun had noticed the red roses crushed throughout the living room when he first entered.

"He kissed me, even when I told him no. He wouldn't listen. He never does! I thought he was going to do it again! I thought he was..."

She trailed off when her sobs came full force. Calhoun wrapped his arms tight around her as if to shield her from pain.

"I won't let this guy get to you," Calhoun promised. "I won't."

When she let up, her voice was steadier and her face wet. He wiped the tears from her eyes and smiled.

"You can trust me," he assured her. "I won't let him or anyone hurt you. Ever."

She turned her face to blink at him, still trying to contain her emotions. His heart bled for her.

"Listen, Taryn, you're a strong woman. That guy's only preying on the fear of the fragile woman he *used* to know. But that woman doesn't exist. At least I've never met her."

"Until now," she stated, clearing her throat.

Elliott pulled away with a soft groan, and he grabbed her waist to pull her back to him, so they were face to face.

Her face was close enough to his, he could smell the fragrance of her shampoo. Her lips were moist and luscious.

He wanted to taste them.

"I've never seen that fragile woman," he repeated hoarsely.

Before she could respond, Calhoun took her lips to his. Elliott seemed taken by surprise—at first. She wrapped her arms around his

The Murder of Manny Grimes

neck so she could sink deeper into the moment.

He continued to kiss her until he pulled away.

Elliott's eyes flashed with annoyance.

"Why are you stopping?" she breathed. "Don't stop."

"Are you sure?" Calhoun asked. He wasn't sure he spoke. It seemed as though his voice had been removed from his vocal cords.

"A fine time to be asking me if I'm sure," Elliott demanded. Her sad eyes returned to their normal fire and ice. "You've been wanting to get in my pants since the day we met."

"I just think..." Calhoun began. He knew this could be his only chance to be with her. He didn't want it this way. He liked easy. But he didn't like... "You're too vulnerable."

"But I want—."

"I'm sorry, El. I have to go." He pushed by her. "I'll see you later."

Elliott let out a round of curses. "Where do you think you're going?" she demanded as he opened the door.

"Home," he told her, as though it was supposed to be obvious. "I'm going home. I'll talk to you later."

Calhoun padded into the apartment hallway, shutting the door tightly behind him.

He was sorry Elliott was hurting.

He hated that Jonas guy.

No matter how much he wanted to be with her, he knew they'd hate themselves afterward if they'd continued.

At least now, their unspoken game of hard-to-get moved into overtime.

And the ball was finally in his court.

Chapter 52

His mind heavy, Calhoun arrived at his apartment and grabbed a Bud Light from his fridge. After taking a couple of swigs, he preheated his oven for his frozen pizza. His moment with Elliott settled in his mind.

He surprised himself that he found it easy to walk away.

Calhoun wanted her, no doubt about that. He wasn't sure what drew him to her, but he found himself wanting more than just getting her into bed. It had been so long since he felt this way about a woman. He wondered if he had ever felt quite this way about a woman.

There was one, a long time ago. He'd even asked her to marry him.

But even Janice didn't melt his spirits. Not in the way that pleased him, anyway.

No, Janice was different.

Janice was calm and preferred no confrontations. She wanted to keep things simple.

Elliott, on the other hand, challenged him. She was unafraid to tell it the way she saw it.

And she had that spark in her eyes.

She wanted him too.

There was no doubt.

But Newman was right. He needed to tread carefully. In no way did he want to hurt Elliott.

Calhoun's oven beeped, so he inserted his pizza and set the timer.

Stepping over to the window, he stared out at the cloudless night, staring at the full moon.

He half hoped he'd be able to meet this Jonas guy. Nothing would give him a more pleasurable experience than punching his fist in his teeth.

"Don't worry, Taryn," Calhoun said into the night. "I won't let anyone hurt you anymore."

* * *

After Calhoun left her apartment, Elliott locked the door and dead bolted it for extra protection. She didn't think Jonas would come back so soon, but just in case, she slipped her gun into the back of her jeans.

Cleaning the apartment, she scolded herself for allowing herself a moment of weakness. Especially since Calhoun, of all people, was a witness.

She vowed it would be the only time.

Elliott didn't want to be weak. She had spent plenty of time teaching herself to be strong and independent. She didn't need anyone to fight her battles.

Certainly not Calhoun.

Why did he have to show up like that?

Why did he have to kiss her like that?

Why?

She threw the rose petals she had gathered into the trash can, and in spite of herself, kicked the can.

No.

Absolutely not. She did not want to go there.

Elliott put her hands on the counter, her mind replaying the kiss.

She didn't want to think of Calhoun that way. He wasn't her type at all. He liked having a new woman every night.

He couldn't be interested in her, unless he wanted to have a one-night stand.

Even as she thought it, she knew it wasn't true. Calhoun hadn't even looked at another woman since they'd met. At least not that she noticed.

And if a one-night stand was all he cared about, they'd be in bed right now.

But he stopped the kiss.

She didn't want him to, but he did.

What were his intentions?

What were hers?

Why couldn't she stop thinking about the kiss and how her knees felt like jelly?

Chapter 53

Sarah Benson clutched a box underneath her arm as she shuffled the boys to her brother's front door. It was early on a Saturday morning, but she couldn't wait. It was hard enough having to wait throughout the night because Kincaid and his wife were having another work dinner.

She banged on the door as she fumbled through her handbag, desperately searching for his house key. She banged again and rang the doorbell as his wife hollered through the door that she was on the way. Her voice was edgy and tired.

Her sister-in-law opened the door and after seeing Sarah, she narrowed her eyes.

"Do you have any idea what time it is?" she asked as she released a yawn.

"Julie, I'm sorry to wake you. I need to see Kincaid. It's important."

It was evident Julie saw the urgency in Sarah's eyes when she ushered them inside.

"Thank you," Sarah said. Kincaid came out of their bedroom at the end of the hall, tying his bathrobe against his waist.

"What's wrong?" Concern etched his voice.

Sarah held the box in front of her. The contents shook as her hands trembled. She hadn't yet removed the lock. She needed someone to be with her when she looked inside.

"I found it," she said, her voice soft and weepy.

"What is it?" Julie wondered.

"Manny did come by the house," she said. "He left this. Hid it."

"Where?" Kincaid inquired as he took the box, inspecting it with interest.

"'Where it will always be under the boys.'" She tried to steady her voice but failed.

Julie put her hand on Boyd's head and said, "Why don't you and your brother go raid the kitchen?"

Boyd hesitantly obliged, guiding his little brother away as Julie linked her arm around Sarah's shoulders.

Sarah felt a single tear fall from her eyelids and she knew she was cried out. Her emotions were becoming numb. She wasn't sure anymore if this was her life. None of it felt real. She wasn't even angry anymore.

She felt...dead.

She was dead inside.

Sarah shook her thoughts away as she tried to focus on the here and now. She'd found a box Manny had buried. She didn't know what she would find inside. Did she really want to know? Earlier, Lieutenant DeLong had asked her about some sort of proof Manny had found.

Would she find out who the man was that murdered her ex-husband?

The loving father of their children?

"Manny came by the house and I never knew." Her voice seemed far away and dull. Kincaid put a hand on her shoulder as though she would be shielded from any kind of pain she'd have to endure. Julie listened, apparently waiting to be told what was going on. "He buried that box under the tire swing. The boys found it last night."

Kincaid, still inspecting the box, disappeared into the kitchen

The Murder of Manny Grimes

and returned with an ice pick. He worked at removing the lock as Sarah rested her head on Julie's shoulder.

Once the lock popped loose, Kincaid looked at his sister. "Are you sure you don't want to give it to the police?"

"Not until I know what it is. Not until I see for myself who murdered my husband."

Kincaid laid the box on the coffee table and lifted the lid. Inside was an SD card.

He picked it up and inspected it curiously. "Hold on a minute. Follow me."

The women followed him through the kitchen, where he had a small, built-in office.

The room housed an all-in-one touchscreen computer sitting on top of a desk, two tall gray file cabinets and a small wastebasket. He took a seat in his chair as the women crowded in the space.

Kincaid slipped the SD card into a small slot on the side of the monitor. When a prompt popped on the screen, he tapped *view files*. A folder opened, and a single file appeared: *MC.avi*.

Sarah swallowed hard.

What was she going to see?

She held onto her brother's shoulders for strength and Julie's arm hugged her tight for additional support.

Her brother clicked on the file.

And they watched.

Chapter 54

Sarah left the boys with her brother so she could take the box and the SD card to Lieutenant Jim DeLong.

Her heart was still hammering with anticipation.

When she couldn't get DeLong to answer his phone, she thought her heart would burst its way out of her chest. She called the Columbia County Sheriff's Department and asked to speak with him.

"Lieutenant DeLong is on leave," the desk sergeant told her.

"On lea—what do you mean?" she exclaimed. "He's supposed to be investigating my husband's murder. Manny Grimes. How can he be on leave?"

"I can transfer you to Russ Calhoun. He's our consultant and Lieutenant DeLong's former partner in that investigation."

"But I just spoke to him."

"You did? Well, I'm sorry, but it's Russ Calhoun who's in charge of the case now. Would you like me to get him?"

Sarah stammered some more until she gave in and agreed. She needed to hand this over to someone. She wanted it to be DeLong because she had trusted him ever since their first conversation. He seemed genuine in wanting to find out who murdered her ex-husband.

How could he choose to go on leave now, when Manny's body was hardly even cold?

"This is Calhoun."

"Yes, this is Sarah Benson. Lieutenant DeLong isn't available to take my call?"

"Uh, no ma'am," Calhoun replied. "Is there anything I can do for you?"

Sarah let out a heavy breath as she went around an 18-wheeler. "I hope so. I'll be in town shortly. I found the box my ex-husband brought to my house."

"A box?"

"Yes. He buried it under the tire swing my sons are always playing with. It was locked, but my brother popped it open. Inside was an SD card, containing a video file labeled *MC*. We watched it. Ugh, my mind is still reeling from seeing it. I think I've seen one of the faces before, but I can't place it right now. I can't seem to think. Is this the killer?"

Calhoun was silent. She was almost convinced she'd lost him.

"You said you're on the way here?"

"Yes. I'll be there soon. Maybe another thirty minutes or so. I'm coming as fast as I can."

"Don't rush, Ms. Benson. I don't want you to have an accident or anything. I'll be here for a few more hours. I'll wait for you. I'll tell the desk sergeant I'll be expecting you."

"Okay, thank you."

Sarah threw the phone in the seat next to the box containing the SD card her husband had put inside. Rather than heeding Calhoun's warning, she sped toward Augusta.

* * *

After Calhoun ended the call with Sarah Benson, he relayed the information to Newman and Elliott.

"We have a little time before Walker is arraigned," Elliott said, glancing at her watch. "We can mention the conversation to Walker, see what he says."

Calhoun agreed.

When they went to the holding cells, Walker was lying on the top of his double bed, head propped on his hands.

"We have new evidence," Calhoun informed him.

Walker sat up and stared at him. "Oh, really? Does this mean you're letting me go?"

"Not a chance, Walker," Elliott scoffed. "We haven't seen it yet. It's on the way. We're giving you one final chance to come clean."

Walker let out a groan.

"I don't know what you people want from me. I told you. I didn't kill anyone. I don't know what evidence you think you may have against me, but it has nothing to do with me. You aren't even supposed to be talking to me without my lawyer present."

"Suit yourself," Elliott replied. She turned to walk away.

Newman and Calhoun hesitated.

"Do you know anything about an SD card?" Calhoun asked him. "Had Grimes ever mentioned it to you?"

"No," Walker replied. He slid off the top bunk and stepped over to the bars. "Why? What did you find?"

"We're not sure yet," Calhoun admitted. "Sarah Benson was the one who found it. She's on her way. You don't have any idea what's on it?"

Walker shook his head.

Calhoun watched him for a few minutes, trying to figure out what Walker knew, if anything. In the beginning, he seemed to have been withholding what was true. But now it seemed Walker finally understood the gravity of his situation. The evidence they had so far pointed directly at him.

Calhoun couldn't shake the feeling something about the case against Jonathan Walker didn't fit. It seemed too convenient.

Too black and white.

"Listen," he said. Calhoun stepped closer to Walker so he could be sure he had his undivided attention. "DeLong went back to Grimes' house. Behind a *Mona Lisa* painting, he found two threatening notes and a stuffed bear's head. His eye had a white patch. Does that sound familiar?"

Walker lifted his gaze to Calhoun's eyes.

"I'm not sure." Walker paused and glanced to the side, eyes dancing around the cell. It was clear he was debating about whether or not to speak his mind.

Calhoun leaned in close to Walker's ear. "Listen to me. I'm trying to get to the bottom of this. If you know something that'll clear your name, now's the time to say. Manny Grimes was your friend. If you really didn't kill him as you claim, then don't you want to help find the person who did?"

Walker walked to his bed, his head lowered to the ground. He rubbed his neck with his hand. He let out a round of soft curses.

"I'm sorry, Manny. I've failed you."

The words were soft, still Calhoun had no doubt Walker said them. He watched as he returned to the bars.

Walker gripped the bars with his hands.

"Tommy had a bear like that. It belonged to his father when he was a boy. When Alan died, Tommy was devastated. He threw the bear in the trash. That was the last time I saw it."

"Thank you," Calhoun replied.

He and Newman stepped away, waiting until they were out of earshot before conferring.

"What do you think?" Newman asked Calhoun.

"If Walker didn't kill Grimes and didn't send him the bear," Calhoun began, "then that leaves—."

"Claire Walker," Newman finished. "Do you think she could have done it all?"

"At this point, I can't really say what I think. Except they're pointing fingers at each other now. Walker's told so many lies and half-truths, I'm not sure what to believe. Right now, I have to wait for Sarah Benson to arrive with the evidence she found. Go to Claire Walker's house and interview her again. See what she says about the bear."

Newman nodded his agreement and grabbed his jacket as they made their way out the building.

* * *

Sarah Benson turned off the exit, nearly scraping the front end of a

Cadillac as she did so. She told herself to slow down. That it was still icy in some places of the road, and if she wasn't careful, then she could easily slide off and kill herself. That wouldn't do her ex-husband or her sons any good. With reluctance, she pressed the brakes slightly as she continued to her destination.

* * *

DeLong finished a five-mile run. As he entered his house, he stretched his legs. During the run, his mind, despite his best intentions, went to Manny Grimes.

He had promised to wait for Calhoun to call before doing anything.

But he was anxious to be involved. He didn't want to just be involved. He wanted to be in charge. He tried to forget about the case by being more attentive to his daughter and wife, but his mind always drifted back to Manny Grimes.

So much evidence, so few answers.

* * *

Sarah Benson reached the sheriff's office, parked, and with the box tucked underneath her arm, she went inside. The desk sergeant led her to where Calhoun stood. As they walked toward him, Sarah remembered where she saw the face on the video.

And froze.

Chapter 55

It couldn't be, could it?

Sarah's heart drummed against her ribcage. She knew she couldn't stay there. She couldn't talk to Calhoun. She thrust the box in the confused desk sergeant's hands and begged her to give it to Lieutenant Jim DeLong.

And only him. She found herself unable to trust anyone.

Anyone except for Jim DeLong.

After the lady finally promised, Sarah apologized and told her she needed to leave. She didn't offer any concrete excuse. Sarah needed to get out of there.

The lieutenant knew how to reach her. So she decided to go home where it was safe. Maybe stay with Kincaid until Lieutenant DeLong contacted her.

Sarah hurried back out into the cold and she slipped, nearly falling on the icy road.

* * *

MC caught Sarah Benson before she fell to the ground. After she found her footing, she turned, and her eyes grew wide.

"You killed my husband," she hissed.

"Very good," he appraised her, gripping her arm. He glanced over at his companion, then back at Sarah. "We're going to go for a little ride. It's such a nice day for a ride. Wouldn't you agree, Miss Benson?"

She cursed him, loud enough for him to whip out his weapon. He pointed it at her stomach and motioned for her to walk toward the parking lot.

"I killed your husband, Ms. Benson," he said softly. "Nothing's to keep me from killing you and the rest of your family. Now, if you just do what I say, we might be able to work out our problems."

Sarah swallowed hard and slowly turned.

"Please," she whispered. "Leave my family alone. I'll do whatever you want. Just don't hurt them."

"Well, that will depend on a few factors," MC informed her as he guided her to the car. He popped the trunk, looking around. Thankfully it was clear. "Get in."

When she hesitated, he hit the side of her face with the weapon. Sarah gasped and held onto the car for support. He helped her into the trunk and slammed it shut. No one else was around. Good.

MC nodded to his companion, who slipped in the driver's side.

"See you in a little while," he said. "I've got to make sure everything's covered." He patted the hood with his hand as he stepped away. He saw Sarah Benson hand over a box to the desk sergeant before she ran off. He needed to find out what it was.

* * *

Calhoun had seen Sarah Benson hightail it out of the building. He began to chase after her when Nancy stopped him.

"She left this box for Lieutenant DeLong. She wanted me to give it to him. But since he's not on the Grimes case..."

Glancing toward the door, Calhoun accepted the box and opened it.

Inside was an SD card. He picked it up and turned it over as though it would reveal the secrets it held.

"Thanks, Nancy," Calhoun muttered.

The Murder of Manny Grimes

He found an empty computer and slipped the card into its slot. He double clicked on the file and watched the video play on the screen before him.

His eyes widened, and he leaned forward to the monitor.

"Is that...?" He fell into the seat.

The audio was low and grainy. Calhoun had to strain to hear, but he heard every word. After the video ended, he let out a round of curses. He stared at the empty video screen, trying to grasp what he saw.

It didn't make sense to him.

But then again, murder never made sense.

Calhoun realized his fists were balled so tight, his knuckles turned white.

"We've got him," Calhoun muttered, his tone dark and distance. "We've got the son of a—."

Calhoun shook his head as though he'd be able to empty out all the confusion, all the anger. He couldn't jump on this.

No, he needed to be smart about it.

He decided he needed to regroup with everybody. Newman, Elliott, DeLong. And they needed to figure out how to bring the man who murdered Manny Grimes to justice.

Chapter 56

DeLong had taken time to visit the florist, and once he settled on the silkiest batch of red roses, he returned home, preparing to coax her into another lunch.

As he walked in the door, DeLong hid the flowers behind his back and searched the rooms for Samantha until he found her in Bella's room, playing Chutes and Ladders.

Her back was to him as she sat on the floor, helping Bella move her game piece to the correct spot on the board. Samantha clapped when Bella finished her move.

"Hey," DeLong announced.

Samantha positioned herself so she could see him.

Her mouth dropped when DeLong revealed the roses.

"These are for you."

"Jim! Those are beautiful," Samantha replied, her face brightening. She pushed to her feet, accepting the flowers. She took a deep breath to take in the fresh aroma. Her eyes were closed as she sighed softly.

When she reopened her eyes, she smiled.

"Thank you, honey," she said. "I could get used to this, you know."

"You should." DeLong leaned over to kiss her cheek. "Things are going to be a lot different around here. I promise you."

"Daddy, want to play?" Bella's eyes sparkled.

"Not right now, sweetheart, maybe later, okay?" DeLong promised, kneeling so he could kiss the top of her head. He turned back his focus to his wife. "Why don't you go put those in water while I take a quick shower? I think I could use a little distraction. The babysitter next door is expecting us to drop Bella off. I thought you and I could go for another lunch date."

Samantha smiled. "That sounds nice."

DeLong kissed her again before heading for his shower.

After he was finished, he grabbed a towel and wrapped it around his waist. Searching his closet, he found a navy blue dress shirt and black pinstriped pants. DeLong changed, dried his hair and opted to spray a little bit of cologne. Next, he found Samantha in the living room. She had set the roses on the mantle above the fireplace and was smiling at them.

She looked over at him. "Wow, you look nice." Looking down at her sweatshirt and velour pants, she said, "Guess I'll shower and change, too."

"You don't have to," DeLong replied, catching her arm as she breezed past him. "You look beautiful." He took the chance he'd been yearning for and kissed her. Her lips were soft and moist. She melted into him and they seemed to mold perfectly together.

When they parted, Samantha licked her lips. Her eyes remained closed as she relived the moment.

"No way am I showing my face anywhere where I look like a homeless person being taken in with sympathy by a dark, handsome businessman."

She giggled. "I won't be long." Samantha took one final look at her roses and then hurried up the stairs for her shower.

* * *

Samantha took a sip of her Diet Coke to wash her ravioli down.

"This is really nice. I mean, really, really nice. I honestly can't say I remember when I've had this much of an enjoyable time."

"I agree," DeLong said, taking a bite of Olive Garden's famous buttery garlic breadstick.

"We haven't had a nice time out in more than a year," Samantha continued. "Maybe more than two. I really miss it." She stabbed another piece of ravioli, lifted her fork to her mouth and set it on the table. Tears filled her eyes. "I miss you."

DeLong reached his hand out to his wife's. "I miss you too. I think we can make this work. I know it. We'll just keep going to counseling and make a point to spend a little time together. I don't want to lose you, Sam." He squeezed her hand. "We both made mistakes. We can't change that. But I think if we stick with each other, our mistakes will only make us stronger."

His phone began to vibrate in its holder on the side of his jeans. When DeLong glanced at it, he saw it was Calhoun.

"Do you need to get that?" He thought he heard a hint of disappointment in Samantha's words. "Because if you do, it's fine."

DeLong wasn't sure about needing to answer the call, but he wanted to. Calhoun wouldn't be calling unless it was a break in the case.

Did he want to answer it?

But—.

"No," DeLong answered, shaking his head. He pocketed the phone.

"Not important."

Samantha lifted the corner of her lips in a smile.

"Something changed in you, Jim. I mean, really changed. You ask me for lunch, bring me a dozen beautiful red roses and we're here, at one of our favorite restaurants, eating lunch, laughing, just having a good time. Something changed."

DeLong smiled. "'And now these three remain: faith, hope and love. But the greatest of these is love.' Sam, I have faith in us. Over time, I've lost it, but I found it again. I have hope to die in your arms when we're old and gray, after many, many fights we will have through the years. And most of all, I've loved you, Samantha, before I ever knew you." He paused, allowing his words to settle. "So, what

do you say? Will you do life with me? No matter what?"
　　Samantha's eyes clouded with tears she fought back.
　　"Yes, with everything I have, I will."

Chapter 57

When DeLong didn't answer, Calhoun left a message, requesting he either return his call or come to the apartment. He also sent texts to Newman and Elliott.

Calhoun popped open a Pepsi and slowly sipped the contents as he watched the rain pour from the darkened sky. Thunder cracked, and lightning ripped through the sky, sending the darkening town more light than the street lamps could put off.

His mind replayed the video file over and over again until his head hurt.

He gulped the last of his Pepsi and looked back outside, glanced at his watch, then the door. Where was DeLong?

Of course, the answer was obvious. He was spending some time with Samantha.

Calhoun was glad for that.

If DeLong was able to save his marriage, maybe, just maybe, Calhoun could free himself from the guilt.

But, right now, they needed to talk.

The Murder of Manny Grimes

Calhoun wanted to scream out loud.

How could he have missed it? The answer was staring in front of him all this time. But he missed it. They all did.

His heart skipped when there was a knock at his door, interrupting his deep thoughts. He walked to the door, unlatched the lock, then turned the knob, expecting it to be DeLong.

What he saw in the doorframe made his heart skip several beats.

Elliott was drenched from the rain, her white blouse clinging tightly to her body. She was buttoned until cleavage showed and he saw the slight curve of her small breasts. Her black dress pants clung tightly to her long legs.

His mind was clouded, unable to think coherent thoughts.

They stood face to face in the doorframe in silence.

"So much for my shower," she muttered.

He couldn't speak just yet. She stood there, a light at the end of the dark tunnel they'd been traveling through the past week.

"It's been a long week, Calhoun," she told him as she finally pushed past him.

Calhoun felt his knees weaken as she brushed by.

He shut the door, trying to push away the feelings he had for her.

Now wasn't the time or the place. She turned to face him.

"DeLong coming?"

"I don't know. I left messages. For him and Newman."

"I called Newman. He started talking about him and his wife finding out they're pregnant."

"That's great!" Calhoun exclaimed with a beaming smile. "Man, did we need good news! I know they thought they'd never have a child."

"Yeah," she agreed. "It's great. I didn't tell him I was meeting you. But he did tell me he went to see Claire. She claimed she hadn't seen Tommy's bear for a while now. She didn't even know he threw it away."

"Of course, she did," Calhoun replied. "That family lies more than the boy who cried wolf. How are we supposed to believe anything any of them says?"

He brushed a strand of damp hair out of her eyes, letting his finger linger on her cheek. Without thinking, he leaned in to kiss her. She warmly welcomed him.

He heard the ringing. It was so distant, he wasn't exactly sure if it was the doorbell, or even his ears.

"You gonna get that?" Elliott's voice was soft and breathy.

The doorbell rang through the apartment again, this time, more insistent.

He forced himself to step away. Elliott's eyes had clouded over.

Running her fingers through her damp hair, she let out a nervous snicker.

"I'll, uh, I'll go fix myself up. Can I use your hairdryer?"

"Yeah," Calhoun said as the doorbell sounded again. "On the dresser."

"Coming!" he hollered through the door as she disappeared into his bedroom. He closed his eyes tightly.

Of course, DeLong just had to show up now.

The man had impeccable timing.

Calhoun opened the door of his apartment. Before he had a chance to react, three gunshots echoed in his ears. He heard a distant scream as he stumbled back, in shock.

* * *

Elliott's heart leaped as the shots echoed through the apartment. The hairdryer fell through her fingers and crashed to the floor. Her breath caught as she ran to the door of Calhoun's bedroom. When she did, she attempted to let out a cry, but sound wouldn't leave her lips.

* * *

Calhoun fell against the coffee table, crashing through the glass. Pain exploded through his body, and he couldn't feel anything except the excruciating burn. He blinked, breathed hard, trying to catch his breath. His vision clouded as the assailant hovered over him. He didn't see anything, just the barrel of the gun.

* * *

Elliott rushed the shooter, an effort to save Calhoun. The intruder clocked her on the chin. She fell to the floor, her forearm rubbing against the carpet. She was kicked hard in the side. Elliott gasped for breath and she could see Calhoun's mouth moving.

He was telling her to run.

The intruder approached her with his weapon pointer toward her. She kicked his knee, scrambled to her feet and stumbled for the door.

She'd find help.

But, when she pulled open the door, her head jerked back as he forced her inside the apartment tugging at her hair. The door slammed shut.

Elliott through a punch in his direction, but he blocked it and pushed her into the corner of the door to Calhoun's room.

Elliott fell back against the bed, her heart thrumming in her ears.

* * *

Calhoun couldn't move.

He tried to will himself, but his back and both legs felt pain as he tried to stand.

He heard two shots that would silence the screaming in the other room, and a second later, he heard the final shot before seeing darkness.

Chapter 58

MC searched the living room until he found the SD card. Knowing he was running short on time, he slipped the microchip inside Calhoun's laptop. The computer wasn't password protected, so he was easily able to view the file. He clicked on the video and watched as he saw himself with Claire Walker.

The video was low, but he knew the crime lab would be able to raise the volume a notch. He didn't want the lab to hear Claire tell him how they could be together since he'd killed her husband. No, he didn't want anyone to hear.

More importantly, he didn't want them to hear later on in the video about how they burned a body fifteen years ago to keep some nosy ensign from turning them in for smuggling drugs to Thailand.

Enough time had passed, so MC removed the tiny card and slipped it in his pocket. Soon, the building would be swarming with police.

MC tilted his ball cap over his eyes as he stepped out of the room. He saw the door of one of Calhoun's neighbors open a crack. But MC wasn't worried. He had pulled on a black jumpsuit, and his

The Murder of Manny Grimes

cap covered his face.

He didn't have any reason for concern.

He smiled to himself as he shut the door.

If he wanted things done right, he would have to do it himself.

All by himself.

Before the day was over, he would have the last bit of his loose ends taken care of.

Finally.

Then he could be sure his and Admiral Matheson's secret would never be revealed.

* * *

Samantha handed DeLong a cup of hot chocolate as she snuggled with him under the wool blanket. They were watching old films on Turner Classic Movies. Bella was playing with her building blocks, stacking them high, before knocking them back down again and restacking them.

For the first time in a while, DeLong felt a peace with his life. Ever since lunch, he felt things were beginning to fall into place.

The best thing was he had no desire to drink.

All he wanted, all he needed was his family.

Watching *It's A Wonderful Life.*

He kissed the top of Samantha's head.

"Can we stay like this forever?" he muttered. "Let's never leave this spot. Ever."

Samantha giggled. "That's a nice thought. Let's try it."

Wrapping his arm around her tightly, he planted another kiss on her forehead.

DeLong's phone rang for the umpteenth time. He heard a moan escape Samantha's throat.

"I'm going to smash your phone against the wall," she complained.

"Maybe if I answer it, he'll go away," DeLong suggested.

He stretched his arm to grab his phone from the coffee table. The caller ID told him it was Captain Stewart.

"DeLong."

The background noise sounded busy.

"I'm sorry to disturb you, Lieutenant, but I'm glad I got you," Stewart said.

"What can I do for you, Captain?" DeLong asked.

"I thought I should be the one to tell you," the captain's solemn voice said. It took a full minute for him to continue.

The hairs on the nape of his neck rose and DeLong braced himself.

"It's Calhoun. He's dead."

Hearing the captain's words, DeLong pushed Samantha off him and he sat up on the couch.

Samantha's eyes grew wide and she mouthed, "What's wrong?"

He blinked as if it would help him understand what he heard. Maybe he heard wrong. After all, he had been hearing things as of late.

"How—what do—what happened?" he stammered.

"He's been murdered in his apartment, three shots to his stomach, one to the head. Taryn Elliott is dead as well."

"I'm on my way," DeLong told him, tapping *end call* before the captain could protest.

He wasn't sure what to tell Samantha, who still stared wide-eyed with worry. "I need to go out, sweetheart."

"Wait," Samantha pleaded, grabbing DeLong's arm. "Tell me what's happened."

He knew he'd have to give her the news eventually, and he didn't want her to find out from anyone but him, so he sat on the couch, an arm around her shoulders. He swallowed, but his throat felt raw.

"My investigator, Taryn Elliott, was murdered."

Samantha's mouth opened in shock. "Oh no!" Then she narrowed her eyes. His expression must have given him away. Samantha knew he cared for those under him, but he wasn't close with Elliott. "What else?"

"Russ was with her."

Tears filled her eyes. "No."

He looked away from her. She grasped his arm.

"He's not—please don't tell..." Her words trailed off as her voice shook. She leaned against his shoulder. "I'm so sorry, Jim."

"I have to go. I'll let you know as soon as I find out information." With that, he darted out of the house.

The entire drive to Calhoun's apartment, DeLong's mind raced.

Who killed them?

Why?

Was it some random murder?

He cleared his head of the thoughts. His heart beat hard against his rib cage, ready to burst through. DeLong blasted the air conditioner to get rid of the beads of sweat forming on his forehead.

The road was amassed with vehicles on the stormy night. His wipers barely kept up with the raindrops and fog. Up ahead, cars were stopping at the red light. Agitated, DeLong stepped on his gas, pulling into the suicide lane so he could zoom through just as the light changed to red. He heard the faint sounds of angry motorists blowing their horns, but he didn't care.

He saw the ambulance and police cars before arriving at Calhoun's place. His heart skipped several beats as he parked behind an unmarked car across the apartment complex.

DeLong chose to leave his umbrella in the car when he climbed out into the pouring rain.

Onlookers were huddled together, talking amongst themselves, wondering what was going on. Police officers wearing black raincoats held back the reporters trying to sneak through for the next breaking news.

Once safely in the building, DeLong headed to Calhoun's apartment on the second floor. A few cops were teamed with neighbors, asking questions and jotting the information given them.

DeLong stopped and hovered just outside the room, unable to bring himself to step inside. He grasped the side of the wall in case his knees betrayed him.

"It's a mess," Officer Harrison John stated behind him. "It's unbelievable. I just saw him at the station a few hours ago."

DeLong cleared his throat a few times and turned to face the officer.

"What's the story?" he asked. His voice sounded weak to his ears. He hoped it didn't to Officer John. Just in case, he cleared his throat.

"The medical examiner says she believes Calhoun was shot first, then Elliott. She'll know more after the autopsy. But the neighbors, the couple over there," he motioned toward an old man and his wife down the hall, "heard shots fired. At first, they thought it might have been a car backfiring. But they came out, saw a man exit the room. They said they knocked, didn't hear anything inside. The man tried the knob. The door was unlocked, and when he went inside, he saw...the vic—I mean, Cal—they saw the bodies." John fidgeted with his coat collar.

DeLong nodded and took a breath before stepping under the police tape, and into the apartment.

Calhoun lay sprawled on top of the glass table, eyes open, body lifeless. Spattered blood graced the broken glass, the couch, the wall. He looked around the room, hardly able to stand the sight of his best friend's body. How could it be? Why Calhoun? DeLong couldn't make sense of it.

"Elliott's in the other room," Stewart said from besides him.

"Has anyone informed Newman?" DeLong wondered.

"No. I called his cell, then his home number. Wife said he went to the store for her," Stewart told him. "Apparently they're expecting."

"I should be the one to tell him, Captain," DeLong muttered.

"Very well," Stewart agreed. "I'll leave it to you." He hesitated a beat.

"I'm sorry, Lieutenant. I know despite whatever's been going on with you and Calhoun, you were friends."

"Who's going to lead the investigation?"

"I'm assigning Oglethorpe. I can't have you or Newman working..." Stewart trailed off.

"I'm not sure I'd want to be," DeLong assured him, stepping toward the body. He stared at the shell that used to be his friend. "Then again, I'm not sure I'd want anyone other than me to catch the guy who did this."

"Jim," Stewart said forcefully. "You can't. It's too personal."

Reluctantly, DeLong nodded. "Unfortunately, I think you're right, Captain. But I would like to be kept informed."

At first, it seemed Stewart was going to protest. But to

DeLong's shock, he nodded. "I'll allow that."

DeLong cursed. "He'd been trying to find me for hours. If only I answered his call, I might have prevented this."

"You don't know that," Stewart replied.

DeLong shook his head slowly. Though he was seeing it, he couldn't believe it was really true.

He went into the other room to find Elliott lying half on the bed, soaked and bloody. Her eyes were open, lulled to the back of her head.

He felt a wave of sickness.

DeLong ran out of the room, pushing past Officer John. He had to get out of the apartment, out of the nightmare he was living.

Chapter 59

When DeLong arrived at Newman's house, he was greeted by a man with excitement in his eyes.

The investigator offered him Coke or water, but despite his thirst, DeLong declined, unsure about whether he'd be able to keep anything in his stomach.

"Jeff," DeLong said.

Newman narrowed his eyes. "Something wrong?"

"It's Calhoun and Elliott." The words seemed to be lead in his throat. "They're dead."

For a second, Newman froze, unable to speak. Next, he cursed under his breath.

"How?"

"Shot in Calhoun's apartment."

"I can't believe it."

Newman clutched the edge of the kitchen table and sat, the drone of the television in the other room carrying through the air.

"I saw it and I still can't believe it," DeLong mumbled.

"Who would do this?" Newman asked. "Whoever killed

Grimes?"

"I don't know, Jeff. But the captain said they'll keep us informed. I'll make sure of it." His eyes felt heavy and his muscles ached.

There were so many things he wanted to tell Calhoun.

Despite the animosity as of late, DeLong knew things would have eventually have found its way back to normal. He knew both of them wanted that. They'd been through enough together to not forgive and forget.

Hadn't they?

Did he really just lose the chance at reconciliation?

DeLong wanted to toss the table on its side. He saw the Bible on the cabinet by Newman's wine glasses and felt like throwing it across the room. And then filling the large glass with a good wine. Or even bad wine.

He stood and began to pace the kitchen, trying to loosen his tightened muscles. It had been two hours since hearing the news.

"Calhoun had been trying to get me," DeLong admitted. "I ignored him because I wanted alone time with my wife."

"Same here. We just found out we were pregnant. I was on cloud nine with the news, I forgot about anything else. I didn't even care." Newman cursed. "That's not only selfish but unprofessional."

DeLong put a consoling hand on Newman's shoulder. "You guys have been trying for eight years. I think you're allowed to be unprofessional and selfish this one time."

Newman didn't respond.

"Did he leave you a message?" DeLong asked, taking another seat.

"Yeah. Just that he needed me to call or stop by."

"Nancy called as I was coming over here. Sarah Benson was at the office. She was going to give the evidence she found to Calhoun but changed her mind. Didn't give a reason. Just had Nancy promise to give it to me instead. Nancy gave it to Calhoun anyway since I was off the case."

They let the silence surround them for a few minutes.

"I found out Jonathan Walker is out on bail. Do you think...?"

"I don't know what to think. But if he's out, I do know I would like another chat with him."

"I'm coming with you," Newman replied as he pushed his chair to stand. "Just give me a second to gather everything."

* * *

One look at Jonathan Walker's weary face, DeLong decided he was definitely innocent. A part of him still wondered whether or not Walker had any part in Grimes' death, but he doubted it. Walker looked as though he'd aged a great deal during the short time he spent in jail. DeLong found himself feeling sorry for him.

When he and Newman arrived, Walker accepted them in his house with a sigh, not protesting, not saying anything. He appeared to feel defeated despite being let out on bail.

After they settled in the living room, Walker sat on the couch and put his elbows on his knees.

DeLong heard the sounds of the boys upstairs, but they didn't come down. He wondered if Walker had told them to remain out of sight. And where was Claire? Upstairs with the boys? Or running errands? He didn't ask. Instead, he chose to break the awkward silence and jump into the why of them returning.

"Two of our people were murdered recently," DeLong began. "Russ Calhoun and Taryn Elliott. Two of the lead investigators in Grimes' murder."

Walker stared him down. DeLong tried to read his expression.

"What? When?" Walker shook his head as he spat out the words. "I don't get it. Manny, what did you get yourself into?" He looked at DeLong, his face full with confusion. "What was my brother into? Was Alan even a part of this?"

DeLong nodded. "We're pretty sure it had something to do with him. Before he died, Grimes found something out. We're not sure what it was. But whatever it was, he was killed for knowing."

"We have reasons to believe that when Alan was in the Navy, he did something bad. Something that includes two men: Admiral Matheson and Ensign McCoy."

"I don't know who they are."

"Are you sure?" DeLong asked.

Walker nodded. "Yeah. I'm sure."

Rather than waiting for another awkward silence, DeLong rose, Newman following suit.

"Well, you know how to contact us if—."

"I won't need to. I don't know anything."

Dissatisfied, DeLong had no choice but to show himself out. Once he and Newman were settled in his truck, he backed out of the driveway.

"What are you thinking?" Newman wondered.

His voice sounded drained. DeLong imagined his did as well. He wasn't even sure how to answer the question.

After a long pause, he sighed.

"Walker's innocent. That much I know. But I'm not so sure he doesn't know more than he's letting on."

"His brother's dead, Grimes is dead. Who's left?"

DeLong let Newman's question linger in the air. After he dropped him off and headed home, he considered the question.

Who was left?

Chapter 60

DeLong woke from a much-needed nap although "awoke" was relative; he hadn't exactly slept. Samantha was lying next to him, her back facing him. He climbed out of bed.

She stirred anyway, turning to face him.

"Can't sleep?"

"No," DeLong answered with a sigh. "How can I? I'm nowhere near finding out who killed Manny Grimes, my friends and colleagues were murdered." He looked hard in the still darkened room. "Were their deaths connected to Grimes?"

"You'll find something, Jim," she assured him. "You always do. That's why you're so good at your job."

He paused before speaking again. When he did, he stared at the window.

"I asked God for help," he told her.

"Yeah?"

"When I was leaving the motel to come back. I asked Him for help."

He scoffed as he turned to face her. "Instead, He lets Calhoun and Elliott die. Guess I'm not worthy enough of His help."

"That's not true, Jim. God didn't kill them. Just because He didn't answer right away doesn't mean He won't."

"Why did He let it happen, Sam? If He's really there, why did He allow Taryn and Russ to be murdered? Why did He allow Grimes?"

"I can't tell you why any of them were murdered, any more than I can tell you why the Earth revolves around the sun." She swung her legs over the side of the bed and reached for his hands. When he pulled away, she sighed. "What I can tell you is that there is a purpose to everything. We just have to be patient and let Him work in our lives. We have to trust Him."

"It's hard," DeLong told her. "I'm not sure I can be so patient."

"I know. But it's possible. Times like now are when you should pray to Him and just do what needs to be done. He prevails. He always does."

He regarded her face, searched her eyes. He saw peace within. "You really believe that, don't you?"

Samantha smiled. "More than ever."

She rose and stood on her toes to kiss him. Then climbed back into bed with a short yawn and put her head on the pillow, closing her eyes.

DeLong gazed at her, then lay next to her. He felt sleep coming on and he didn't want to miss it.

* * *

The next time DeLong woke, the sun had begun to go down, and his phone was ringing. He felt for the phone on his bedside table and looked at the caller ID. It read *unavailable.*

"DeLong."

"Lieutenant DeLong, this is Dr. Gordon. I finished reviewing my tapes and there's something I think you may want to know."

"I'm listening." DeLong rose from the bed and slipped on his robe.

"On one of the tapes, Manny was talking about a Master Chief and a couple of guys named Matheson and Greene."

"Go on," DeLong urged the doctor after he hesitated.

"Well, he mentioned that he called a reporter...a...a Kelly Partain. She wrote a story for the papers a few years back, but retracted the next day."

Kelly Partain. He remembered seeing her name in the article he and Newman found at the library.

"Why did she retract it?" Now, DeLong held the phone between his shoulder and ear as he slipped on a pair of jeans.

"He didn't say. He just said he needed to get the proof on tape. That was a few days before he called me and said he was in Birmingham. By that time, Manny was acting very erratic and not making much sense."

"So, this reporter told him something?" DeLong asked.

"When he was on the phone with me, he was going on about why he couldn't let it go. That he needed to make sure justice was served."

"Master Chief, huh?" DeLong repeated. Then a light bulb flicked on in his head. "Oh my goodness. That could be it!"

His mind reeled, and he almost forgot Dr. Gordon was on the line.

"Master Chief—that could be MC. Are you *sure* you didn't hear him say a name or anything else?"

"Yes, I'm quite sure, Lieutenant," the doctor replied. "I listened to that particular conversation over and over. He kept saying something about going to IA."

"IA? Internal Affairs?" DeLong creased his brow. He rose and paced the bedroom. "So MC's a cop?"

He paced, fully aware his wife had entered the room and was intensely focusing on his movements. DeLong stopped to peer through the window at the rain, trying to piece the puzzle together.

MC.
Master Chief.
Master.
Chief.
Then the answer struck him like lightning against water.

Chapter 61

The evidence had fallen into place like pieces to a complicated 3D puzzle.

How could he be wrong? DeLong knew he was once in the Navy. And his rank was Master Chief.

He paced around the room while Samantha sat on the edge of the bed, watching him.

According to Nancy, Sarah Benson had given her evidence that she had wanted DeLong to receive instead of Calhoun. But since DeLong was off the case, she ended up handing it over to Calhoun. Then he and Elliott were both shot to death shortly afterward.

No.

He grabbed his phone and called Sarah's cell. When she didn't answer, he tried to call her house phone. After that failed, he called the operator and urgently requested the number of Kincaid Benson in Birmingham, Alabama. When he got the number, he punched it in.

DeLong was well aware of Samantha's eyes following him as he quickly paced around the room.

"Benson Household."

"Mr. Benson, this is Lieutenant Jim DeLong of the Columbia County Sheriff's Department in Augusta. I'm trying to reach your sister, Sarah."

"I haven't heard from her. She was supposed to be going to see you," Kincaid said. "You haven't seen her?"

"No, I haven't. Actually, I've been out of the office, but she was supposed to be meeting with my partner. But at the last second, she seemed to have changed her mind," DeLong told him. He decided to not include that Calhoun had been killed. There was no reason to worry the man unnecessarily. "Listen, if you hear from her, please have her give me a call."

Kincaid said he would and DeLong ended the call.

"Sarah Benson's missing," he told Samantha.

His mind reeled and went into overload. Calhoun and Elliott found out the truth and were killed for it. They had to have been. It didn't make sense to DeLong any other way.

Sarah Benson was missing.

Lieutenant Oglethorpe had already informed him there was no trace of anything vital in Calhoun's apartment.

It was the last piece of hard evidence.

The killer must have found it and destroyed it for good.

He hurried out of the bedroom and downstairs. He passed Bella, who tried to snatch his attention. Samantha picked her up, muttering something about Daddy having important work things he needed to take care of.

He did a search on the computer and finally found what he was looking for.

DeLong called the number of Kelly Partain.

"Partain."

"Yes, Ms. Partain, this is Lieutenant Jim DeLong of the Columbia County Sheriff's Department in Augusta, Georgia." He ran through the reasons for his calling.

"Yes, I remember talking with Mr. Grimes," Kelly told him.

"Can you relay to me what you told him?"

"I don't know. I mean, didn't I hear on the news he's dead? I can only assume it's because he knew the truth. I have a family. I'm not sure I should risk talking."

"Please, Ms. Partain. Too many people have died because of this. It needs to end."

He listened to the breathing on the other end of the line. DeLong watched the seconds tick by until she spoke again.

"All right. I'll tell you everything I know."

Chapter 62

After DeLong heard the testimony from Kelly Partain, he ended the call and snatched his car keys from the table. He shouted to Samantha that he had to leave. She yelled down the stairs to be careful. He said he would, then when he stepped outside, he hesitated before shutting the door. He called over his shoulder that he loved both her and Bella very much.

He heard her reciprocate as the door slammed shut.

When DeLong pulled onto the road, he called Newman to let him know he was coming to pick him up, then went into detail about what he'd found out.

As he did, his heart fluttered with anticipation. After spending the entire week feeling flustered and frustrated they weren't going anywhere, he was anxious to close the case.

He stopped at the traffic light. The Christmas lights and the glow of the street lamps broke through the night. The leftover snow had melted. He could see parts of the road where black ice reflected the lights.

His mind drifted back to the investigation as he stepped on the gas to continue on his way. He not only closed the case. He ended up unraveling a secret that had been rooted in the hearts of all involved over the past fifteen years.

His mind switched to Sarah Benson as he turned onto Newman's street. He found himself praying she was all right. Had she been kidnapped? Was she still alive? He gripped the steering wheel until the natural color of his hands turned white.

He pulled into Newman's driveway, glad he was already outside, waiting for him. He was gripping a travel coffee cup.

"Whew," Newman said as he climbed inside. "Cold. Come on. Let's bring this SOB down."

"Yeah, let's," DeLong muttered.

* * *

MC finally arrived home. His partner's car was parked in the garage as planned, so he could easily retrieve Manny Grimes' ex-wife from the trunk. As he unlocked the front door, he wondered if Sarah had given him any trouble.

He opened the door, the light of the moon shining across the massive living room. He preferred to live just outside of town, where there weren't a lot of houses around. This way, if he ever needed privacy, he knew the chances of being bothered was slim to none. Now was a good time for the seclusion. He still had things to take care of in order to finish cleaning up the mess.

He heard a scream coming from a room upstairs, then a very clear, "*Shut up!*"

MC rolled his eyes as he climbed the stairs, slowly putting one foot in front of the other. The boards underneath the carpet creaked with each step, but he'd lived in the house long enough to not notice anymore.

MC followed the sounds of sobbing until he reached the master bedroom. Turning the knob, he pushed open the door.

Sarah Benson lay across the bed, hands and feet cuffed to the posts.

Tears streamed down her face. His partner had his hand clamped over her mouth. Sarah's chest heaved in quiet sobs.

"Max," he said. "Let her go."

Max Greene twisted his body so he could face him, but kept his hand over Sarah's mouth.

"She'll scream," he growled.

"Then let her. No one's around to hear. Let her scream."

Greene hesitated, and with a frown released his hand. Sarah whimpered but didn't scream. Instead, she begged between sobs to be let go.

"I won't tell anyone," she cried. "Please. Let me go."

"You know we can't do that, Ms. Benson."

"I have a family. I have children."

MC ignored the statement and focused on Greene. "Did you even try to get anything out of her?"

Greene shook his head, tossing his fedora between his hands. "No, she's refusing to speak."

MC rolled his eyes, sitting on the corner of the bed. He stroked Sarah's face as though he wanted to console her. She cringed and tried to get out of reach, but of course, she couldn't.

"Sarah," he said softly. "I'm so sorry you had to be involved. Really, I am." He gave her a smile. "I'm going to ask you a question, now. And I need you to answer truthfully. Okay?"

MC took her whimper as a yes.

"The SD card. Did anyone other than you see the file?"

She didn't answer, only cried harder. She struggled against the cuffs, but they remained intact. Sarah let out a scream. Greene stood to the side, watching.

Annoyed, MC raised his hand and brought it to the side of her face, connecting his palm to her cheek with an amount of force that made even his palm sting. She gasped, and her breath quivered as she attempted to control her sobs.

"I'm going to ask you one last time, Ms. Benson. Did anyone else see the video file?"

She quickly shook her head.

"Are you sure?" He stroked her shoulder, his thumb rubbing against her throat.

"Yes," she cried, her voice thick with tears. "I'm sure."

"Good."

He patted her shoulder and rose.

The Murder of Manny Grimes

"Now what?" Greene wondered.

MC smiled. "Now we finish taking care of business."

Greene flashed him a smile, his pearly white teeth showing. "Can I?"

MC shrugged, stepped aside, gesturing with his hand. "Be my guest."

Greene tossed his fedora to the chair where his overcoat rested and rubbed his hands together as he sat on the edge of the bed. He placed both hands on Sarah's throat and squeezed. She tried gasping for air as she fought against the handcuffs but was unable to get loose.

MC opened his bedside table, slowly. Greene was too involved in his own task to take notice. When Sarah was finally still, he waited for a few beats, then MC held the gun against Greene's temple and squeezed the trigger. The bullet exploded out the barrel and imprinted itself on the side of Greene's head. At the force of impact, Greene's hand released from Sarah's throat and he slumped over her body.

Now, he'd taken care of the mess.

"Thank you for your service, Max," MC said to the empty shell of his old friend. "I'm sorry it had to be this way. But as you can see, there was no other choice."

Chapter 63

Newman and DeLong watched the house for fifteen minutes for a sign of activity. The house was silent, but they knew the killer was home. His car was parked in front of the garage and the dim light in the room upstairs was on.

They waited but decided enough was enough. Newman called Oglethorpe, who was in charge of investigating the murders of Russell Calhoun and Taryn Elliott. He filled him in on everything they knew.

After hanging up, Newman slipped the phone into his shirt pocket and frowned at DeLong.

"He's on his way, but he doesn't like it."

DeLong continued to stare through the glass at the house. "Neither do I," he muttered.

They waited until the investigator pulled up behind DeLong's truck.

For the sake of remaining undetected, neither vehicle had their headlights on.

They climbed out of their respective cars.

Newman walked around the car and they waited as Lieutenant Dan Oglethorpe padded toward them. He was a man in his late fifties, thick brown beard with specks of gray, and eyes round and close together.

For anyone who didn't know him, they would believe his glossy eyes were due to the cold weather, but rather, they are always glossy. He wasn't skinny, nor was he fat. His laughter was always silky and smooth. DeLong knew Oglethorpe was invested in the Boys and Girls Club, as well as a shelter downtown that helped battered women escape from their abusive husbands or boyfriends. He remembered Samantha once saying Oglethorpe seemed like a giant teddy bear.

"Jim," Oglethorpe acknowledged. He clucked his tongue. "Are you gentlemen sure this is a good idea?"

"You wanna make an arrest, don't ya?" Newman asked.

"Yeah, but *him*? I'm sorry, but I truly don't think so."

"Just trust me," DeLong pleaded.

"Well," Oglethorpe said, hesitantly. Although he'd grown up in the Midwest, his accent was as southern as they came. He sucked in a breath and pushed it out. "Okay."

As he said the words, they heard a gunshot coming from within the house. Instinctively, they all drew their weapons and hurried toward the door. DeLong put a finger to his lips, motioning for the others to be as quiet as they could. He surveyed the premises and signaled Oglethorpe to check out the back of the house. With a short nod, he ducked into the shadows.

Weapon in one hand, DeLong tried the door. Newman stood on the opposite side, aiming his weapon. The door opened easily, and Newman stepped inside.

* * *

MC was about to move Greene's body when he heard the creak of the door downstairs. As silently as he could, he moved to the bedroom door and peered out. He saw the light from the moon peeking through. MC let out a silent curse. He glanced around the room as his mind reeled.

Well, he was just going to have to wing it.

MC stepped out of the bedroom and into the bathroom. He held his gun in front of him, ready for anything.

* * *

Oglethorpe cut himself when he brushed by the thicket bushes underneath the back window. When he reached the back door, he tried the knob and found it was locked. So were the windows, which was fine by him. He didn't relish the idea of climbing over the overgrown thicket bush.

Instead, he hurried through the shadows back to the front door.

* * *

DeLong and Newman surveyed the downstairs before meeting at the foot of the stairs. They listened, but all was silent in the house. Oglethorpe met them and wordlessly informed them there wasn't anything to see in the backyard and everything was locked. DeLong put one foot on the stairs.

* * *

The creak of the steps told MC his uninvited guests were making their way to him. Slowly, MC inched his way out of the bathroom.

Showtime.

Chapter 64

DeLong was the first to see him. "Put your hands up!" He leveled his gun at the man moving in the darkness.

"Whoa, whoa!" the man exclaimed. "Don't shoot!"

DeLong kept his gun pointed. Oglethorpe and Newman followed suit.

"Mike Stewart, you're under arrest for conspiracy to murder."

"Wh-what?" Stewart stammered. "No, you've got it wrong. It's not the way it seems." Stewart carefully set his weapon on the floor and kicked it toward the other officers. "Please. I'm being framed."

"Explain," Oglethorpe said as Newman retrieved the weapon.

"Sarah Benson. She's been murdered. Max. I thought we were friends. But he was using me as the fall guy. I-I killed him. I had to. Don't you understand? He was going to kill me. Frame me for Sarah's murder, and probably set me up for Grimes."

DeLong exchanged glances with Oglethorpe and Newman.

"Why would he do that?"

"Because a long time ago I did something bad. We all did: Greene, Matheson, Walker, me. I think Greene knew you were getting close. So, he came up with the plan to frame me."

"Where's Sarah?" DeLong demanded.

Stewart tilted his head toward the bedroom. "She's dead. I tried to save her. Really, I did. Greene strangled her. I shot him, but I was too late."

DeLong's heart rose in his throat.

Could he really be telling the truth? DeLong shook his head free of the questions and slowly continued up the steps. He continued to hold his gun on the captain.

When they were face-to-face, he asked, "You said you did something bad. What was it?"

Stewart swallowed. "When we were all in the Navy, we were smuggling drugs to Thailand. An ensign found out what we were doing."

"You killed him?"

Stewart nodded. "Well, to be fair, Admiral Matheson killed him. Then, Greene tossed his body into the furnace to burn."

Sounded about right. Except—.

"Do you know a reporter named Kelly Partain?"

Stewart shook his head and narrowed his eyes. "I don't believe so."

"It seems Kelly was the author of a news story some fifteen years ago," DeLong explained. "She wrote about Alan Walker being blamed for the murder, but the next day printed a retraction. I spoke to Kelly. According to her, Admiral Matheson paid her off a good deal of money. But now, she wants justice to be done."

DeLong hesitated before continuing. He wanted his words to sink in and observe Stewart's reaction.

"She told Grimes what she knew. Now Grimes is dead."

"It was Greene, Lieutenant. It was all him. He wanted to try and set me up."

DeLong decided to try a bluff.

"Then there's Calhoun. He called me and said Sarah gave him the evidence. And that evidence implicates you were the mastermind, the one in charge from the time the ensign was murdered, to now."

"Wh-how—." Stewart stammered, eyes blinking in disbelief. He shook his head slowly, then swung his arm to knock the gun loose from DeLong's hand. He kneed the lieutenant, who fell backward into Newman and Oglethorpe.

Stewart grabbed the gun DeLong dropped and ran into the bedroom.

DeLong hurried to rush him, knocking the captain to the floor. They struggled until someone kicked DeLong hard in the back.

Chapter 65

DeLong cried out as he toppled over. He was kicked in the face once before finally he heard a familiar voice.

"Stop it now. Why are men such violent creatures?"

Ribs exploded with pain in DeLong's side as he squinted to look at the speaker. She stood, arms crossed, glaring at Stewart and the second man.

Claire Walker.

She held a gun in her hand, pointing it at Oglethorpe and Newman.

"You, go over to that corner."

They obeyed, hands held in front of their chests in an effort to keep from being shot. DeLong forced the pain out of his mind, which was not easy. He slowly moved to a sitting position and eyed Claire.

"Mike was right, Lieutenant," Claire stated in her syrupy voice. "You really are a good investigator. Too good." She clucked her tongue. "It's a shame. I really liked you."

"You were in on it this entire time?" DeLong asked, struggling to control his breathing. His side was throbbing.

"Yes and no," Claire replied, nonchalantly. She flashed Stewart a smile. "Mike and I are lovers. But I didn't know he'd killed someone before. Not until my idiot husband confessed his sins to me one dreary night. I couldn't let my baby go to jail. You know? I love him. You protect those you love, right?"

"How could you?" It was Newman. "The father of your children was murdered. How could you be so heartless?"

"That man was going to turn Mike in," Claire said innocently. "I couldn't simply let that happen. I'm sorry he died, I really am. But when it comes to choice, Alan and I stopped loving each other years ago." She cleared her throat after a short pause. "Actually, to be perfectly honest, Mr. Newman, I'm not sure Alan and I ever really loved each other. See, I was pregnant with Tommy before I was married. So, I asked him to marry me. It isn't natural for someone in my family to have a child out of wedlock."

"But murder is?"

"Oh, I've never killed anyone," Claire said, directing her attention to DeLong.

"No, but you've helped cover it up," Oglethorpe put in. "That's just as bad."

"What I'd like to know is," the mystery man said, speaking for the first time since arriving, "how did you figure it out?"

"Obviously, *Admiral Matheson*," Stewart said heatedly, narrowing his eyes. "Neither you nor Greene are very good at your own jobs. Had you had done what I—."

"I'm sorry," Matheson interrupted with mock regret. "If only I suggested we kill Walker ages ago—oh, wait. I did. But no. You thought we'd have too much blood on our hands and thought we could quench him." He motioned his arm toward DeLong and his companions. "Now look where we are, *Captain*."

"It doesn't matter anymore," Claire snapped. "So, cool your testosterone." She looked at DeLong. "How did you figure it out?"

"Manny Grimes," DeLong said simply. "He told his therapist about Master Chief and that he was going to go to internal affairs." He stopped and stared at Stewart. "Now, Captain, I believe Professor Plum did it in the schoolyard with the revolver. But, unfortunately since you murdered Calhoun and stole whatever evidence Sarah Benson gave him, probably destroyed it, we don't have proof of anything," DeLong gave them a smile. "Not to say we don't have *any* proof, mind you. After all, we do have Manny Grimes on tape."

"And the therapist will unleash the tape to IA," Newman put in, seeing where DeLong was headed. "We found out the truth. It's only a matter of time before others find out."

DeLong saw Claire swallow. She looked back at Stewart. "Is that true?"

"He's pulling our legs, sweetheart," Stewart told her. "There probably isn't really a tape."

"Oh, there is, Captain," DeLong taunted. He stood slowly, though the pain took hold of his body. "And even if there isn't, we have Kelly Partain. She saw the whole thing."

"What? Who's Kelly Partain?" Claire demanded.

"I have no idea who he's talking about." Stewart glared at DeLong.

Claire continued to huff at him.

"She's that reporter."

Both Stewart and Claire stared at their companion.

"What are you talking about, Matheson?"

"The reporter. Remember? She noticed Ensign McCoy had vanished. She wrote that article about his disappearance. But nobody ever said—."

"She saw the whole thing," DeLong repeated. "She was with McCoy when you were hiding the drugs in the boiler room. He'd told her to stay where she was. McCoy confronted you, so Matheson killed him. I'm guessing Stewart suggested tossing his body in the furnace. No body, no crime. No crime, no jail. Everybody walks away."

"But not everybody walked away," Newman added. "Alan Walker felt guilty for fifteen years for what he'd done. It ate him up inside. Finally, he decided to come clean. Obviously, you couldn't allow that. So, you staged his suicide. My guess is Christy wasn't supposed to be there."

"No," Claire confirmed. "But it worked out. Alan had left me weeks before, because of my affair. Christy confronted me. Of course, I denied it, but then she started spending more time with Alan. I can only guess he told her everything."

"Grimes had shown Alan proof of the affair. He'd been following you so he could show it to your husband."

"Yes," Stewart admitted.

"Did he know who you were?" Newman put in.

"He knew I served with Alan. Before I became captain, we met. I liked to keep tabs on Alan. I always knew he was weak. I knew one day he'd want to come clean. So, I needed to watch him carefully. We had dinner together from time to time. Alan, Grimes, Claire and I. Guess that's when Grimes started noticing something was going on between me and Claire."

"Did he know you became the captain?"

"No. Not until the very end. Well," Stewart said. "I'm getting a little bored with all this truth talk." He aimed the gun directly at DeLong.

Just then, a gunshot came from behind Stewart. He dropped his own weapon in shock, stumbled a few steps before hitting the edge of the bed, onto the floor.

DeLong dove for the weapon at the same time as Stewart. They struggled while Oglethorpe and Newman went for Claire Walker and Admiral Matheson. Once DeLong managed to loosen the gun from Stewart's grip, he knocked it out of reach. He managed to push Stewart away enough to throw a kick at his face. Stewart fell to the ground and DeLong hurried to retrieve the weapon. He aimed it at his captain.

He glanced up and saw a horrified Admiral Matheson and an angry Claire Walker against the wall, arms up.

Stewart's shooter was Jonathan Walker. He stood by the bed with Sarah Benson. She had at some point during the struggle woken up.

That was a bit of good news they needed.

Tears streamed down her face and she still struggled against the handcuffs. DeLong leaned down to the captain and searched him for the keys. When he found them, he tossed the keys to Walker, telling him to uncuff her.

"Mike Stewart, Claire Walker and Ozzy Matheson," DeLong

said, looking at each of them. "You are under arrest for the murders of Manny Grimes, Alan Walker and Christy Walker, and conspiracy to covering the murder of Ensign Lawrence McCoy."

Oglethorpe was already on his radio calling for backup.

Chapter 66

After the police carted their murder suspects away and they marked the house as a crime scene, DeLong padded toward Jonathan Walker, who stood, shielding his body from the cold, leaning against his car.

"Hey." DeLong waited for a beat as they watched the police walk inside to do their job and gather evidence.

"I figured if I was going to be in trouble, I might as well do something to earn it," Walker said finally.

DeLong chuckled softly.

"I'm sorry for the trouble you've had the past few weeks," he said. "I can only imagine what you've been through."

"No, you can't," Walker muttered.

It was true, DeLong decided, he couldn't even imagine.

"Why did you come here?"

DeLong waited until Walker decided to speak. It seemed as though he was considering whether to confess or not, but finally, he did.

"Well, after they came to me about Tommy's bear head, I began to wonder. Then when I was released on bail, I started going through my wife's journals," he began. "In the days before they were killed,

Christy and Alan spent a lot of time together. I had suspected that maybe they were having an affair. But I didn't want to let Manny know he'd convinced me. Then I just thought I was crazy." He let out an incredulous laugh. "I told myself they weren't sleeping together. Even though I knew they spent an awful amount of time with each other. My wife loved writing, you know? She'd write short stories because she wanted to escape this world. She'd write in a journal to either revel in joy, or unleash anything that bothered her."

Walker paused, reached into his jacket and pulled out a leather-bound book with the initial "C."

"You can have it," he said. "If it'll help put them away. I don't know if it'll be admissible in court. But at least through Christy's writings, she will be able to speak for Manny. And Alan." Another pause. Walker breathed in the cold air and pushed it back out. "At first, I wanted to protect Claire. She was all I had left of my brother. But then, I realized I wasn't protecting his memory. So, I followed her here."

DeLong held his hand out and Walker accepted.

"I'm glad you did." DeLong assured him. "You did a good thing, Mr. Walker."

"I hope so, Lieutenant DeLong. But please don't become offended when I say, I hope my family and I don't see you ever again."

DeLong lifted the corner of his lip in a smile. "No offense taken, Walker."

He watched as Walker climbed into his car and left Stewart's house.

DeLong skimmed through the journal and read the vivid tellings of what Alan Walker had told Christy. It was hearsay, but he wondered if the district attorney could figure out a way to enter it as evidence.

"Been a long night," Newman said, shattering DeLong's thoughts.

He nodded. "Yes. It has."

So much had happened since he'd heard of Calhoun's and Elliott's deaths. So much had happened since three preteens entered the police department, blue from trekking through the winter storm.

DeLong yawned, eyes beginning to droop. All he wanted to do now was go home, be with his family, and sleep.

"Let's get together for lunch tomorrow," DeLong said to Newman. "As a sort of tribute to those whose lives were lost."

After Newman agreed, DeLong stepped over to where Sarah Benson was being checked out by the EMT. She was protesting against going to the hospital.

"I'm fine, I promise," Sarah was telling him. "All I want to do is get home to my family."

The technician sighed and agreed, only if she waited until the morning before heading back to Birmingham.

"That's fine. Actually," she looked over at DeLong, "I was hoping tomorrow, you could show me Manny's house. I want to see the work he was doing. Would you mind that?"

"It would be my pleasure, Ms. Benson," DeLong said. "Newman and I are headed home. Would you like us to take you to a hotel ?"

"Yes, that would be great."

She smiled at him, the first smile he'd ever seen coming from her. It radiated her face and Sarah Benson appeared to have had a major weight lifted off her shoulders. She'd been through a lot, he knew, but maybe now she could start to find peace.

* * *

After he dropped Sarah off at a hotel and took Newman home, DeLong headed back to his family. When he entered the house, he went upstairs, first to check on Bella. She slept peacefully, arms drooped over the edge of the bed. Her favorite pink elephant had fallen to the floor.

DeLong picked it up. Lifting his daughter's arm slightly, he slid the elephant close to her. She squeezed the stuffed toy and turned to face opposite him. He leaned in to kiss her cheek and whisper that he loved her.

Turning around, he saw Samantha standing, half-asleep in the doorway.

He guided her to their bedroom.

"What are you doing up?" He looked at the clock and realized it was nearing one thirty in the morning.

"Waiting for you," she said with a yawn. "I want to hear what happened."

He helped her lay down. "I'll tell you everything in the morning." He kissed her cheek. "But we won."

She smiled lazily and fell asleep.

DeLong changed, lay his head on his pillow, but couldn't sleep. His mind was still sorting everything that happened over the past week.

Chapter 67

The next afternoon, DeLong woke up, feeling more refreshed than he had in a long time. Samantha's left arm was draped around his waist, her soft, rhythmic breathing in tune with his own. He realized the anxiety he'd been feeling had almost gone away. He considered making breakfast, but a glance at his bedside clock told him it was almost time to meet the others for lunch. After he'd dropped Sarah off at the hotel, he invited her to join them. Then he'd take her to have a look at Grimes' house before she retrieved her car at the police department.

His cell phone rang somewhere in the distance. As carefully as he could, he slipped out of bed, trying not to wake his wife. Then, he went in search of the phone. He followed the sound to Bella's room.

"'Lo?" he heard her say.

DeLong stepped into the bedroom to find Bella sitting frog style on the floor with her Care Bears. She wouldn't be able to hear who was on the other end, he knew, because the phone was upside down. When Bella saw him, she smiled, leaning backward and reaching out her arm.

"Daddy for you," she said with a giggle.

"Oh, it is?" DeLong replied. He leaned down to tickle her. Her giggle warmed his heart. Taking the phone, he said, "Thank you. You'll make a fine assistant someday."

"I don't want to be an assistant!" she cried out with a laugh.

"Oh, you don't? What do you want to be?"

"I want to be a lieutenant! I want to solve mysteries like you!" She leaned into him and hugged his neck.

The corners of DeLong's eyes began to well up as he wrapped his arms in a hug. He almost forgot someone was on the line.

"DeLong," he said as Bella positioned herself in his lap, holding a purple Care Bear against her chest.

"Hey, man!" It was Harry. "I was just checking in on you. Seeing how you're doin'?"

DeLong considered all that had happened in the past week. The search for Manny Grimes' body. The search for his killer. The falling off the wagon and conspiracy they'd unraveled. The discovery of his wife's affair with Russ Calhoun and the murders of his best friend and Taryn Elliott. All things considered, he could tell his sponsor he was doing awful. That all he wanted was to be alone with a bottle of whiskey.

But, no. That wasn't how he felt at all.

He'd solved the murders. He awoke in the same bed as his wife, and his five-year-old daughter wanted to be just like him.

"Actually, Harry, I couldn't be better."

They'd made plans to see each other again at the next Alcoholics' Anonymous meeting. They ended the call with Harry reminding him to take each day one at a time. He spent a few minutes talking about random things with his five-year-old, then went to wake Samantha, who was already taking a shower.

"We've got to hurry," Samantha called to him through the curtains.

"What's the hurry?" He slipped his pajama bottoms off and opened the curtains. His heart fluttered as he stared into his wife's eyes. "Got room for one more?"

With a smile, she nodded, and he stepped into the shower.

* * *

"Okay, we need to propose a toast," Newman said, picking up his

The Murder of Manny Grimes

wine glass. The restaurant was busy, so he had to raise his voice just a notch. Newman's wife, Christina, took her glass and held Newman's empty hand with hers.

DeLong and Samantha sat across from them and Sarah Benson sat on the end.

DeLong picked up his freshly filled Coke and took a sip.

"Hey, man," Newman complained. "You need to drink *after* we toast."

DeLong snickered softly as Samantha squeezed his hand. She knew it always made him uncomfortable at the beginning stages of being on the wagon while he was with others drinking. But he knew his discomfort was only a state of mind and mentally told himself to get a grip. After all, he wasn't the only one staying away from alcohol. Christina was pregnant, and Samantha was being a supportive, loving wife. "All right, what do we toast to?" DeLong asked.

"How about the brilliant police lieutenant who cracked a major case?" Samantha suggested, beaming at her husband.

DeLong chuckled and leaned over to give Samantha a quick peck on her cheek. "As much as I would love to grab all the credit, it was truly a team effort."

"I wasn't the one who cracked it," Newman pointed out. "It was all you."

"Oh, I'm sure you're just being modest, dear," Christina replied, swatting his shoulder.

"Okay, then I guess we need to toast Sarah. If it weren't for her finding the evidence her husband left, this case would be cold," DeLong suggested, winking at Sarah, who blushed.

"I'm down with that," Newman replied. He raised his glass in the air.

DeLong, Samantha, Christina and Sarah tapped their glasses to his softly.

"To Sarah," they said in unison.

"Thank you," Sarah told them shyly. "But it wasn't—."

"No sense talking yourself out of this, honey," Samantha told her. "These guys are stubborn. They usually get their way."

"That they do," Christina laughed, rubbing her stomach.

"And how about a toast to Russ and Taryn," added DeLong,

"for their effort not put in vain."

"Calhoun and Elliott," Newman echoed.

They tapped glasses again.

"And to Newman and Christina, may they have a wonderful pregnancy," Samantha said.

They echoed the toast and drank. DeLong placed his glass on the table and focused on eating his steak and potatoes.

They chatted about everything except the last few weeks. Then when the conversation moved into the Newman's unexpected pregnancy, Samantha leaned into his ear.

"They look happy."

"Yes. Being dad-to-be suits him."

"I want another baby. Will you have one with me?"

DeLong took a few minutes to pretend he was thinking about it.

"Actually, I was thinking of having one with her." He pointed to a random girl who stepped into the restaurant. Sam swatted his shoulder. Leaning into her, he said, "There's nothing I want more."

After they finished their lunch, the group made their way through the parking lot.

"So, what will happen to Jonathan Walker?" Samantha asked as they walked. She moved in close to DeLong in order to shield herself from the cold. Sarah followed them, a few steps back. She had a faraway gaze on her face, but DeLong decided to let her alone with her thoughts.

"We're not charging him," DeLong said. He looked at the brightly lit sky. The wind pushed against his face and he felt a chill crawl up his spine. "He made the mistake of obstructing justice, but in the end, he did the right thing. Those boys lost two people in their lives. No sense in taking him away from them."

"I wonder what he'll do," Christina said, "now that his life's been turned upside down."

"He said he'll probably plan on staying here in town. The boys already made their friends. They don't have any other family," DeLong replied.

"I feel bad for that family," Samantha said. "They've been through so much."

"All because of that mother of theirs," Christina agreed.

"Well, I, for one, am glad it's over," DeLong muttered. He

glanced back at Sarah. He wondered what she was thinking. He decided to ask.

She smiled at him and shook her head. "I'm trying to figure out what I want to do with Manny's house."

"You don't have to decide right away," DeLong told her. "Take a look at it. Discuss the options with your brother."

"I just want to do right by him."

Christina and Samantha stopped to drape their arms across Sarah's shoulders. "From what I understand, he's always loved you," Samantha said. "Whatever you decide to do, that's what he wants for you."

Sarah didn't respond.

"What are you going to do on your vacation?" Newman asked DeLong as they reached their vehicles.

DeLong looked to see Samantha chatting with the other women.

"I was thinking of spending time with the family. Reconnect with them." He shot Samantha a crooked smile. "That okay with you?"

"More than okay," she beamed.

DeLong and Newman shook hands.

"Don't be a stranger, and I'll see you soon."

"You got it," Newman agreed. "It was a pleasure working this investigation with you."

DeLong shook his head, protesting. "No, the honor was mine. You're a wonderful investigator, Newman. Keep at it." DeLong looked over at Sarah and said, "Ready to see the house?"

Sarah was gazing out the window. She sighed. "To be honest, no. I'm not sure what to expect. I don't know how I'll feel being so close to him, but knowing I can't touch him."

As he drove, DeLong reflected on her words. He tried to imagine how he'd feel if he were in her position. But he couldn't. He glanced toward Samantha, who kept her focus on the trees and cars going by. He hoped he would never have to find out.

When they pulled up the long, circular driveway of Manny Grimes' home and parked, they climbed out the SUV.

Standing in the chilly December weather, he stared at the house.

Sarah mimicked him and with a deep breath decided to walk inside.

Samantha walked around the SUV to wrap her arms around his waist.

"I wonder what she's thinking," she said quietly.

Her words faded away as he slipped into his own thoughts. Manny Grimes had helped him solve his murder. No one knew that. No one would ever know Grimes gave him the push to keep at it. He wasn't sure if it was Grimes himself, or DeLong's subconscious. Either way, he decided to give the credit to Grimes.

It was even safe to assume, DeLong considered, that Manny Grimes had even saved his marriage.

"Thank you," DeLong said, his voice slightly above a whisper.

"What?" Samantha asked.

He smiled at her and kissed her. "Nothing. I'm just talking to myself. Want to go inside?"

When she said yes, they walked inside to find Sarah staring at the things-to-do note Grimes had posted on the refrigerator. Tears trickled down the corners of her eyes.

"I'm sorry," she whispered to the empty air. Turning to face the DeLongs, she said, "Thank you so much for never giving up on him."

He stepped toward her to give her a consoling hug.

"I get the feeling he wanted my help. That he would have haunted me or something."

He heard her giggle against her sobs.

He pulled away and she wiped the tears from her face and smiled at him. "I mean it, though. Thank you."

"You're welcome," he told her. It was times like now DeLong was reminded why he became a cop. He'd wanted to make a difference in the world. He supposed it was the same as his AA group motto, take one day at a time. In order to make a difference, he needed to make the difference one person at a time.

Somehow, the large house didn't seem nearly as eerie as he once thought. They listened to the silence. Sarah breathed in and out as though she were breathing her husband into her soul. DeLong listened for sound, waited to see if there were breezes with Manny Grimes' fingerprints.

He had seen him. Had felt him.

It didn't matter whether he actually imagined it. He told himself

The Murder of Manny Grimes

Manny Grimes spoke to him.

So much had happened since the three boys stumbled their way into the sheriff's office, cold and frightened. But it seemed more like an eternity ago.

The murder of Manny Grimes changed him. In more ways than one.

He was thankful for the change. He was thankful for the second chance.

He had made many mistakes in his life.

DeLong shook his head. He shouldn't be looking at the past any longer. He needed to look forward to the future. He still had his family.

They were his future. He and Samantha would continue to work on their marriage. After all, *love is patient, love is kind. It does not envy, it does not boast, it is not proud. It does not dishonor others, it is not self-seeking, it is not easily angered, it keeps no record of wrongs. Love does not delight in evil but rejoices with the truth. It always protects, always trusts, always hopes, always perseveres.*

He'd remember that.

And he'd remember that above faith, hope and love, the greatest is love.

And he had love. He felt it.

Sarah's sigh broke through his daydream. "I'm ready to go now." She looked around the kitchen. "But I'll be back. I'll bring the boys. If they like it, I'll save it for them. I'll finish what Manny was doing." Her voice caught in tears. "It was my dream."

In silence, they walked back to the car. Before DeLong climbed behind the wheel, he took one more look around to see if maybe he would see the ghost of Manny Grimes. But there was nothing. Only DeLong's own shadow reaching out across the earth.

It was then he realized Manny Grimes was gone for good.

* * *

Lieutenant Jim DeLong returns in *Blood Runs Cold.* Read an excerpt on the following pages.

Angela Kay

Read an Excerpt from *Blood Runs Cold*

Chapter 1

The sky was still murky from the heavy storm the night before, the dew lingering in the early morning air. The leaves on the trees sagged toward the ground, droplets of water rolling to the earth. The crisp spring air brought enough of a chill to require a light jacket. It seemed almost perfect for the occasion for which Lieutenant Jim DeLong parked his car.

He released an inward groan when his new dress shoes sank in a soft spot on the grass, then scraped off the mud as he stepped onto the concrete. He drew in a breath and pushed it out, letting the smoke from his cigarette evaporate into the air. DeLong tossed it onto the ground, thinking it was time he quit. Lately, his wife had been hounding him about it, and in all honesty, smoking was a nasty habit.

Surveying the premises, he noticed the police cars scattered in the area, lights glistening against the puddles.

One officer searched the inside of a mustard-yellow Kia, dusting for fingerprints. Another pulled a light blue dress with frills on the bottom from a Dillard's bag. He made a comment that his daughter would love the dress. When he spotted DeLong nearby, he cleared his throat and returned the dress to the bag.

DeLong paid little attention to him as he noticed the caution tape blocking off the back of the building leading to the river.

He made a beeline in that direction, pushing through a small crowd of bystanders trying to see what was happening. A man was taking videos with his cell phone. As he neared, DeLong heard an officer request he put the phone away. Reluctantly, the onlooker muttered something underneath his breath, slipped the phone into his pocket, and took a small step backward, frowning at his companion by his side. When the officer focused his attention on another onlooker, the young man retrieved his cell for more videos.

Slipping underneath the tape, DeLong scanned the area. To his left was an officer standing near the building's entrance, speaking to a young couple. The woman's breathing was erratic, her face white. Her long, dirty blonde hair clung to her skin and her velour outfit. The man kept his right arm wrapped around her waist, drawing her near to his chest as he responded to the officer's questions.

"Hey, Jim."

DeLong glanced sideways to see Jeffrey Newman, his lead Crime Scene Investigator, walking his way.

It had been a while since DeLong last saw Newman. His wife had given birth to a premature baby girl, so he had taken his leave to take care of his family. Three weeks ago, DeLong received a text that they were expecting a second baby.

"Jeff," DeLong acknowledged, "how's Christina and the baby doing?"

"They're good," Newman replied, his expression stoic. "Her sister came into town a few days ago to help while I'm working. Christina's worried about this pregnancy since we almost lost Joanie during labor."

"Sam's available if you need anything," DeLong offered.

Newman smiled. "Thanks. Remind me to show off photos later."

The gleam in his eyes was unmistakable. DeLong was happy for his friend, but still, envious. After months of trying and running tests, he and his wife realized a second child wouldn't happen. He found it frustrating that a couple like the Newmans could try for so long to no avail, and then it happened back-to-back. And then there was Samantha, getting frustrated at her own infertility. As an only child, she wanted their daughter to have a brother or sister to enjoy.

But the doctors informed them last week it wouldn't happen.

"What do we have?" DeLong forced himself out of his daydream.

"The couple over there," Newman nodded toward the man and woman DeLong saw earlier, "were running along the trail. They spotted something in the water, went to check, and found the body."

"Any ID?"

"No. No ID, no purse, no phone."

"Could it have been a robbery gone wrong?" DeLong wondered as they made their way to where the crime scene was sectioned off.

Newman sighed. "I don't think so, Jim. You'll see why."

The body was discovered at the Augusta Canal, which was part of the Savannah Rapids Pavilion. Depending on the time of day, the trail circling the Savannah Rapids was busy.

The trees were full of luscious green leaves, the creek to the side, whispering, showing its white teeth as it powered against the rocks.

All-in-all, it was a peaceful area, and now murder only darkened it.

DeLong took notice of the building he'd walked by before meeting with Newman. Reporters had arrived, forcing their way through the crowd of bystanders. He was sure cameras were rolling, but the officers were doing well in keeping anyone from crossing the tape.

The building was out of view of where DeLong and Newman were heading. If anyone saw anything, then they were likely running or walking along the trail.

As they neared, DeLong observed the body of a woman lying in the water. She was roughly five foot six, wearing a black t-shirt. Her arms and legs had deep gashes and bruises. It appeared as though she put up a good fight.

Her jeans were ripped, but DeLong wasn't sure whether it was a fashion statement or a result of the struggle. He assumed she wasn't sexually assaulted, but he wouldn't know for sure until the coroner performed the autopsy.

DeLong made his way toward the water and knelt by the body, taking in the strong fragrance of sunflower and mud. She lay on the ground, her legs and arms askew, a red handkerchief placed over her face.

No, it likely wasn't a robbery. If the murder was random, they wouldn't have bothered covering her face. It was always possible the couple who found the body did. He made a mental note to find out.

Hand marks were visible on her arms, telling him someone had grabbed onto her tight. Her neck had discoloration as though her killer had strangled her.

After slipping on latex gloves, DeLong removed the cloth and found his victim's head facing the dry land. Dried blood clung to her skin from a deep wound on the side of her head. He glanced around, wondering if the weapon still remained at the scene.

He inspected the handkerchief, noting the gold flowers design and the words "love always." With care, DeLong folded the handkerchief and placed it in an evidence bag.

During his time on the police force, he had seen many ways for a murderer to kill his victims. It always troubled DeLong, knowing human beings had such disrespect for life. A part of him thought he needed to get out of the game. But when he analyzed crime scenes, he wanted nothing more than to find justice for the victims.

DeLong brushed the wet blonde hair with care from the woman's face.

He let out an angry curse.

He angled his head to the side, snapping his eyes shut, then forced himself to turn back with a daunting sigh.

Her too-familiar face was pale and bruised, almost to the point of being unrecognizable. Her eyes closed to the world.

"You know her?" Newman's quiet concern was clear.

Pulling back, DeLong rose, finding himself unable to take his eyes away.

"Yeah," he replied, his voice dry. "I know her."

Newman waited a few beats before he opened his mouth to speak. However, DeLong wasn't in the mood for questions he didn't want to answer. So he turned away and headed to where the witnesses stood.

As they walked toward the couple, the coroner went down the steps to retrieve the body.

The young woman had stopped crying though her lips quivered and her eyes gleamed with tears. She still clung to her friend for support.

"I'm Lieutenant Jim DeLong," he told them. "Can you tell me what you saw?"

"We were running on the trail when we saw her." The man's face revealed no angst, yet his voice betrayed him.

"Do you come here often?"

He nodded. "Every morning, we run five miles."

"Did you see anything or anyone out of the ordinary? Maybe someone seemed nervous, angry?"

"No. We didn't see anything until we saw her."

"Who spotted her first?" Newman asked.

"I-I did." The woman's voice was timid, her eyes hollow. "She was just laying there. So still." She shivered and leaned in closer to her companion, who wrapped his arms tighter around her body. A small sob escaped her lips.

"Did you put this handkerchief over her face?" DeLong held the evidence bag for the couple to see.

"No," they replied in unison.

"Can we go now?" he asked. "I should get her home."

DeLong nodded as he reached into his jacket pocket for his business card. "We'll contact you if we have any more questions. In the meantime, if you need anything, or remember anything, call me. It doesn't matter how big or small."

As the couple walked away, one of Newman's investigators called out from the wooded area.

"I think I've found something!"

DeLong and Newman jogged to where the investigator knelt. He was partly hidden by overgrown tree branches. The investigator donned a pair of latex gloves and reached underneath a shrub for a large gray rock.

DeLong made his way over, Newman following close behind.

"Look at this. Could be a murder weapon."

The rock was smooth and covered with a dried red substance. The investigator opened the kit he had placed next to him and pulled out the Luminol and a cotton swab. He rubbed the dark stain and dropped the clear liquid onto the swab. They watched as the color turned pink.

Next, the investigator dusted the rock and captured a partial print. After gathering all he could from the evidence he found, he packed it away.

DeLong looked around the canal, deep in thought. They still had to confirm the blood on the rock belonged to the victim, and a partial print wouldn't reveal much. But, it seemed they already got lucky. Most other evidence would likely have been destroyed due to the heavy overnight rain.

As he glanced around the premises, DeLong felt a slight surge of hope amid his churning stomach.

Newman cleared his throat to get DeLong's attention.

"You wanna tell me how you know the victim?"

A few heads bobbed their way, and DeLong motioned for Newman to follow him. What he wanted to say, he wanted to keep private.

Even though he'd eventually have to come forward and tell the whole story.

But until then, it'd be a secret among friends.

A Note from the Author

When I first started writing *The Murder of Manny Grimes*, I was in college, taking a novel writing course. Our assignment was to write the first two chapters of a novel. I wrote thirty pages each for those chapters. Of course, though I've always been a writer, I was still a novice. I was pleased that the entire class *loved* those two chapters. Even my professor, whom was a hard to please type.

Eventually, I used those two chapters, along with a one-act play, as my exit portfolio.

After college, I continued to write *The Murder of Manny Grimes*. Then I stopped. I changed every. single. word. of the book. Including those two chapters. Why did I do that? Well, not only is writing rewriting, but I'd come to the realization that while the writing was pretty good, people won't care about the plot. I had Manny Grimes a cold-hearted, evil man, that even the three boys who found him cheered when, to quote one of them, "the wicked witch is dead."

Facepalm. I don't know about you, but I'd like to care about the victim. At least care enough that I want the detectives to solve his murder. So I made Manny Grimes into a good guy—a good guy who has made mistakes in his life that he regrets. A good guy who didn't deserve the end he got.

It took me seven years to write my first book. I honestly never thought I'd finish. But I did.

After I finished the final draft, I was glad to have solved The Murder of Manny Grimes.

If you haven't already, pick up a copy of the second book in the series, *Blood Runs Cold!*

Printed in Great Britain
by Amazon